THE PARISIAN CHAPTER

ALSO BY JANET SKESLIEN CHARLES

Miss Morgan's Book Brigade: A Novel

The Paris Library: A Novel

Moonlight in Odessa: A Novel

THE PARISIAN CHAPTER

A Novel

JANET SKESLIEN CHARLES

ATRIA PAPERBACK

New York Amsterdam/Antwerp London

Toronto Sydney/Melbourne New Delhi

An Imprint of Simon & Schuster, LLC
1230 Avenue of the Americas
New York, NY 10020

First Atria Books trade paperback edition May 2026

ATRIA PAPERBACK and colophon are registered trademarks of Simon & Schuster, LLC

Interior design by Kyoko Watanabe

Manufactured in the United States of America

3 5 7 9 10 8 6 4 2

Library of Congress Control Number: 2025942652

ISBN 978-1-6680-8312-3
ISBN 978-1-6680-8313-0 (ebook)

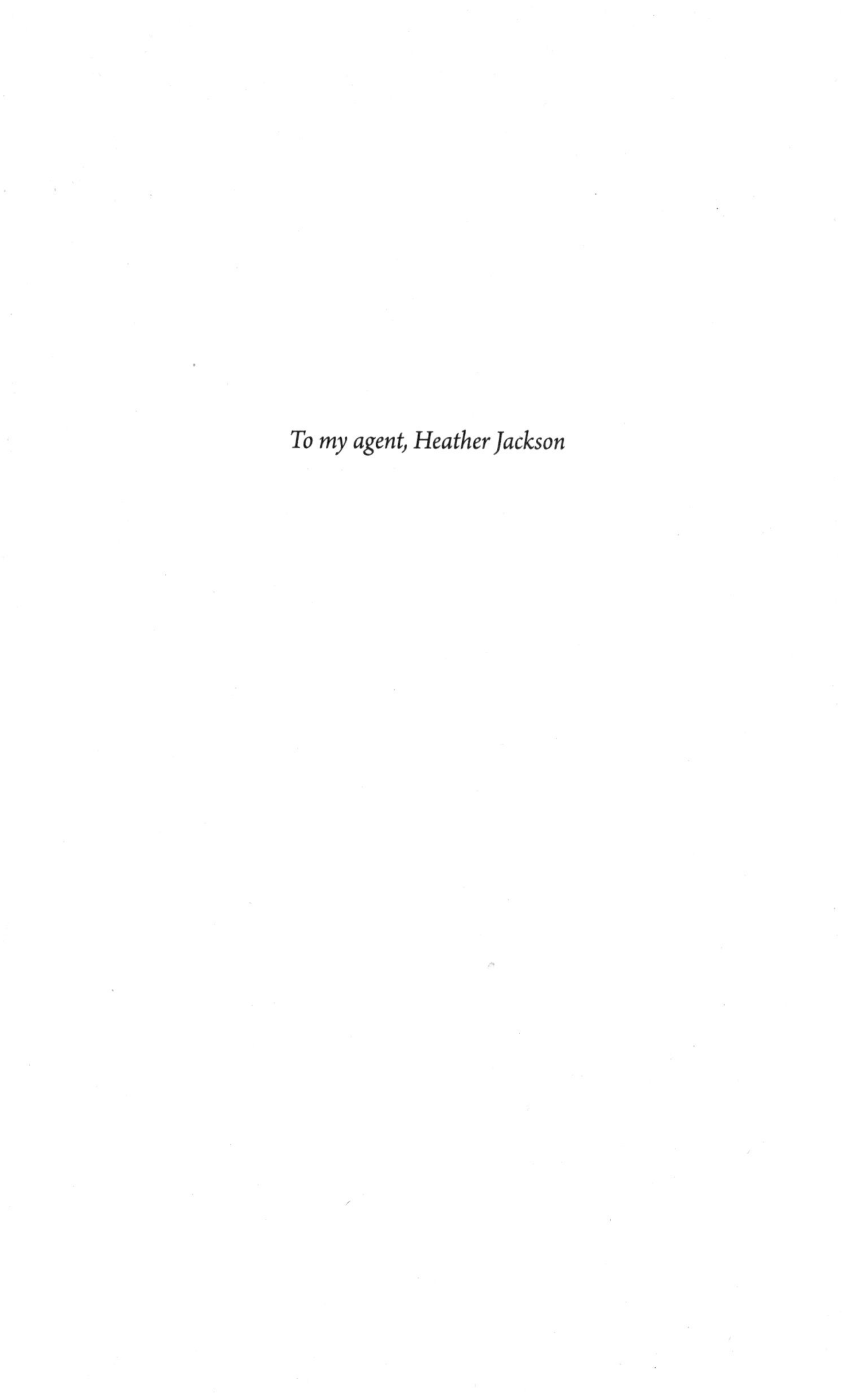

To my agent, Heather Jackson

But what if we let time pass, looking at an incident in the rearview mirror rather than at the moment of impact? We can wave goodbye to it, but still see it so clearly, captured in a pristine reflection. And what do we gain? Perspective, wisdom, and perhaps not acceptance—some things do not deserve to be accepted, after all—but at least a sense of calm.

—JAMI ATTENBERG,
I Came All This Way to Meet You: Writing Myself Home

Chapter 1

JANUARY 1995

Lorenzo Bruni—head librarian

I'm on the Front Line, the first librarian that people encounter when they enter the American Library in Paris. And let me tell you, people are pains. My colleagues and boss, Quentin Hayes III, have no idea what it's like to deal with the public. Day after day, year after year, I stand at attention behind the circ desk, waiting for patrons to ambush me. Like today. Katie Hunt slinks over to return a pile of torn magazines. Her kid ripped the *Family Circle* to shreds, and she wants all to be forgiven. I want to shout that we're in a foreign country—we can't just go to the store to pick up another copy. But Hayes gave strict orders not to yell. While I'm taping pages, old Mike Roth saunters in with a baguette sandwich sticking out of his book bag. Hayes won't let me kick him out because *he paid for his membership like everyone else.* Before I can inform the loudmouth that the library isn't a picnic area, Jennifer de Narp storms over. Using her Louis Vuitton clutch as a pointer, she calls my attention to a burned-out lightbulb in the reading room and orders me to change it. I want to say that our handyman will handle it, but Hayes won't let me refuse her. She's one of the Select Few, insanely rich donors. While I dig the ladder out of the broom closet, Mazie Chester sneaks past in her neon-green greatcoat. It's been a decade since she paid for a membership, but Hayes won't let me confront her. His logic: if we're nice to her, she'll leave her fortune to the library instead of to Morris Templeman, her cat. This place is a revolving door of loons.

And speaking of revolving doors, another program manager left without a goodbye. Lizzy cleared off her desk and spelled out "I QUIT" with Saul Bellow paperbacks. We weren't surprised by the resignation—not many can hack the job, or Hayes—but the choice of Bellow puzzled us. She only lasted six months before she huffed home to Auckland.

Contrary to what you might think, some people don't *want* to be in Paris. Perhaps their spouse got transferred here for work, and they trailed behind. Countless writers have followed in the soused footsteps of F. Scott Fitzgerald, and they stick around because they have more pride than brains. Or like me, they came to study at the Sorbonne and stayed for love. Bound by a passion for the same subject, many of us fell for a French classmate. Reciting your vows by the light of a hundred flickering flames during a candlelit Mass at Notre-Dame seems romantic. And it is, until the love of your life cheats. By then, there are children. The French divorce court won't allow you to leave the country—not if you want to go with your kids, anyway. I long to move back to my native Sicily to be closer to family. But until my twins turn eighteen, I'm stuck in Paris. Ten more years to go. In my parenting support group, we call it a prisoner-of-war situation.

When you live abroad, eventually—no matter your age or situation—catastrophe strikes back home. Say your mom gets cancer. You're torn between returning to nurse her for a few months or staying put to reassure your kids, who are back to bed-wetting because of the split. You choose your children, which means your siblings—who bear the brunt of caretaking—hate you. Your mother passes, *and you weren't there*. For the rest of your life, guilt is an acid that eats at you.

Any wonder people in this town are wound so tight? To escape the whiny patrons and nagging phones, I follow the nonfiction stacks from 355 (*The Art of War* by Sun Tzu) to 970.3 (*Trail of*

Tears by John Ehle); skirt the spartan back office, where unlike me, support staff work without constant interruption; sneak past the land mine of Hayes's corner office; and climb the clanging metal stairs to the Afterlife.

On this deserted mezzanine, a wingback chair and gray couch bathe in the gentle light that filters through the cracked plexiglass ceiling. Three walls teem with musty classics, while the fourth holds unpublished manuscripts. Encased in matching blue boxes, each tale is an unexpected gift. The engrossing account of a female firefighter who battles blazes and sexism, or the Algerian baker who "rises" to fame when his bread wins the premier prize in the city of Paris's best baguette competition. I've read all but three manuscripts. I just want to sink in the chair to savor a story—and ten minutes of peacetime—before returning to the battlefront.

But I see that moron Roth left half of his ham sandwich on a shelf, the butter soaking into *David Copperfield*'s spine. I fetch a paper towel to mop up his mess.

"Hell is other people," Sartre wrote. Certainly while sitting in the American Library in Paris.

Chapter 2

JANUARY 1995

Lily Jacobsen—job applicant

Six years ago, when my best friend and I landed in Paris, our first stop was the Eiffel Tower, where we savored our escape from wheat fields and church socials. In daydreams, I'd pictured us alone, the vast esplanade ours. But there were thousands of people, more on this city block than in our entire hometown. I breathed in the buttery aroma of crepes from *le snack-bar*. Even the air was different here—filled with energy, with the sound of taxis (taxis!) honking, siblings laughing as their cameras clicked, lovers murmuring to each other. Milling under the latticed iron legs, some folks gaped at a pair of shiny-faced soldiers on patrol, each carrying a Kalashnikov; others bought trinkets (Eiffel Tower key chains or bottle openers) from street hawkers; but most were like Mary Louise and me—they peered up in absolute awe.

After jostling between busloads of tourists to board the elevator, she and I lingered on the top. First, we soaked in the view of the city, which seemed to go on forever, like the plains back home in Montana. Then, she sketched the people in the park below, while I penned a postcard to my neighbor Odile, the Frenchwoman who'd set us on this path. *We're here, we're here, we're here! Following our dreams, seeing where you lived and loved and read.* I slid the card into the yellow mailbox so it would have a postmark from la Tour Eiffel on July 14, 1989, the bicentennial of the French Revolution.

Mary Louise and I crossed over the invincible lawn of the Champ de Mars, where Parisians picnicked on park benches. Near a trellis of jasmine, a group of girlfriends in bright bustiers clinked champagne glasses—maybe to celebrate Bastille Day, maybe just happy to have a day off work. Looking closer, we noted their guillotine earrings, a playful, macabre commemoration of *La Révolution*. Everything was astonishing to us—flowers, food, fashion. We didn't know which way to turn our heads.

Continuing along, we found ourselves in front of a pastry shop. The window display was as intricate as any painting in a museum. We only meant to pop in, but the cakes—small pieces of perfection—deserved our full attention. The customer in front of us couldn't make up his mind. Who could blame him? The éclairs were long and slim; the Paris-Brest, named for the famed bicycle race, were shaped like wheels; and the *réligieuses* were plump, like the nuns who'd inspired them. When it was our turn, I said, *"Deux éclairs au chocolat, s'il vous plaît."* The words felt as good on my tongue as the chocolate.

Following the shadow of the Eiffel Tower, Mary Louise and I turned onto a side street and headed down the block, toward the banner that heralded the hallowed American Library in Paris. I touched the blue canvas, needing to feel concrete proof that we were actually here.

When I was a kid, listening to Odile's stories, especially of her time working at the ALP, had made me want to live in France. Mary Louise and I hatched a scheme to study at the Sorbonne. With Odile's help, we figured out the application process and the visa paperwork. Though I was the one who wanted it the most, I wouldn't have been brave enough without Mary Louise.

Now, her eyes met mine. "Ready?" she asked.

"Oui, oui, oui!" I gushed. Some people burst into song when they are happy; I burst into French. Fortunately, Mary Louise was used to my weird ways.

I tugged on the brass door handle. Beyond the deserted welcome table I spied tall racks of magazines, a scraggly palmetto that reached toward the window, kids playing with blocks in the children's room. Mary Louise followed me to 820, where we opened Odile's favorite books, *The Priory* and a dog-eared copy of *Persuasion,* to scour the cards for her signature. In the reading room, I ran my fingertips along a scarred table and wondered if the backward braille of indentations had been formed by her pen. At the circulation desk, I searched for Odile in the eyes of the dapper librarian, but at the mention of her name, his expression remained blank.

I asked him about Odile's long-lost friend, Margaret Saint James. They'd worked together at the ALP during the Occupation, but war and betrayal had separated them.

He raised a brow. "You expect to find employees from fifty years ago?"

Mary Louise opened her mouth, probably to say something conciliatory like *Not expecting, just hoping,* but I cut her off. "The Arc de Triomphe and Café de Flore are still here," I shot back in the same snotty tone he'd used with me.

"Why are you always so rude?" Mary Louise chided when we were back on the boulevard.

"He started it."

She grimaced. "As always, you ended it."

~

On my own, I tracked down Margaret's old atelier, which was located near the Montparnasse Cemetery. The current owner told me she'd retired and gone to South Africa to be with her daughter. I wrote to inform Odile and asked if she wanted me to keep digging. *It's a blessing to know she's with family,* she penned in elegant cursive. *I don't want to get my hopes up again. No more talk about the past. Let's look to the future. Tell me about the Sorbonne.*

The classes were challenging. Marie Louise and I tried to take notes, but the professors spoke more quickly than we could write. Luckily, there was respite on weekends. In the leafy allées of the

Tuileries, we shared picnics of baguettes and rotisserie chicken with other students—Yuka from Tokyo, Claudio from Seville, Mireille from Mulhouse. Even though we met new friends from all over the world, I still found Mary Louise the most interesting, the one whose opinion mattered the most, the one I wanted to spend time with.

At the tip of Île de la Cité, an island in the middle of the Seine, she balanced her easel on the cobblestones, sketching the willow tree whose slender branches licked at the river while I scribbled in my notebook, inspired by couples holding hands, by the accordionist playing "*La Vie en Rose*," by the wistfulness of the clouds. She and I got lost in the labyrinths of the Louvre—the museum map was little help in navigating nine miles of corridors. *Can you believe we're here?* Our eyes would meet, and we wouldn't have to say a word. We roamed narrow streets until our feet throbbed, then we jumped on random city buses to admire chic *quartiers* in stop-and-go traffic. There was the blue bistro, its waiters in smart tuxedos; the mime breakdancing before the bronze statue of Ben Franklin; the melancholy shopgirl who stared out the window. Sometimes, I thought Mary Louise resembled her. When she thought I wasn't looking, her mouth puckered the same way it did when she was about to cry. I worried she didn't want to be here, that I'd pressured her into following me to France.

At the end of our first semester, late one night, curled up on our futon with only the dregs left in the bottle of red, I worked up the courage to ask, "Do you regret coming?"

"What makes you think that?"

"I miss my family, too." I leaned forward, hoping she'd confide in me. "I wouldn't blame you if you want to go back."

She rolled her eyes. "To what? Cruising Main Street? That place is a dead end."

I frowned. "I wouldn't go that far." Now that we lived thousands of miles away, I missed our small town.

"It was different for you." Her fingers twitched, which meant she was dying for a cigarette. "You were the smart one, I was the fuckup."

"That's not true."

"In high school, you talked me out of doing dumb stuff."

"Like what?" I demanded.

"That custom cutter whose eyes were as green as his John Deere combine."

I snorted a laugh. "He was cute. But I said 'what,' not 'who'!"

"Same dif. When Billy and I ditched class to make out under the bleachers, you talked sense into me. Without you, I might have been a teen mom, a dropout stuck cleaning motel rooms. You believed in me and made sure I graduated. You showed me the possibilities of the future. My possibilities. My future. No one in my family went to college. No one even had a passport. No one dreamed big for me like you did."

"Tu es fantastique." I didn't say that her parents didn't know her like I did.

Paris represented a fresh start for both of us—one where Mary Louise would find her path, and I would no longer be the tongue-tied teen who couldn't talk to boys. I even spoke up for Mary Louise, who struggled with French. I would pen my debut novel, then return to my hometown a literary success. I wanted so much for us—fame, happiness, great boyfriends. Together, we'd accomplish what we could not alone, I told myself, without realizing that she'd responded to my question without answering it.

We were in France to be *artistes,* even if we often felt homesick and lost. I felt eclipsed by the city's literary greats, so she talked up my chapters. What started as a tale of a girl running away from a suffocating small town became the story of a young woman seeking love in the world's most romantic city. Between Jean-Luc, who stood me up; Pierre-Antoine, who put me down; and René-Charles, who used me to correct the wonky English of his dissertation, then dumped me when he was awarded his Ph.D., I wasn't making much progress on finding that great romance. Neither was

Mary Louise. André dated her in the hope of getting a green card. Mickael had a goal of sleeping with a woman from every country. She was an unsuspecting character in chapter 43 of *Around the World in 80 Lays.*

Still, we didn't give up—on our art or on finding boyfriends. On Saturday nights at the Basement Brasserie, over bottles of inexpensive Bordeaux, we hung out with a handful of friends. Whenever one spoke in French, my gaze flitted to Mary Louise, who nodded along. I always ensured she was able to follow, sometimes whispering snippets of the conversation in English. When she responded in pidgin French, I listened, always interested in her opinion. A classmate had called our friendship "*fusionnelle*," as if Mary Louise and I had been fused together, forged from small-town life.

As we scoped out Frenchmen, I joked that we should contact Guinness to find out if Mary Louise or I held the record for crap dates.

"It would be a tie," she told the others.

"What was your worst date?" I asked her.

She stiffened. "I don't want to talk about it. And you shouldn't write about my failures."

I wanted to argue that the dates weren't failures—those guys were jerks, and it wasn't her fault. But when she used that stilted tone, I knew not to argue.

An author's apprenticeship is a million words. I wrote during every spare moment—on the bus between tutoring sessions, on nights that Mary Louise spent with one of her on-again, off-again boyfriends. I'd planned to write a romantic comedy, but the novel had too many disappointing first dates and false starts. Though it meandered more than I'd intended, the plot was coming along. I couldn't say the same about my career. After graduation, it had taken months of sending out résumés to finally receive job offers.

Mary Louise worked as a receptionist at an upscale American dental clinic, while I was hired at Wall Street English. Teaching corporate jargon was not how I envisioned my career. Each time

I entered the classroom, my middle-aged students winced. The bankers insisted that my English class was a "hostile takeover" of their beloved French. The realtors complained that they were forced to "speak le business" in order to kowtow to international clients snatching up the best Parisian properties. I'd been certain my love of language would win them over, but after twelve months and fourteen days of their steaming resentment, I accepted my failure. Resigning had been a relief. To cover my share of the rent, I tutored enthusiastic pupils after school and on Saturday mornings. With the freedom to write during the day, I'd told myself it would take two months to polish my novel, and two more to sign with an agent. That was a year ago.

In Paris, almost everyone I knew wanted to publish a book. We came from Perth or Birmingham or Fargo with our Fitzgerald dreams and Hemingway aspirations, certain that the City of Light would nourish us.

Outside the university cocoon, Mary Louise and I soon learned that Paris was a big city like any other. Expensive. Agitated. Aloof. Even years after our arrival, she and I still shared a studio on the fifth floor of an old building. There was no elevator, but the steep servants' stairs kept us in shape. If we peered out into the courtyard through our only window, we could look down on rich people—the portly CEO who brought home a gorgeous man every Friday night, the heart surgeon on the fourth floor whose lips were always pursed. It wasn't much of a view, but we told ourselves it didn't matter, we had all of Paris.

Our linoleum flooring was peeling, and the brocade wallpaper had bald spots, but we covered them with Mary Louise's pastel painting of the Eiffel Tower. Her other canvases leaned against the walls. My manuscripts and accompanying letters of rejection were stacked in the corner. We used the pile as an end table; coffee rings stained the cover page of *French Kisses*, the chronicle of our misadventures with Parisian men. "We write to taste life twice," Anaïs Nin said, and I took the adage to heart.

~

Today, on the way home from my final tutoring session of the day (triplets with wealthy parents), I splurged on some flowers for Mary Louise to commemorate the fourteenth, the date of our arrival in France. Marcelle, my favorite character in *The Library Card*, insisted that if you keep a bottle of champagne in your refrigerator, you'll always find something to celebrate. Life is hard, so it's vital to mark each victory. Thus, on the fourteenth of each month, Mary Louise and I commemorated our rebirth in Paris, our French-iversary.

Recently, she'd been withdrawn. We'd known each other since kindergarten, and for the first time in our lives, I couldn't discern what she was feeling. We ended up having what I called wordless fights: we'd talk until she retreated behind a wall of silence. Was it something work-related? Mary Louise didn't love answering phones in the dental office. When I suggested finding a better job, she retorted that the money was good. When I asked if she and her ex-boyfriend had a fight, she told me to mind my own business. Maybe she was still down because of what that obnoxious art dealer said about her paintings. Or maybe it was last night.

We'd attended our friend Paloma's going-away party. Despite the sangria, the gathering felt like a funeral. She was leaving us for a job in Miami. Since she could only take two suitcases, she divvied up her Parisian life, bequeathing books to me, an easel to Mary Louise, pans to Mireille, a futon to Yuka. Our group had been through bad grades, a pregnancy scare, bouts of homesickness, and more and more goodbyes. Though Paloma promised to return, Mary Louise and I knew that Paris was a trampoline town—once students bounced, they were gone for good.

"Another one bites the dust," Mary Louise said glumly as we trudged home.

Our social circle was tightening like a noose around the neck. Soon, our friends would all be gone. A thought bubbled up inside me: maybe Mary Louise thought we should leave, too; maybe she was unhappy because she didn't want to be here anymore.

Now, I stared at the bouquet of mimosas I'd bought for her. If only she'd tell me what was wrong, I could fix it. If only she would confide in me.

Arriving home, I dumped my messenger bag onto the floor, next to sheets of paper and bits of charcoal. I grinned at the half-formed figures that Mary Louise had drawn. This was a good sign. After she'd pitched her artwork to Parisian galleries, she quit painting.

"What do you think?" I heard her say. She stood in the doorway, probably returning from the bathroom down the hall, which we shared with a Turkish journalist and an Italian singer. She'd braided her curly red hair in a crown, so it wouldn't get in her face as she sketched.

Peering at the drawings, I saw her father, snuff crammed in his cheek, and could practically smell the grease on his shirt after a long day at the garage.

"You captured him perfectly."

She shrugged. Maybe my praise didn't mean much.

I proffered the mimosas.

Mary Louise looked at me askance. "What's this?"

She had to ask? For our French-iversary five months ago, she'd signed us up for a group lesson on how to do *le cancan* at the Moulin Rouge. When I tried to raise my leg above my head like the dancer showed us, I tumbled backward onto the foam mat. Mary Louise joined me there, her belly laugh echoing throughout the theater.

"Something to celebrate the fourteenth," I replied.

"Oh! I guess I forgot."

She put the flowers in our only vase while I spooned some Carte Noire into our French press. I poured the milk, she the coffee, and we curled up on the futon with our mugs. She reeked of cigarettes, which meant she had a new boyfriend, and that he was French. I recalled Julien, who arrived exactly an hour late for every date, as if his watch were set on Greenwich time. Or Louis, a creepy fashion photographer who took pictures of her while she slept. The one thing the men seemed to have in common was their smelly Gitanes cigarettes. I bawled her out every time they stunk up our studio. Consequence: It had been a while since she'd introduced one of her dates to me.

I hated that she smoked. I resented her secrecy. But fights about both had led nowhere, so I kept my mouth shut.

"I've been wanting to tell you something," she said.

Your latest guy? What's his name, Romain or Pierre? I wanted to tease, but lately she'd been so sensitive that I didn't dare. As I sipped my coffee, I gauged her tone. Concern. "Did something happen at home? Is your sister okay?"

She gnawed on her bottom lip, probably weighing her words. "I'm moving out."

"What?" My hands started to tremble, so I set my mug on my stack of manuscripts. Café au lait sloshed over the rim, turning the type into a milky gray cloud. The announcement had a similar effect on me, blurring my emotions and stirring up questions: Where was she going, and when? Why was she leaving me?

Coffee continued to creep across the page, taking with it any meaning. On any other day, I would have jumped up and dabbed the manuscript with fistfuls of napkins like an EMT performing CPR. After all, my words were my life. But now . . . I sat frozen as Mary Louise sopped up the mess with a cloth. I wanted to tell her not to bother, that the draft was lost, the mood ruined.

A month ago, she'd mentioned apartment hunting, but I hadn't realized she was serious.

"When are you moving out?" I didn't intend to sound angry. "When?" I demanded in a softer tone.

She wouldn't meet my eye. "As soon as you can make rent."

Mary Louise earned good money, and could afford to live on her own, unlike me. I loved teaching teens with my part-time tutoring gigs, but the pay barely covered my share of rent and food.

"What changed?" I turned away, focusing my attention on the bookcase so she wouldn't see how upset I was. No need for her to feel as bad as I did.

"I need more space. We both do. Everyone our age is either getting married or getting their own place."

Since when do we care what "everyone" is doing?

She arranged the drawings in her portfolio, careful not to smudge them. A way of giving me privacy as I absorbed the seismic shift in our relationship. Was it something I'd done—talked on the phone too much, smacked my cereal when she tried to sleep in? Something I hadn't done—the dishes, taking out the garbage?

"It's nothing you did or didn't do," she reassured me.

A part of me was heartened—as always, she read my mind. Another part was devastated.

We'd always been inseparable.

"I'll only be a few métro stops away," she said.

My head shot back. "You already found a place?" Somehow this news stung more than her initial announcement. "I'll pick up more tutoring hours, or find a second job. I certainly don't want to hold you back."

"Don't be like that."

Words can reveal or conceal. To hide my hurt, I grabbed a copy of *FUSAC* (*France-USA Contacts*) and held it to my face. I skimmed the headlines—PRESIDENT BILL CLINTON INVOKES EMERGENCY POWERS. O.J. SIMPSON ON TRIAL FOR MURDER—before moving to the personal ads. Usually, we delighted in the random desires of strangers. ("Can you believe it? This one wants a woman who'll nibble his toes!") Coming from a straitlaced town, where folks had a tough time articulating their desires, we admired anyone who could admit what they wanted.

Now, Mary Louise ignored my ignoring her and plunked down beside me. She flipped to the next section, which happened to be job listings.

"You're certainly eager to turn the page," I muttered.

She looked like she wanted to say more. I waited for her to confide in me about her mystery guy. Or her future studio. Something.

"I'm worried about leaving you to pay rent on your own," she said. "Just read."

> HLC, France's second-best business school (source: *Finance Times*), seeks English instructors. Salary commensurate with degree. Travel costs reimbursed.

"Second-best" instead of "ranked second" brought a bitter smile to my lips. I was feeling second-best myself.

"Clearly, they need you," Mary Louise said.

"You're saying that because you want me to take any old job so you can move out."

"I'm saying it because you're a good teacher," she responded in a low, even tone.

"No more business English."

She handed me the charcoal, and I blacked out the entire ad.

> The American Library in Paris is recruiting for a part-time Program Manager. Must be able to work evenings. Modest salary.

"Oh, là, là!" I drew five exclamation points beside the ad—a sign, a dream.

This was the first time I'd seen an ALP job advertised. On our visit there, we learned that a yearly membership cost a hundred bucks. I couldn't justify paying that much, not when the Sorbonne library had a large English-language section.

"There's probably tons of downtime there, so you'll be able to write *and* research," Mary Louise reasoned. "You'll save money by using their printer. As an employee, I bet you can check out all the books you want and never pay any fines. And Odile will be so proud."

She was selling me something I'd already bought. Glancing at Mary Louise's canvases propped against the wall, I realized that the sooner I had a steady paycheck, the sooner she'd be free to move out and hopefully resume painting. Last spring, in sundresses we used to wear to church, we'd schlepped six of her sixteen-inch canvases into the métro, zigzagging under the city from gallery to gallery. Ten owners rejected us immediately, but one accorded Mary Louise a chance. Her voice sang as she spoke of inspiration and Cubist techniques, of the esplanade of la Tour Eiffel meeting the plains of our native Montana. Listening to her broken French, I felt a burst of affection. There was no way he could say no.

"Conventional," he said with a dismissive sniff. "Boring."

I opened my mouth to rip him a new one; Mary Louise told me, "It's fine," even though I could see it wasn't. I placed my foot over hers, our shorthand for *I love you and everything will be okay*.

She didn't speak the whole way home.

When I'd dreamed of Paris, I imagined us in Montmartre, in apartments we'd bought. Over sparkling mimosas on my balcony, we'd watch silver clouds settle around the dome of the Panthéon. But we still lived in the studio that was supposed to be temporary. The only things more depressing than the rejections I received for my writing were monthly bank statements that whispered, "Failure." But I was willing to do what it took and knew Mary Louise felt the same.

I reread the program manager job description. My chances were slim. Everyone here was more qualified than me: I'd studied French, but Parisians learned two foreign languages in high school, plus many had college degrees in fields such as research analysis or public relations. I didn't want to go back to forcing bratty bankers to learn English, the sludgy bottom of the job barrel. And I didn't want anything to change our friendship, but I knew that Mary Louise was right: we needed to get on with our lives.

The next morning, I mailed off my résumé and cover letter. Four days later, as I opened a letter from a literary journal and absorbed the not-what-we're-looking-for-at-this-time rejection, the ALP secretary called to schedule an interview.

~

On my way to the library, I strolled up Avenue Rapp, famous for its Art Nouveau building. A cold rain drizzled, and I tugged the beret that Odile had given me down over my ears. There was almost no one on the tree-lined sidewalk. Parisians were either ensconced in their offices or sunning themselves on the Riviera. I swallowed. It had been a while since I'd been able to afford a trip, even a weekend getaway. Now I might not be able to make rent. How had I let things become so bad? What if I botched the interview? I felt my heart hammer and told myself, "Breathe. Stay in the now." I reached out to grasp a tree and closed my eyes. Just touching the damp bark calmed me.

When I opened my eyes, I spied a forty-something blonde striding in my direction. She carried a turd-brown Louis Vuitton purse in one hand; in the other, a cigarette. We reached the crosswalk at the same time. As we waited for the light to change, her smoke wafted into my face. I swatted it away and muttered, "Gross."

She took a long drag and flicked the cigarette onto the sidewalk. It lay there between us, smoldering. Parisians—whether French, Moroccan, or American—assumed street sweepers in green overalls would tidy up behind them, their own personal manservants. Any fifth grader writing a school report could inform you that cigarette butts took up to a decade to decompose, and that each year, Parisian sanitation workers swept up 350 tons. City of Light? No, city of lighters.

My world is not your ashtray, I wanted to tell the blonde, but when I became angry, a colossal drop cloth covered the vocabulary in my mind. I couldn't find the word for "ashtray" in French. The smoke from her cigarette unfurled, up and away. The acrid odor continued to fill my nostrils, as it had days earlier when I arrived home to find Mary Louise and the stench of Gitanes. The blonde didn't care what she discarded, like Mary Louise with me. Why couldn't smokers acknowledge the damage they wrought? Why couldn't they treat people—or rather, Paris—with respect?

I had no French words to express my frustration but needed to take a stand. I stepped closer to the blonde, intending to ground out the butt with my heel. At least that's what I told myself as my loafer connected with her shin.

She yelped, which gave me pause. I'd actually lashed out at a person. A litterer, but still.

"Ça va pas?"

What is wrong with you? the woman's tone screeched.

I pointed to the cigarette, then to her. The traffic light changed, and as usual, several drivers ran the red. No one respected rules. In Paris, you had to look after yourself, because no one else would. The smoker crossed the street, hobbling away from me, bobbing between cars, clutching her overpriced purse to her chest like I was going to rip it from her hands.

I ground out her cigarette with my heel before continuing toward the library. I had to acknowledge that I hadn't exactly cleaned the street—not like my stepmom, who collected empty beer cans from the ditch on her morning walk. Ellie would have picked up after the smoker with no fuss, no muss. I couldn't believe I'd kicked a stranger. When had I become so on edge and angry? What was Paris doing to me?

But I had to stay focused. *Hold it together,* I told myself. *You can do this.* In the foyer, I tucked my beret into the pocket of my slicker and approached the welcome table, where a pale woman with a white crew cut greeted me. Though the hairstyle suited her, emphasizing her graceful neck and high cheekbones, I couldn't help but wonder if she'd recently gone through chemo and hoped that she'd have a clean bill of health. When she asked to see my membership card, I explained that I'd come for a job interview.

"I'll escort you to the director's office."

She walked slowly, and I matched her pace. It gave me time to drink in everything. The palmetto in a cracked terra-cotta pot. The chipped paint on the window casings. The stained green carpet. So much of Paris was appearances. In the Luxembourg Garden, the lawn was to be admired, not to be touched and certainly not to be picnicked upon. Running clockwise on its sandy paths, lanky *joggeurs* sported Lacoste polo shirts, collars popped. *Parisiennes* donned high heels even if they were just dashing into the supermarket to buy canned peas. Rubbing the toe of my loafer over the splotch of ink on the carpet, I felt such affection for these imperfections, the way these stains and scratches underlined, *Real life is messy, and that's okay*. We passed the children's section, the walls decorated with cheery paper snowflakes. A fey brunette recited *The Paper Bag Princess* to little ones gathered in a semicircle. *The dragon took another huge breath, but this time nothing came out. The dragon didn't even have enough fire left to cook a meatball.* The kids leaned forward, the way I did when I reached an engrossing part of a novel. The sparkle in the librarian's eyes made me realize how much she loved her job, made me realize how happy I was to return to this bookish place.

The greeter and I passed the reading room, where patrons pored over books. There were several cute guys, and I couldn't help but wonder about dating one—if I got the job. Continuing past the nonfiction stacks, I searched for my favorite numbers—001.9 (the unexplained, like UFOs or Bigfoot) and 808 (writing and getting published). The greeter boasted about the library's treasures: a pair of Hemingway's tortoiseshell spectacles; a letter from Henry Miller; and books that had once belonged to the Left Bank bookseller Sylvia Beach (the patron saint of impoverished writers) as well as Marlene Dietrich, who scrawled opinions in the margins ("This is without a doubt the worst writing I have ever laid eyes on."). The greeter added that the cavernous safe in the director's office was rumored to contain the lost manuscript of Irène Cohen, a beloved Parisian novelist. I knew all about Professor Cohen from Odile.

"Her Cairo trilogy is incredible!" I replied, practically bouncing at the thought of discovering more of her work. "Is there any chance I can read the manuscript?"

"No one on staff has the key."

"Can't they hire a locksmith?"

"The budget is tight."

Ah yes, *modest salary*. The only kind I've ever known.

"Still," I ventured, "a secret new novel would relaunch interest in Irène Cohen. Her work deserves the attention."

"You know your literature. Too few people are familiar with Irène's work."

After chatting with the greeter, I was no longer nervous. She smelled of hot cocoa, which made me trust her.

"Any advice?" I asked as we arrived at the director's door.

Skipping the bland just-be-yourself nonsense, she said, "Be honest, but not too honest."

"Okay. Is there anything you can tell me about the director?"

"Sure: Hayes is a bean counter and a name-dropper. He has no sense of humor."

Before I could respond, she knocked on his door.

"Come in," came the muffled response.

For a middle-aged guy, the director was handsome enough, with wire-rimmed glasses and a Saint-Tropez tan. In his pinstriped suit, he resembled a stockbroker. On his desk was a framed photo of him with President Reagan. Given the library's homey shabbiness, I knew Reagan's trickle-down theory didn't work here.

Mr. Hayes sifted through a pile of résumés. "Constance Thorn?"

I shook my head. "Lily Jacobsen."

"Take a seat." He gestured to a table and chairs in front of the window, which gave onto a paved courtyard that was more parking lot than secret garden. My back was to the gray safe, which was the size of an upright piano. I wondered how to get my hands on Professor Cohen's manuscript. Odile and I would love to read it.

I answered Mr. Hayes's questions the best I could. No, I'm not a library member. Yes, I have working papers. Yes, I have strong feelings about fonts. No, I'm not familiar with Saul Bellow's prose.

"Saul Bellow, Pat O'Malley, Richard Ford." The director lifted his gaze to the heavens the way our priest back home did when evoking the holy trinity. Mr. Hayes explained that booking A-list speakers for the Entre Nous literary series was *the* key responsibility of program manager. The ALP was struggling financially. The cost of maintaining this old building was considerable, the pipes alone . . . Anyway, big names would entice prospective donors. However, with the relatively small Anglophone audience in Paris, authors passing through usually spoke at only one venue. It was a high-stakes competition between the ALP and Parisian bookshops. So far, those bastards at Piccadilly Books were winning.

Perhaps realizing he'd gone off script, he glanced at my résumé. "So you were a teacher? The job is about dealing with the public. We have many personality types here. You must be patient and diplomatic. It's vital to cultivate good relations, even at your level."

My level?

"How's your French?" he asked.

"I speak fluently, but to be honest, sometimes when I'm stressed, my words evaporate."

He nodded. "We can all relate to that, in any language."

I longed to boast that my friend Odile had worked here—and faced the Nazis—during the war, but the way that Mr. Hayes kept peering at his watch stopped me. When he asked if I had any questions, I brought up salary.

"We're a nonprofit," he reminded me.

Subtext: minimum wage. I couldn't help but wonder if that was his BMW I saw parked in the courtyard.

He asked if I was planning to stay in Paris. "I don't want to hire someone who can't commit. The previous two program managers lasted less than a year apiece."

I should have asked why they'd resigned. I should have seen the red flag he waved in my face.

Chapter 3

JANUARY 1995

Jennifer de Narp—trustee

Gripping my second-favorite Vuitton handbag to my chest, I limped into the ALP, where as usual, Meg manned the wobbly welcome table. "I was nearly mugged, by a woman! Can you believe it?"

"Never underestimate women, they can be just as violent as men."

Meg was correct: one should not underestimate women. At my all-girl boarding school, I often sought refuge in the stacks after cruel pranks by classmates. And now, at the ALP, I had to deal with my nemesis, Pam de Laney.

"Are you all right?" Meg asked.

I gave a little shrug, though honestly, the encounter had shaken me. "At least the mugger didn't get my money. Isn't Paris supposed to be safer than Dallas?" I lifted my pant leg to show Meg the bruise that had formed.

"Poor thing," she tutted. "Let's get some ice on that."

I followed her to the kitchen. At the Formica table, I sank onto a chair while she took ice trays from the fridge, which mostly served to hold bottles of wine.

As she placed the bag of ice on my purplish shin, I murmured, "You're a dear."

It was nice to be fussed over, especially since my own mother never cosseted me. She spent more time with her charities than at home. Nonetheless, she instilled in me at a very young age the need to serve. My entire adult life, I've supported educational organizations: Libraries Without Borders, which provides books to schools in developing countries, and another favorite, Reid Hall's steering committee. At the turn of the twentieth century, Elisabeth Mills Reid created a clubhouse for women artists. After World War I, this feminist Garden of Eden became a study abroad program for women. Junior year there broadened my horizons—the language, the food, the culture, the distance from my native Texas; now, I relished raising money for scholarships so that women from modest backgrounds could experience the same life-changing opportunities.

Though I wanted to be a lawyer like my father, he and my mother were more concerned with me marrying well. When he came to Paris to visit a satellite of his law office, he took me out for lunch. Before the waiter could bring our crèmes brûlées, he threw a wad of francs on the table and stormed out. Once again, I'd given him indigestion by bringing up law school. That evening Mrs. Kinchlow, the director of Reid Hall, invited Daddy and me for chamomile tea in her airy office. Girded by a tweed skirt and a pastel twinset, she listened as he informed her that my year in Paris was a way for me to collect recipes for future dinner parties and find a titled husband.

"Yes, of course," Kinch agreed blandly. "That's why young women attend classes here."

I didn't know how she said it with a straight face. Kinch was certainly used to dealing with demanding fathers ranting about their uppity daughters. With her hair bound in a tight bun and a pearl necklace that made her appear as demure as a debutante, no man would ever guess how subversive she was, how far she'd go for her girls. Several of us were convinced she'd buried some bodies beneath the cobblestones of the cloistered campus courtyard.

"Nonetheless, it's flattering that she wants to be like you," Kinch said. "What is your practice?"

Daddy explained that men in our family had a tradition of "community service"—cutting their teeth in the role of district attorney to "put bad guys away for life"—before moving on to lucrative private practice at an international firm.

Kinch gushed about how wonderful it was that he valued schooling for his daughter, and that research had proven that the brightest boys had educated mothers who could advocate for them.

"I'm sure Jennifer will raise a brood of strapping sons," she continued. "But what if her aristocratic husband passes away? His younger brothers might inherit the money *you* bestow on Jennifer and her children and bleed them dry. In the great state of Texas, in times of tragedy, families might come together to support a foreign widow. In France, however . . ." Brow knit in concern, she paused to let him imagine the lawsuits and custody battles. "Wouldn't you want your daughter to be able to provide for your grandsons, in that case? I'm sure we can agree that Jennifer is a gifted debater. She might as well be paid for it, for example, as a lawyer."

Sons, inheritance, ensuring wealth remained in the family. Kinch and I watched the pieces click together in his brain. Soon, he was imploring her to write a letter of recommendation to ensure I would get into *the* top French law school. When he took his leave, he shook her hand heartily, thanking her for looking out for our best interests.

I loved my parents, but I needed an ocean between us. Studying law in Paris had allowed me to stay at Reid Hall. And later, my background in tax law helped me stay one step ahead of my "noble" husband and his venomous parents, *le baron* and *la baronne*. At least my wedding to a Frenchman had afforded me a *carte de résident*. When my marriage eventually disintegrated, I clung to my identity as a lawyer and to Kinch. I would owe her forever, so when she beseeched me to help the ALP, a "sister" educational organization, I joined the board.

Sadly, the library was starting to feel like a lost cause. Under

Hayes's "leadership," membership was down. Fewer members meant fewer fees. There was barely a budget to buy books and pay staff. These days, the trustees' mission was to find a way to keep the lights on—but we disagreed on how. Unlike those of my other boards, ALP meetings were full of blowhard men and strife.

Fed up with being the token woman, I would have loved to see a member of W.E.—wives of executives—on the board. These trailing spouses were intelligent, hard workers who'd left behind their own aspirations to support their husbands. But the W.E.s were unable to accept paid positions because the French government refused to grant them work visas like their husbands got. Sexism at its finest.

So when I'd heard that a woman was joining the ALP board, I was elated. Until I learned who—Pam de Laney. What she'd done was bad enough. Now she had the audacity to join the board—my board. Was nothing sacred?

At monthly meetings around the conference room table, she tried to impress me with announcements of the thousands she and her current husband donated for the children's room remodel and the writer in residence program. Nonetheless, I did my best to rebuff her. But two years ago, during the search for a new director, ignoring her became impossible. I wanted a woman, an actual librarian, but damn Pam put forward her own nephew, an accountant who she insisted would balance the books. I glared at her. She pretended not to notice.

When just the two of us were left in the room, I hissed, "You have no morals. Adultery, nepotism, it's all the same to you."

"I told you at the time that I was sorry," she shot back.

The chairman didn't care for either of our candidates, though. He insisted the ALP needed "a name" like Quentin Hayes III, who I happened to know from my undergrad days. The lightweight sailed through life—and our debate team circuit—thanks to his prep school connections and illustrious family name. After what had happened, I kept tabs on him—and didn't like what I saw.

Before the vote, over a boozy lunch at Le Bristol, I raised my concerns about Hayes and took the opportunity to praise my candidate, who was actually qualified.

"Librarians care too much about books, and not enough about the bottom line," the chairman argued between bites of foie gras. "Paltry book fines aren't enough to cover exorbitant heat bills."

When the ballots were tallied, I saw the other trustees hadn't even considered my candidate. On the bright side, damn Pam had been voted down, too. Even so, that left the ALP with Hayes. He was a cheater, a fraud. And I wanted him gone.

Chapter 4

FEBRUARY 1995

Lily Jacobsen—program manager

Dear Ms. Jacobsen,

Thank you for your submission of French Kisses. *There are more than enough books and movies about naïve Americans in Paris. The world does not need one more.*

Sincerely,
The Lerner Agency

After reading the rejection letter, I went through the writer's stages of grief: disbelief that my manuscript hadn't been snatched up, an afternoon of wallowing on the futon, sucking down large quantities of chocolate, anger at the literary agency and the world at large, and finally, denial about the state of my career—there were other agents and editors to query, and I was ornery enough to write and publish the book just to prove the naysayers wrong.

Despite my trying to be chipper, deep in my soul, anguish from another rejection festered. These past weeks, Mary Louise had absented herself. I missed her, missed being able to share life's ups and downs with her, especially when word came that I got the job as the program manager.

When she returned home on the fourteenth, I was heartened—

she remembered our day. Before she could say hello, I thrust my ALP work contract under her nose. She squealed and hugged me. She set two glasses on our kitchenette table and poured the bottle of bubbly that had waited patiently in the fridge.

She raised her glass. "Just like Marcelle said, we need to celebrate the wins. Congratulations on your job!"

I loved that she talked about my favorite characters like they were real people. As we touched our rims together, I tried to tell myself that change was good. Mary Louise was only moving across town, not to a different country. And I'd be following in Odile's footsteps in a dream job. Even so, it was hard to fight the doubts. *You're a nobody. How will you ever convince big names to read at the library? Your writing isn't brilliant. Time to quit daydreaming that you'll ever be an author.* Seeing me struggle with my thoughts, Mary Louise said, "You will publish. You will."

She knew how I felt. When she'd applied for jobs, the only offer she received was from an American dental practice. She'd said accepting it felt like she was giving up her dream of showing her artwork in Paris. I insisted that she could paint on the side, and that receptionist work would be a way to improve her language skills and that her French co-workers might become friends. Over a year later, they were still just co-workers and her French still sucked. Unlike me, she'd built up a nest egg.

Mary Louise slipped her foot over mine as I signed the contract, which dictated the details: minimum wage, twenty hours a week, no overtime pay, dressing in a "*classique*" manner, and the first three months were a trial period, in which I could be fired at any time.

When I reported for duty at the welcome table, a smile illuminated the greeter's wan face. "Congratulations, Lily! I'm glad that you're the one he hired."

"Me, too." I was a little embarrassed that I hadn't caught her name.

At my desk in the back office, she gave me the lay of the open-space land. Near the window was Marius, the collection manager, a gaunt Frenchman. As he mended bindings, his papery hands moved with the grace of an orchestra conductor's. At the next desk was the secretary, Odessa, who greeted me with a distracted nod before returning to mounds of files.

"She's the one who really runs things," the greeter said.

"I thought that was me," said a tall, trim man who'd thrown open the glass door and entered from the courtyard. In a sweater vest and checkered pants, he nailed the homicidal golfer look.

"This is Lorenzo, the head librarian," she said. "He offered to help out tonight."

"'Helping out' is the library's genteel euphemism for 'work for free,'" Lorenzo said. "Meg and I will train you since the previous program manager quit on the spot."

"Quit on the spot?" I echoed. "Why?"

"Let's just say Hayes isn't the best boss," Meg replied.

"She didn't even last a year. Some people can't hack working here." Lorenzo smirked. "I'm sure it'll be different for you," he added, sounding entirely unconvinced.

On the wall behind my desk, there was an oversize, jam-packed calendar, where I would keep track of book clubs (green ink), support groups (blue ink), and Entre Nous literary events (red ink). Meg showed me examples of invitations sent to speakers, as well as the follow-up correspondence on when to arrive (6:30 p.m.) and how long they should talk (no more than forty minutes). It hit me again that I had no idea how to lure writers.

"What's the budget for an event?" I imagined that hotels and meals could get expensive.

Lorenzo snorted. "Budget!"

He explained that for tonight's event with Cal Gaige, the program manager had tracked down his French editor to find out if he'd be in Paris to promote the translation of his latest book. The publisher financed his trip and booked appearances on French television and radio; the library just asked for some of the author's time, positioning the reading as an opportunity for authors to share their work.

That didn't sound too bad.

"You must book A-listers," Lorenzo continued. "If you don't, Hayes and the trustees will be breathing down your neck. And even if you do, they'll be right behind you, second-guessing."

Meg shot him a warning glance. "Don't worry. This is an interesting job. You'll meet amazing people."

"What are some of the challenges?" I asked.

"In this role, you have to do some . . . appeasing." She measured her words carefully, the way my stepmother measured the ingredients of a complicated recipe. With care, Ellie poured flour into the measuring cup, then ran a knife over the rim to get the exact amount. No more, no less.

"And I suppose Hayes neglected to mention that the program manager must 'freshen up' the restrooms before events," Lorenzo said.

Freshen up. I frowned. In high school, I'd spent summers as a hotel maid. I didn't mind cleaning, but the unexpected return to scrubbing toilets felt like a step back.

I followed Meg to the supply closet. She knocked on the door. Did she believe the place was haunted, or that a gremlin lived inside rolls of toilet paper?

"Twice, I've walked in on the assistant director snogging the writer in residence."

A little thrown, I didn't reply. The prim quiet of a library pitted against Paris, a city renowned for its lovers. Clearly, assumptions about libraries being dull were wrong.

We each grabbed paper towels and a spray bottle of bleach. I told her she didn't need to help out, but she insisted and even let me take the women's restroom while she tidied the men's.

She suggested I get started in the reading room, that she would join me shortly. *Get started doing what?* I wondered as I headed down the hall, fingers grazing the stacks. I repeated everything I needed to retain. *Find French editors and ask them to loan us their writers. Clean the bathrooms. Knock before entering.* Now, I observed patrons working studiously at round tables and wondered where we'd store the tables during the event. Should I ask everyone to leave, like a lifeguard bellowing, "Everybody out!"? I felt submerged, as if I'd been dropped into the deep end of the library pool.

In the corner, a cute guy with book head drew my attention. In the same genus as bedhead, it's a condition caused by holding fistfuls of hair while inhaling a gripping novel, or by a long stint of studying, elbow on the desk, hand digging into the scalp, eyes on the page. Such pure concentration made me long to know what he was reading. Perhaps *One Flew over the Cuckoo's Nest*, or a translation of Camus? Squinting at the books fanned out before him, I tried to glimpse a title. He glanced up. Watching him watch me, I felt a jolt.

Lorenzo sidled up beside me. "Closing time in fifteen minutes!" he hollered way too close to my ear.

I willed Book Head to stay for tonight's event, but like most patrons, he slid his notepads and pens into his briefcase and headed out.

Meg showed me how to fold the legs of the tables and slide them into the stacks, while a wiry man moved the chairs into rows. "This is David, one of our best volunteers," she said.

He regarded me with serious brown eyes. With his button-down shirt and graying corkscrew hair, he reminded me of the steadfast men back home, the ones who volunteered on the ambulance crew. They didn't say much but were always there for folks.

"Nice to meet you," I said. "How long have you been volunteering?"

"Since I got here, two years ago. I don't know what I'd do without Meg."

I had a feeling I'd soon be saying those very words.

In a tiny kitchen, she grabbed bottles of wine and juice; I brought the napkins and plastic cups. At the refreshment stand near the entry, David sliced the Brie and baguettes on a wooden board. All in all, we created an inviting aperitif.

"Make sure volunteers serve the wine," Lorenzo advised. "You don't want attendees filling their cups to the brim themselves and getting sloshy drunk."

"And cut the Brie immediately," David added. "Last week, Mazie Chester slid a wheel of Camembert into her tote when she thought no one was looking. Rich people are weird."

At the welcome table, Meg greeted people by name and asked them to sign in.

"For statistics," Lorenzo explained to me. "We count the number of attendees. In December, you'll present a report to the trustees, and you must show that attendance improved."

"What if it doesn't?"

"Remove some names from March and add them to November," he said. "Voilà!"

The French publisher and author arrived. In a tony three-piece suit, the publisher was all smiles as he introduced Cal Gaige, a twenty-something American in jeans and plaid flannel. His eyes darted about, unable to take in everything. I could empathize—Mary Louise and I had experienced the same sensory overload when we first got to Paris. Meg and I whisked our guests to the director's office, where he shook their hands and offered them a drink. While my boss praised Cal's work, I poured wine into plastic cups. Mr. Hayes scowled and dismissed me with a curt "That will be all."

At the entry, I greeted people who strolled in. Lorenzo approached with two cups filled to the brim. Handing me one, he said, "See, there are some perks! Be grateful you can drink on the job."

I asked him what I'd done wrong in the director's office.

"Just like in airplanes, first-class donors and authors are served with wineglasses, while folks in economy are disposable—I mean, use disposable cups."

Orientation continued. He gestured to a group he called "the

Faithful," longtime residents who appreciated the fellowship of bread, wine, and books, then to a handful of young women with backpacks slung over their shoulders. Like Bambi, these were "Yearlings" from the junior year abroad program. From September to June, the reading room was their second home.

"You're looking at future Supreme Court justices," Lorenzo finished.

At exactly 7:00, Mr. Hayes escorted the author and his publisher to reserved chairs in front.

Gripping the podium, the director scowled at the empty rows of seats, then at me. I'd misjudged how many attendees there would be. To bolster the numbers, I gestured for Meg, David, and Lorenzo to join me in the back.

Mr. Hayes presented Cal Gaige, "the literary Wunderkind of the West," before adding, "The Entre Nous literary series is free and open to the public. If you appreciate fine events like these, please consider supporting the ALP by purchasing a membership. If you're already a member, consider donating."

The author adjusted the mic. His gravelly voice broke through the silence, and it seemed as though the lights dimmed. Audience members stopped fidgeting. Cal said he didn't write in the summer because he worked as a fishing guide for uptight East Coast anglers. He said that when he did write, he wrote slowly, taking his time to understand life. Glancing around, I could see we all found his words heartening. He read an excerpt set on the Going-to-the-Sun Road, which switchbacks its way to Hidden Lake. Joe, the main character, struggled with booze and solitude, but thanks to his neighbor Lacy, there was a moment of grace—both in his story and here in the reading room. The author transported us to the Rocky Mountains, where July is cold. Like Joe, we shiver and pull our denim jackets tighter. When he climbs into the pickup and revs the engine, we join him in the passenger seat. It's been a long day at work, and we're ready to go home. He eases out of the parking lot, and we bounce over the "warshboard" bumps. There is dirty snow in the ditches as we drive in the direction of the Garden Wall, a narrow ridge of rock that separates two valleys, two possible futures. With the windows rolled down, the mist of the weeping wall hits our faces. Joe confides that the spray of snowmelt reminds him of the way the priest anointed parishioners with holy water. And don't we all, somehow, want to be blessed? Farther down the road, trees line both sides of the highway. We breathe in deep. The cold air makes our lungs ache, but the smell of pine soothes us. Joe pulls up to Lacy's house. He takes a swig from his flask and passes it to us. We down the whiskey, and taste the caramel notes of regret, followed by the salty undercurrent of longing. As Joe summons the courage to talk to Lacy, we hear his lonesome heart beat. All he wants is love. All we want is love.

When Cal finished, the audience remained silent. We were mesmerized, still inside a fictional setting that felt real. And now that the story was over, we were bereft. This was what I wanted to do with my life—create worlds to give readers respite. But in the meantime, I felt gratitude for my job as program manager, for being the one to foster this joy. I clapped my hands together and other attendees joined in.

During the Q and A, they asked questions, from how nature inspires artists to tips on writing. Meg then led him to the circ desk, where the bookseller had stacked Cal's short story collections. The Faithful chatted as they stood in line to purchase a book. I bought one and asked Cal to make it out to Mary Louise. She'd appreciate his work, with its nods to Mother Nature and human nature.

At 10:00 p.m., as I bid the audience members goodbye, David stacked thirty chairs before the wall of books. In the morning, the carpet of crumbs would be vacuumed; the furniture put back in place. When I tried to pitch in, David waved me off, saying he needed the exercise. He was pretty thin. I thought he could use a good sandwich.

Lorenzo gestured to Meg and David. "Volunteers keep this sinking ship afloat. Imagine doing setup and takedown alone."

It would have taken triple the time. Maybe I could ask Mr. Hayes about organizing a volunteer appreciation day, if there wasn't one already. I peered down the hall and saw light seeping from under his office door. "Is he holed up at his desk? Doesn't he mingle with patrons?"

Lorenzo looked at me with pity. "My naïve little noodle. He's long gone. Most people don't realize it, but after his introduction, he slithers out."

He didn't stay? This seemed as sinful as a priest slipping away after communion.

"Hayes keeps the lamp on to give the impression he's burning the midnight oil," Lorenzo continued. "Probably learned the trick from his stockbroker days. Anyway, the last thing you want is Hayes trailing you, complaining that you wrapped the leftover cheese wrong."

He helped me carry the empty bottles to the recycling bin outside. Meg was already there, throwing away tonight's garbage, so the sour stench of cheese rinds and wine didn't permeate the reading room.

"Did David leave?" I asked her. "I wanted to thank him."

"He's not one for goodbyes."

Behind the circ desk, she flipped off the lights. In the dark, the stacks were eerie. I followed her and Lorenzo down the hall toward the back office exit. Above us, we heard a loud thump, like the boom of a hefty dictionary falling from a shelf and hitting the floor, our ceiling.

"What was that?" I clutched Meg's arm.

"The ghost of the countess," Lorenzo replied grimly.

"Whatever," I said.

From Odile, I knew he was referring to Clara de Chambrun, the countess from Ohio. During World War II, though she was seventy years old, she directed the library and dealt with the Nazis.

Meg shot him a look. "Don't be ridiculous."

"After the way she was treated, who can blame her for being disgruntled?" he said.

"I'm sure Clara has better things to do than haunt us," Meg replied.

We three donned our coats and stepped into the pitch-black courtyard. While she locked the door, Lorenzo said, "In all seriousness, there is one patron you have to be careful of."

Meg handed me the key. I took it, but she held tight.

"Yes," she said. "Lorenzo's right. Watch out for Mike Roth. He's dangerous."

~

A week later, it was moving day. Mary Louise had packed her clothes, paintings, and art supplies. She bequeathed me her books—too heavy to carry—and her first watercolor of the Eiffel Tower, which had graced our wall since the day we moved in. The painting was my prized possession. Growing up on the plains, often feeling like an outsider in my own family and longing for my life to begin, la Tour Eiffel had been my beacon, my lighthouse, a solemn promise that things could be different. And things were different, just not in the way I'd expected.

Her life fit into two suitcases (one mine, one hers), which we lugged to the métro station, down the steps, and into the carriage. She was moving eight stops away, the farthest we'd ever lived from each other.

When we entered her new place, I stared at the marble fireplace, at the pristine white couch that I would swear no one had ever sat on, at the gold drapes that framed the windows, where an easel faced the Luxembourg Garden, my favorite park. This was prime real estate. Faulkner had stayed in this neighborhood on a visit. John Travolta and his wife had honeymooned here. How could Mary Louise afford it on her own? Earlier, I'd pressed for details, but she'd remained vague, saying it had good light and was closer to work. In fact, her apartment was three times the size of ours. Did she have a different, better roommate? Was she shacking up with some guy? I thought she wanted to live alone so she could paint. I didn't understand. Anger simmered inside me and moved from my belly up my throat to my brain. I could no longer think, no longer speak. I stared at her with my mouth open.

"I'm getting a deal on rent," she rushed to say. "This apartment belongs to a patient. Well, a patient's mother. She's getting up in years and can't travel, so it sits empty."

The explanation reassured me. On evening strolls, we glimpsed many shuttered windows. Tons of foreigners bought pieds-à-terre, used for two weeks per year. It saddened us that the apartments went to waste. Of course, we couldn't help but think that their owners had so much while we were crammed into a studio. At least now, one of those homes would be filled with life.

Mary Louise saw me to the door. I felt panicked at leaving her, at being alone.

"Can I treat you to dinner to celebrate?" I asked.

"I need to unpack."

"How about a reading at the library? Every Wednesday. Promise you'll come."

She regarded me without blinking. In her Psych 101 class, she'd learned that liars don't make eye contact, so when she fibbed, she met your gaze with a weird intensity.

"Soon." She closed the door gently in my face.

Chapter 5

FEBRUARY 1995

Marius Moreau—collection manager

Parisian born and bred, I assure you that the best time to visit is August—inhabitants leave and the city becomes an oasis where you can traipse along empty boulevards. The rest of the time, it's a nightmare of jackhammers and honking horns, of narrow sidewalks overrun by people elbowing their way past. When you cross the street to escape them, taxis speed up to mow you down. My daily commute is an obstacle course.

Libraries are the only place I've ever felt safe. Working in one is all I've ever wanted. I crave the quiet of books, their promise of calm. In grade school, the other boys taunted me. "Petit Marius, pale and frail!" When I stood up for myself, they chortled, "Listen to the baby wail." During recess, they shouted and laughed as they played with marbles; I assisted the librarian, a serene man who seemed to hold the answers of the universe in his dappled hands. The silence was a refuge, a relief.

After graduating from lycée with *mention très bien*, I attended France's prestigious École Nationale des Chartes for librarians and archivists. I was the top of my class. The other students came to me for answers, that is, until the exit exam—an oral Q and A before a three-man jury. My classmates and I learned about books—which to buy; how to catalog them; techniques to repair them—but never how to communicate or give presentations. The whole reason I chose library work was to avoid people.

On that fated day, in a stately room with engraved paneling, I was alone with the trio of elderly archivists. They remained quiet as they sized me up. For the first time in my life, silence felt oppressive. To stop myself from fidgeting, I laced my fingers together, hands folded as if in prayer. Perhaps subconsciously, I was begging: like me, pick me, want me.

Finally, the one with the bushy white mustache asked a question.

Perspiration trickled down my sides. I blinked hard to keep my tears from falling. I'd never felt so alone, so vulnerable. I couldn't speak. The words stuck in my brain and couldn't be forced out. Even today, I cannot remember how I got out of that room—did they dismiss me, did I leave of my own accord?

In those days, there were no second chances, no reprieves. Words failed me. Or I failed myself. Without this diploma, no Parisian *bibliothèque* would hire me. Though I don't recall the questions, that feeling of helplessness, of having my fate in the hands of others is seared into my soul.

Needing to pay the rent, I accepted a job as a cashier. I was pitiful, feeling my bookish knowledge was wasted as I rang up yogurt and toilet paper. Beside me, my co-worker—a Slav with ivory skin, whose nobility was in her every gesture, from the way her slim fingers counted back change to how she disregarded smarmy customers who mocked her accent—ordered me to stop pouting. No job is beneath us, she insisted. Later, I learned that Anna was a Russian countess who'd lost everything during the Revolution. She'd started over in France without a centime to her name.

At an employee Christmas party, after hours in the superette, she introduced me to her husband, Boris, the head librarian at the ALP. I inquired about a position. He admitted it wasn't easy to work with Americans; however, the director there felt that ability was as important as diplomas. When he hired me as the collection manager, I nearly wept in relief.

Ever since my inauguration, January 20, 1961, which I shared with John F. Kennedy, I've selected the works that grace the ALP's shelves. To find the latest, I attend book fairs in Frankfurt, London, and Bologna. To find the best, I look no further than our reading room, where I help local authors with research. Their biggest fan, I cheer them on from the sidelines of the stacks. For years, they write and edit before sending their ideas into the world—that is to say, to editors in New York and London. Together, the budding authors and I count the days until the responses come. My favorite part of my job is seeing the hope in their eyes. I'm as excited as they are; I want their books on my shelves. Unfortunately, much of the time, the response is a form rejection letter. Some writers persevere, sending to the next editor on the list; others become too demoralized to continue. There's a certain sadness when a writer gives up, when a dream dies.

I remember too well the stain of failure, that crippling helplessness when others decide you, or your work, is not good enough. I wanted to shield writers from that feeling. Six months into my job, I knew I needed to act—to honor the writers, pay tribute to their talent. Frankly, some manuscripts can be more intense, more raw than published books, which may have had their rough edges sanded off.

My collection started thirty-five years ago, with a library patron's cracking account of Bricktop. Have you by chance heard of the Black nightclub owner and chanteuse who sang her way from saloons in Chicago to Prohibition Harlem to Café Society in Paris? Born Ada Beatrice Queen Victoria Louise Virginia Smith, she was called Bricktop because of her flaming red hair. F. Scott Fitzgerald immortalized her nightclub in his short story "Babylon Revisited": "He passed a lighted door from which issued music, and stopped with the sense of familiarity; it was Bricktop's, where he had parted with so many hours and so much money."

She was a darling of Cole Porter, the renowned composer, who tested his songs in her club. When World War II broke out, she volunteered in soup kitchens organized by Elsie de Wolfe, Lady Mendl (credited as the first interior designer in America) and Wallis, the Duchess of Windsor (credited with inspiring a king to abdicate for love). Later, these friends used their clout to procure a ticket on one of the last ships leaving France, helping Bricktop to escape the Nazis.

After thirty rejections, the biographer chucked the manuscript into the reading room bin. I scooped the chapters out—Bricktop's story deserved to be saved. I bound the pages and laid them in a blue box tied with a white ribbon—a gift for discerning readers. In the Afterlife, I cleared a wall for the manuscript and added photos of the chanteuse as well as a vintage dress by Edward Molyneux, who dressed Bricktop along with Vivien Leigh and Marlene Dietrich.

One day, I found the biographer beaming at the exhibit. By then, we'd become friends.

"I can't believe it," Jim said. "You made my dream come true."

I never intended to create a collection—my initial aim was to support locals. I helped several finish their novels. Jim persisted and got the biography published. He even borrowed my exhibit for his book tour. He insisted he couldn't have continued without my encouragement. Buoyed by his appreciation, I asked a few patrons to consider writing their own stories. Don't we all have secret depths? And different reasons for living in Paris? The Afterlife contains a shelf of memoirs.

Now, a more ambitious goal—to help writers all over the world, and to acquire a manuscript from every country for the Afterlife. I recently ran an ad in the *London Review of Books* asking writers to send their best work. Each unpublished story is fascinating, whether it describes farming in 1910 Nebraska or raising thirteen children in Naples in the 1950s. Naturally, my favorite is the war journal of Margaret Bauer.

Chapter 6

MARCH 1995

Lily Jacobsen—program manager

Dear Odile,

I'm following in your footsteps at the ALP! There's something special about having a key—I feel a thrill each time I unlock the door. Many Parisians' favorite stroll is among the trees of the Tuileries, but I prefer the path from my desk, past the rows of stacks, to the reading room. At the Xerox machine behind the circ desk, I parse out photocopies as an excuse to people-watch. My timing is chosen—when the head librarian skulks off to smoke. He hates it when staff use "his" photocopier.

Each workday is as unique as a sunrise; I watch the library, drowsy at first, awaken. Not unlike zombies, staff roll in through the inner courtyard to the back office. The collection manager starts the percolator, and soon the scent of crisp newspaper pages competes with the coffee in our mugs. Early bird patrons are greeted with a warm bonjour from the volunteer at the welcome table. Students in flannel shirts and Doc Martens amble into the reading room, and I can't help but gawk at Book Head, the boy I like. He has soulful gray eyes, and I want to know everything about him, from his job to his favorite book. Is he an architect or an art historian? French or foreign? Parisian or just passing through?

At my desk, I scour forthcoming titles in French publishers' catalogs to glean which "big names" will promote their books on French radio and television. It's like looking into the future—Amy Bloom and Cristina García will be in Paris in June. On elegant stationery with the ALP motto—"From the darkness of war, the light of books," I send letters to their editors, begging them to loan us their authors. I'm psyched to create my own list of speakers!

At our Entre Nous series, you meet folks from all walks of life, people who in normal circumstances would not cross paths. Millionaires and starving students, nuns and book thieves. I adore the Faithful, my own habitués who attend every event, like the Coolidges from Kent, a delightful retired couple, the first in the neighborhood to install solar panels and a garden on their building rooftop. And a more recent arrival, a redhead like Mary Louise, who everyone calls Tolstoy, probably because he's often reading the Russian novelist. A Gulf War vet, he suffers from PTSD; loud voices and noises startle him. He said he appreciates the ALP because he can count on the calm.

Moi aussi, I adore the sighs of students as they peruse the job bulletin board near the entrance; the squeaky wheel of the book cart; the head librarian shushing a patron who forgot herself and raved to a stranger about her favorite mystery series; the scrape of pencil on paper—it sounds like oui-oui-oui. During my lunch break, I try to capture Paris on paper and hope that one day I, too, will give a talk here.

Don't you miss the city? Will you ever come back? Please write! I want to know how you're doing.

Love,
Lily

I didn't tell Odile that Mary Louise moved out. It hurt too much.

To distract from the pain, I threw myself into my new role. Since Mr. Hayes wanted to host "big names," that's what I focused on and wrote to dozens of editors. Wanting to get everything right, I'd asked his opinion on the publicity material that I created for story hour or Entre Nous events.

He glanced at it. "Chill out. The world doesn't revolve around your posters." Then he looked closer. "Is this . . ." His nose wrinkled in distaste. "Garamond?"

"I thought an updated font would be better."

"Georgia is the only acceptable font."

"It sounds like your favorite song might be 'Georgia on My Mind,'" I gently teased, hoping to create a rapport.

"Is that some kind of joke? Because changing fonts isn't funny. You must respect the rules. Documents must be uniform and professional!"

Each morning, on my desk, I found his complaints in Sharpie scrawl. On Monday, he'd left me a Piccadilly Books events flyer. On John Irving's headshot, he'd written "WHY CAN'T YOU GET A BIG NAME LIKE THIS?" I hadn't even known the author was in Paris and felt terrible for letting the library down.

The mail arrived early each morning, and I hovered near Meg at the entrance, eager to parse the hefty stack of magazines, ads, and bills, hoping for a letter from one of the French editors I'd contacted. It took almost two weeks to receive my first response, an envelope with the raised logo of a prestigious publisher. This could be it, the first famous author who would speak here, sharing her path to publication and her ideas about the world. Maybe Mr. Hayes would finally be satisfied.

Now, I pulled the letter from the envelope. *Dear Mademoiselle Jacobsen, Many thanks for your interest in having Amy Bloom speak. Unfortunately, you are too late. Her week here is fully accounted for, between her appearances at literary festivals and on the television show* La Grande Librairie. *We wish you every success. Sincerely, Folio publishers*

I swallowed. I'd really gotten my hopes up—since I loved the library, I assumed everyone else would, too. Maybe I should have called the editor. Maybe I aimed too high. I consoled myself with the fact that a dozen other responses were on the way. There was still time to book amazing authors. I would show Mr. Hayes that I could do the job, that I could be successful at something.

Despite the stress, I was enjoying learning the ropes. My first weeks were a swirl of patrons, gossip, and unwritten rules. This afternoon, as I stood behind the circ desk at the photocopier, two warring book club leaders confronted me.

"As the longest-running book club, we deserve dibs on the conference room!" Marge from Better Off Read Mysteries argued.

"My group has always met there," Don from A-Politics Now shot back.

They inched closer, and I retreated, until my back was pressed against the control panel.

Returning from his cigarette break, Lorenzo glowered at us. He snapped his fingers and pointed to the Front Line. Marge and Don retreated to the strip of duct tape positioned a foot from the circ desk. Lorenzo claimed that the sliver of silver guaranteed confidentiality while patrons checked out books, but really, it was to keep them at a distance.

Far from loved ones and navigating a foreign country, many patrons—and staff—were homesick and touchy. Book club bickering was an example of little things taking on great importance. I proposed a noon time slot to Marge, sweetening the deal with unlimited wine; she accepted. The book club leaders both thanked me and returned to their groups. I loved getting to know patrons, and finding solutions to these daily dustups was so satisfying. Maybe this was the difference from my previous job—most folks here were appreciative of my efforts.

Unfortunately, staff couldn't solve every problem. Our computers were a big source of contention. The ALP had only two for public use: Gertrude and Ernest (named after the Lost Generation icons, and about as old). Each had a five-day waiting list for a thirty-minute session. Just now, one of our tween users was finishing up a few minutes late; the next patron, a stocky bald man, pointed to his watch and shouted, "Can't you tell time?"

The girl's chin began to tremble as she tried to log out.

Photocopies in hand, I rushed over. Meg migrated from the welcome table and told the man to apologize.

"She should apologize for wasting my time!" he responded.

At that, Lorenzo strode over. "Emma, there's no rush." Arms akimbo, he went from dandy to bouncer in three seconds flat. "I've had about enough of you, Roth."

So this was the guy they'd warned me about at my first Entre Nous event.

"Apologize or leave," Lorenzo said.

"Whatever." Roth stalked off.

"Are you okay, Em?" Meg asked.

She nodded.

"If he bothers you again, yell good and loud," Lorenzo said.

The idea of yelling in a library made her giggle.

"Atta girl!" He tugged gently on the hood of her sweatshirt. "Grab some candy from my drawer."

"The good stuff?" she asked.

"You know it," he replied.

The three of us watched her pick out a chocolate.

"How long has Roth been a problem?" I asked.

Aware of nearby patrons, Meg and Lorenzo inched closer.

"Forever," he said in a low tone. "Each semester, he hits on the new crop of Yearlings who study here. He's the kind of guy who doesn't accept no as an answer. Last term, he cornered one and threatened her, so I filed a complaint with the cops."

"They said that until he attacks someone, there's nothing they can do." Meg shook her head.

Some things were the same all over.

"You!" The word—an accusation—brought us from our huddle.

Across the room, near the entrance, a blonde aimed her Louis Vuitton clutch at me like a gun. Not *a* blonde. *The* blonde, the one I'd kicked in the shin. "I know you," she said, her tone equal parts curiosity and irritation at not being able to place me.

I held the photocopies to my chest like a shield and waited for the past to catch up with me.

"How does she know you?" Lorenzo demanded in a hushed library hiss.

I didn't want to admit the truth.

"How does *she* know *you*?" he repeated, as if inquiring how Princess Diana had become acquainted with a bus station cockroach.

"We've never met," I hedged.

Meg regarded me thoughtfully. "You mean you've never been formally introduced."

Of course she saw through my prevarication.

"Jennifer de Narp is a trustee and one of our biggest donors," she continued.

A trustee? She could probably get me fired. And should get me fired. What had I been thinking? I lifted the photocopies to my chin to shroud my face and prayed she wouldn't recognize me.

"Did you hear the 'de' in her name?" Lorenzo asked. "That denotes French nobility. Her husband's family owns a vineyard. And she's a lawyer who comes from a long line of Texas D.A.s. The kind who demand the death penalty."

The trustee squinted at me as she came closer. I could practically see her scroll through the Rolodex of her mind: *A friend's niece? My accountant's secretary?* She barely noticed when Mr. Hayes greeted her. He followed her gaze to me, puzzled. The director could not envision a scenario in which a trustee would be interested in a lowly program manager.

"I never forget a face," she said.

"Perhaps you met at a county fair in her native Wyoming?" Mr. Hayes said as he smirked.

Ms. de Narp slapped on a brittle smile. How many times had I worn that same mask when dealing with condescending professors and patronizing boyfriends? She surely resented the way he dismissed her intuition—after all, she was right. For my part, I was aware that his crack meant he considered me a country-bumpkin nobody. He couldn't even remember where I was from.

"There's a lot on the agenda," she told him frostily. "Let's get to it."

Mr. Hayes escorted her to his office. After his door clicked shut, I loosened my grip on the photocopies.

"Lily, you're so pale!" Meg said.

"It's nothing. I'm fine." I just wanted to put the unfortunate sidewalk encounter behind me.

Lorenzo raised a brow. "There's definitely a story here. You know Jennifer de Narp. And she knows you. Spill."

"Fine!" I said. "I kicked that woman."

"You kicked a trustee?" For the first time, respect edged out the bitterness in his tone.

"Why would you do such a thing?" Meg asked.

"She threw her cigarette onto the sidewalk and expected some poor street sweeper to pick up after her."

I waited for them to tell me that I was crazy for attacking a stranger. Instead, Meg chuckled.

"Lots of us want to kick trustees," Lorenzo admitted.

"But we don't," Meg said firmly.

"When Jennifer de Narp figures out how she knows you," Lorenzo finished, "she'll fire you faster than you can say 'au revoir.'"

~

Preparing for Entre Nous events was like throwing a party and not knowing if ten or a hundred people would attend. Tonight, when David asked how many chairs to put out, I felt optimistic and suggested forty. Near the door, I stood poised, the toe of my loafer on my favorite ink splotch, which I viewed as a starting block. I kept my eyes peeled for the speaker, a garden expert who'd been invited by the previous program manager, and I imagined an older woman with a sun-kissed face, like the church ladies back home who tended vegetable plots. While sizing up attendees and trying to figure out which was the speaker, I reminded them to sign in—I was already nervous about my year-end statistics.

A woman in a pink pantsuit approached. "I'm Vicki Williams. Thank you for the invitation."

"Welcome! We're thrilled to have you." Taking in her ashen complexion and stick arms, I wondered how she could be known as the "Garden Lady."

"Wait until the end of my presentation before you make such declarations," she said with a friendly wink.

I escorted her to the director's office, where Mr. Hayes introduced her to the Select Few, the library's biggest donors. Three women wore blazes of diamonds; their husbands sported zingy Hermès ties. I lingered in the hope that they'd talk to me. Finally, one did.

"Get the Bordeaux." Mr. Hayes pointed toward the kitchen.

After serving the elite—in wineglasses this time—I resumed my post near the front door.

A brunette charged past. I asked her to sign in.

"Do you know who I am?" She strode to Mr. Hayes's office.

David handed me a cup of wine. "That's Pam de Laney. You'll live longer and happier if you identify the trustees and stay out of their way. Jennifer de Narp is here as well."

I committed Pam to memory—bloodred nails, Birkin bag, rude as hell. And Jennifer I already knew too well.

At seven, only fifteen of the chairs had been filled. Before David and I could discreetly remove a few, Mr. Hayes arrived with the speaker and introduced her to the sparse audience, glaring at me the entire time. I felt incompetent.

But sure enough, Ms. Williams worked her magic, and I left my worries behind as she recounted the life of Marguerite Chapin, an

American who became Marguerite Gilbert Caetani, Princess of Bassiano, Duchess of Sermoneta, when she married an aristocrat in 1911. From the last row, I admired the series of slides illustrating Ninfa, Italy's most lush, romantic garden. Wanting to leave her mark, the duchess planted two hundred rosebushes on her husband's estate. None survived longer than six months. Completely transported, I scribbled in my notebook. *What's the lesson? That desire is not enough? More research, and less obsession? Passion is nothing without knowledge?*

At the end of the presentation, the trustees Jennifer de Narp and Pam de Laney approached and snapped me out of Ninfa's spell.

"Did something happen to the bookseller?" Jennifer asked. "Where are Vicki's books? We all want signed copies."

"Signed copies?" I repeated weakly. I'd assumed that the previous program manager had contacted the bookseller for events she'd organized, but I should have doubled-checked.

"Of course! There should always be books on hand at Entre Nous *literary* events."

"How could you make such a mistake?" Pam de Laney hissed. "You've made the library look incompetent."

"I'm sorry, I—"

"Save it." The trustees stalked over to the Faithful, who loitered near the circ desk, where the bookseller would have set up shop. Seeing them exit empty-handed, I apologized to Vicki Williams, who replied with a stilted "It's fine."

I felt awful. She'd given us such a wonderful gift with her presentation, and I'd ruined her evening.

Meg offered to stay and help close, but I wanted to be alone. Well, what I really wanted was for Mary Louise to console me, but that wasn't possible. Since the move, I hadn't seen her once. I flicked off the lights. On my way down the darkened corridor, wine in hand, I thought I heard the raspy sound of someone breathing. Ghostly moonlight shone through the reading room windows, filling the stacks with shadows. There were plenty of dark corners for lurkers to hide. I tried to shake off Meg's warning about Mike Roth.

At my desk, I entered the statistics:

Date: **March 19**
Program: **Entre Nous**
Attendance: **18 (if you include David, Meg, and me)**
Books sold: **0**
Bottles of wine opened: **8**
Glasses drunk by me: **4**

Chapter 7

MARCH 1995

Felicity Jenner—library member

My family and I have lived in Paris for nine months. Miranda, a friend from my Oxford days, was the twelfth guest we've had. Back in Manchester, no one came to visit in all our two years. But when you move to Paris, suddenly you're everyone's best friend. Or, as my daughter, Ellen, quipped, it's not so much BFF as a free B and B.

Miranda's gold bracelets jangled against her wrist as she pointed to the Eiffel Tower through my window. "What a view!" she gushed. "Your flat is amazing. How did you decide to move to France?"

"Franklin and I knew that a foreign language would give Ellen a step up on the uni application process," I replied.

The truth, not that I ever admitted it, was this: ten months ago, Franklin came home from work, with no phone call to let us know he'd be an hour late. Over dinner, he announced that we were moving. No discussion. Just his decision based on what was best for his career.

Of course, poor Ellen, who'd just turned seventeen, had been miserable at the idea of leaving her friends. I tried to soothe her, but learning French and starting over once again were daunting. Then I realized that I'd be starting over, too. Goodbye, England. Goodbye, family. Goodbye, garden.

"Get good grades," I'd told Ellen with each change of country, each new school. "You're going to uni, and you won't ever depend upon a man."

The evening of the announcement, as Franklin and I got ready for bed, he tugging off his tie, I turning down the counterpane, he informed me that we'd be leaving in a month and that he expected me to deal with "details," such as selling our home and packing up our life.

Franklin had never said "thank you" for organizing our relocation across the Channel, which entailed parsing a dozen bids from moving companies and perusing a hundred listings to find a perfect flat within walking distance of his work, across the Seine to his office on posh Avenue Montaigne. Nor did he show appreciation for the breakfast of eggs and bacon that I prepared for him, and only him, since Ellen and I preferred lighter fare. I'm certain he never acknowledged his assistant, either. She and I were compensated to make his schedule run smoothly—she in francs; I with room, board, and jewelry on my birthday (certainly picked out by said assistant).

This was the lot of the executive's wife, the trailing spouse. Franklin would never put it so crassly, but in his mind, it's *My money, my choice*. What Ellen and I wanted didn't signify, which is why we'd lived in Tokyo, Toronto, and Manchester. With each move, Franklin kept the same job and colleagues, but Ellen and I started from scratch. I'd considered divorcing him. Who doesn't occasionally fantasize about leaving their spouse behind? But in the end, I decided I couldn't do that to my daughter. I worried it would break Ellen's heart if her father and I separated.

Recently the three of us had organized a visit to Oxford, where Ellen would start in the autumn. I was looking forward to giving them a tour, and Ellen was excited for her first college visit. Only as usual, Franklin canceled at the last moment. A merger needed his attention.

We tried not to let it bother us. At dinner in an Italian restaurant, I ordered myself a bottle of Chianti. Ellen stabbed at her spaghetti.

"Mum, aren't you tired of living on his timetable?"

"I am, a bit."

"He never keeps his promises to us. He's never around. I hope you haven't stayed for me."

She's perceptive, my Ellen.

Not wanting her to see the truth in my expression, I bent my head and busied myself with cutting my lasagna. "I stayed for both of us."

"You deserve to live your own life."

She reached across the table and hugged me so fiercely. I tear up just thinking about it.

My friend Miranda was right about one thing, though: our view was spectacular. The flat I'd found, built for the 1889 World Fair, was marvelous—gorgeous moldings and a fireplace in each room. Living in Paris should have been a dream come true, but too often, the flat felt too big and too empty. Friends visited for a week, then returned to England. And my life? I'd splurged on a bottle of real French champagne to toast our move to the city of romance, but Franklin always said he was too busy or too tired. I sent cards to family, but they rarely responded. While Ellen was in class, I took French lessons, one-on-one torture for me and the tutor, a chain-smoker who corrected my mistakes before they were all the way out of my mouth.

The one positive was my weekly trek to the ALP. I first visited to see if they had bilingual study guides for Ellen and me. Once I was inside, nostalgia hit me—the gentle thump of the date stamp hitting a book, the murmur of friendship, books in cellophane gleaming on the new arrivals shelf, spider plants hanging from macramé holders, all things tended and cherished. It brought me back not just to the years I took baby Ellen to story hour but to my own childhood and treasured memories with Mum.

This time, as I loaded up on books (*Cold Comfort Farm, A Tree*

Grows in Brooklyn, and my two Trollopes—Anthony and Joanna), Meg, a fellow Londoner, urged me to volunteer and tucked an application form into *The Warden.* In the moment, I suspected she wanted a fellow Brit around, but later I saw that it was more than that: Meg had a sixth sense for what people needed.

At home, I began to fill out the form. Under the line for profession, I put "lawyer," though I hadn't practiced since we left England the first time, back when Ellen was a baby. Under volunteer work, I put "development," since I'd been active in raising funds for a nature conservancy and a local theater. I wondered what kind of role I could play here.

Chapter 8

APRIL 1995

Lily Jacobsen—program manager

Dearest Lily,

Congratulations on your new job! I hope that you will love it there as much as I did. Have you gotten to know Book Head? What's his favorite novel? And did you hear back from any French editors? I'm keeping my fingers crossed for you. Of course, I know exactly what you mean about squabbling patrons. I used to joke that I needed a whistle to referee my favorite habitués, Mr. Pryce-Jones and M. de Nerciat. And speaking of refereeing, your brothers and I are reading one of your old favorites, Bridge to Terabithia. *If they aren't fighting over the last cookie, they're kicking each other under the table. No matter, I love discussing books with them the way I used to do with you. Joe confided that he bawled at the end of the book; Brumby admitted that he found his own Terabithia, his own haven, in reading.*

It's been a while since you've written about Mary Louise. Is everything all right? I miss hearing about your adventures together. They remind me of the lovely times I had with my best friend—teas at the embassy, long talks in the Tuileries. Please do write! Rereading your letters about your visits to the café with the stern waiter and your strolls along the Seine makes me feel like I'm with you. I confess that the way you describe the city makes me long to visit. Of course, I miss you, but with everything that happened during the war, I never thought I'd miss Paris—proof that you have a way with words.

Keep at it, and soon, you'll be a Published Author with your own Dewey Decimal Number.

All my love,
Odile

At the mention of the boys, a pang of homesickness hit me as hard as a punch to the gut. When I'd moved to France, I'd only considered what I would be getting, not what I would be giving up—time with Odile, my dad and Ellie, and my little brothers. Living with Mary Louise had kept those thoughts at bay, partly because she was an important piece of home, and partly because we were so busy that I didn't have time to think about loved ones we'd left behind. Now, an uncomfortable quiet had set in. No more Friday night drinks with Mary Louise to celebrate the end of the week. No more lazy Saturday mornings listening to her hum as she prepared the café au lait to accompany our croissants. No one bounded in after a Saturday night date, giddy that she'd met *the one*. No more tears after a breakup with Pierre or Edouard. Now it was my turn to sob. She'd broken up with me, and I didn't understand why.

I'd left messages on her machine. I waited for her to call me, but the telephone remained stubbornly silent. I imagined Mary Louise sketching, so focused that she didn't see the weeks pass. Was she getting enough to eat? Sleeping enough? I rang her at work—as a receptionist, her job was to take calls. When she proposed a quick lunch, I couldn't help but feel like a difficult patient she was placating.

At a bistro equidistant between our jobs, we asked for tap water and ordered the cheapest thing on the menu—omelets. From our table near the kitchen door, we could hear the whisks whirling in the pots. Now that I had to cover rent on my own, meals out were no longer things I could afford. But I couldn't refuse her invitation, afraid another wouldn't be forthcoming.

Mary Louise started to speak, but I was bursting with stories about my job. "You wouldn't believe my morning. Today, we had the W.E.s and E.W.E.s."

"The wes and yous?" she echoed.

I explained that support groups like the Wives of Executives and Ex-Wives of Executives met weekly in the conference room.

"I accidentally double-booked it, and the W.E.s almost came to blows with E.W.E.s. Some are big donors, and when they feel slighted, they go straight to my boss. He's not too happy with me."

On the weekend, off the clock, instead of working on my novel, I spent hours perfecting our publicity materials. During the week, before bed, I penned a list of everything I had to do the following day so I wouldn't get bawled out. At night, I lay wide awake, Mr. Hayes's intro rattling in my head like an annoying jingle I couldn't shake: *The Entre Nous literary series is free and open to the public. If you appreciate fine events like these, please consider supporting the ALP by purchasing a membership. If you're already a member, consider donating.*

Now, in the hope that Mary Louise might attend a reading, I handed her the Hayes-approved events calendar. I waited for her to say something nice. Maybe *Great use of negative space* or *Perfect description of the book.* Instead, she shoved it in her purse.

When our omelets came, we scarfed them down in silence. I wanted to prove that this distance between us wasn't real, wanted her to care where I spent my days. When she'd started at the dentist's office, over a year ago now, she'd been glum, like the job was an admission she might not become an *artiste.* Needing to know she was okay, I'd paid a visit. At the sterile white counter, I claimed I had a toothache. To make it appear real to the hygienist listening in, I rubbed my jaw and groaned. Mary Louise swatted me away with a laugh. Or what I'd thought was a laugh. Maybe I'd embarrassed her. Anyway, I'd gone to see her, why wouldn't she pop by the library?

"Come check out the cute guy I drool over. I call him Book Head."

"I'm not getting sucked into 'Lily-land,'" I thought I heard her mumble.

"What?"

"Nothing." She rose from the table and grabbed the frayed strap of her pleather purse. "I should head back."

"You barely said two words."

"As usual, you didn't let me talk."

As usual? Had I been a bad friend? "Sorry. I was excited to share. Stay. What's going on with you?"

She sank onto her seat. "I've met someone."

I hoped he was better than her latest ex, Dave, the lead singer of a punk band who insisted that Picasso didn't paint, he "drew weirdness." In the same vein, I didn't consider Dave's profanity-laced shouting to be music. When the three of us went out, he refused to pay for his drinks. I jokingly asked Mary Louise if he picked up that trait from Picasso, expecting her to laugh, but she slugged me. Hard.

"Where?" I asked.

"At work. I squeezed him in when he showed up with a broken tooth. That was on a Monday. On Tuesday, he sent me a thank-you bouquet. On Wednesday, he invited me to la Belle Époque."

"Wow." I'd never been to a Michelin-starred restaurant before. "What's it like?"

"There was a wall of bloodred orchids. The maître d' hit a button, and the ceiling opened. Suddenly, we were eating by the light of the moon."

Taking in the enormity of her experience, neither of us spoke. By law, French restaurants had to display their menus outside, so I knew that two bites of salad at La Belle Époque cost thirty bucks and that five shrimp cost fifty. Much of Paris was off limits because it was impossibly expensive. And Mary Louise had finally gotten to taste the forbidden.

"I'll always remember every bite," she said wistfully.

"Enough about the food! Tell me about the guy."

She didn't answer right away. Maybe I'd been judgmental in the past, but I was only looking out for her. This time, I promised myself I wouldn't comment.

"His name is Antoine. He's mature . . ."

Mature meant paunchy. And possibly married.

"He owns his own company."

A fossil from the geriatris era.

I was trying to keep it together, but I must have made a face, because she became defensive.

"I'm sick of guys our age who want to split the bill or eat at a crepe stand. I want to be spoiled for a change."

I put my foot over hers. "You deserve the best."

"This could really go somewhere."

We'd been through many tenuous beginnings together. I felt a rush of love for her. My best friend. I prayed things would work out.

"When do I get to meet him?" I asked.

"When you can keep your opinions to yourself." She gestured for the bill. "You sound stressed. I hope you're not upset that I left you in the lurch."

I chugged my water to buy time to think up a decent answer. The truth was, I couldn't afford the heat bill. When I complained about the cold during my weekly Sunday phone call home, my father sent me a pair of long johns. I wore them even in bed and reminded myself that Simone de Beauvoir wrote in her ski outfit during the war because her Paris pad was freezing. I'd added three more teens to my Saturday tutoring roster, which was an additional sixty bucks a week. To save on food, I gobbled down Brie on baguettes during events.

"It's all good," I promised. "Like most starving artists, I'm paying my writing dues."

~

After lunch, I entered the library through the front door, where Meg greeted me with an envelope with gold foil borders. It was from Gallomart, France's most prestigious publishing house. Their logo and return address were printed in elegant embossed lettering. My name was written in calligraphy. It seemed too fancy to be a form rejection. I braced myself. Please, please, please.

Dear Mademoiselle Jacobsen,

Thank you for your interest in our illustrious author Richard Ford. We had no idea that there even was an American Library in Paris. It sounds quite quaint. Nonetheless, Gallomart already has an exclusive, long-standing partnership with the international, esteemed Piccadilly Books.

Sincerely,
The editorial department at
Gallomart Publishers

"Well?" Meg asked.

I shook my head.

"Next time," she said.

It was hard not to despair. I wanted to wad up the rejection, but it was proof that I was trying. I would add it to my stack. I reminded myself that I couldn't control editors' responses, and could only do my best.

To cheer myself up, I peeked into the reading room and felt a burst of happiness at seeing Book Head, his chestnut hair sticking up adorably. Mary Louise had a boyfriend; soon, so would I. Wending between tables, I handed out event flyers as an excuse to approach. Spread out before him, I spied a slew of Texas guidebooks.

"Planning a trip?" I shot for flirtatious, but instead sounded like an overexcited travel agent.

"Not anytime soon. Just dreaming, I guess." He spoke with a slight accent. Why does English sound better when it's spoken by a French person?

"Maybe you should aim higher."

He crossed his arms. "You're criticizing my dream?"

"I didn't mean to." Too often, my mouth worked faster than my brain. "I meant aim due north . . . to Montana. The Rocky Mountains and Yellowstone National Park."

Why was I trying to sell the place I'd left without a backward glance?

"I bet it's stunning," he said. "Is that where you're from?"

"Yes. We have one million cows and eight hundred thousand people. You have space to think. Folks there are kind." A pang of longing hit me. I missed my little brothers, dad, and stepmom. Not wanting to become maudlin, I continued, "You know the song 'The Yellow Rose of Texas'? It was originally 'The Marigold of Montana.' The songwriter bowed to peer pressure."

"Why don't I believe you?" There was a tinge of warm humor in his tone.

"If you don't believe me, ask John Steinbeck. 'I am in love with Montana. For other states I have admiration, respect, recognition, even some affection, but with Montana it is love.'"

He side-eyed me. "Did Steinbeck really write that?"

I held up my hand. "Scout's honor. In *Travels with Charley*."

"Did he spend time in Texas?"

"He did, but if you want Texas, try *The Liars' Club*. It's equal parts hilarious and heartbreaking; it's the story of a family, but also of a time and place."

He nodded as I spoke. "I'll check it out. My name's Christophe, by the way. You can call me Chris. Like Kris Kristofferson, my favorite songwriter."

"I'm Lily."

From the circ desk, Lorenzo gave us the shut-up-you're-in-a-library stink eye.

I wasn't the only one who felt the Sicilian death stare. "I guess we need to be quiet," Chris whispered, "but I'd love to continue our conversation. Want to grab dinner sometime?"

"Absolument!"

"Friday at seven? Meet you here?"

"Oui!" There weren't enough exclamation points in the library's books to express my excitement.

At my desk, Mr. Hayes lay in wait, a crumpled piece of paper in his hand. His suit was rumpled, as if he'd slept in it, yet his face was haggard, as if he hadn't slept at all. "Why can't you book real authors like Saul Bellow, Richard Ford, or Pat O'Malley?" he demanded. "Every week, Piccadilly hosts Pulitzer Prize winners. The only writers you manage to find are locals. Low-hanging fruit, rotting on our branch."

Should I mention that speakers had been booked months in advance by my predecessor? And by "real authors," did he mean men? I held up the letter from Gallomart to show that editors were responding, but Mr. Hayes didn't give me the opportunity to speak. Worse, Odessa, the secretary, and Marius, the collection manager, were at their desks—how humiliating to be criticized in front of co-workers. I felt my cheeks flush.

"No wonder we have a lousy turnout!" Mr. Hayes shook a half-filled attendance sheet at me. "And don't forget to update your statistics!" He stalked off.

Peeking up from behind her binders, Odessa winced in sympathy. "Girl, don't take it to heart," she advised. "We lifers have learned that if Hayes likes you, you can do no wrong. If he doesn't . . . well, nothing you ever do is right."

Hayes didn't like me?

Across from me, Marius had turned his attention to mending a spine. Without looking up, he said, "I've worked here for thirty-five years. Eight directors have come and gone. I've learned that if you wait long enough, problems—both personnel and personal—go away."

Statistics:

Number of months worked: **3**
Events organized: **24**
Authors who turned up late: **2**
Authors who turned up drunk: **1**
Audience attendance: **not good enough**
Events that trustee Jennifer de Narp attended: **24**
Events that Mary Louise attended: **0**

Contrary to what Mr. Hayes thought, there were great novelists who weren't "big names." For example, Wendy Peterson, who'd written an incredible account of 350 women who volunteered just miles from the front in World War I. I'd discovered it in the "Underrated Gem" section of the Red Wheelbarrow bookshop. A work of historical fiction, *The Library Card* recounted the career of Jessie "Kit" Carson, who worked for Le Comité Américain pour les Régions Dévastées (CARD). This modest NYPL librarian changed the literary landscape of France by making reading accessible to all ages, genders, and social classes. Wendy Peterson's book showed how one person could make a difference. I'd given copies to everyone I knew. According to the bio on the back cover, she worked at the New York Public Library, so I was stunned to bump into her at the bookshop. I gushed that I was a fan and asked what she was writing now.

"These days, lesson plans." She explained that in order to get a work visa, she'd accepted a job teaching English in a French executive MBA program.

The black frames of Wendy's glasses set off her tired eyes. Her weary tone reminded me how teaching business English had eaten away at my soul. These *écoles de commerce* charged a fortune in tuition, but teachers were paid next to nothing.

"I've been there," I said. "My students compared me to a hostage taker. It was demoralizing."

"Exactly. Their companies pay them to take English classes, yet somehow they're victims."

I felt a quiet thrill that she understood. "Right? I'd kill to learn a foreign language on the clock."

I asked how long she was planning to stay in Paris. She said at least a school year. When I asked if she'd had family over to visit, she replied, "My dad thinks I'm nuts for coming here. He never visited me in New York, he sure as hell won't come to France."

God, I could relate to that, too. Some friends had nonstop visitors who squatted in their studios, used all the hot water, emptied the fridge, and left a mess. Others were like me—no company ever. For my loved ones in Montana, Paris might as well be the moon—distant and unattainable. It had started to feel lonely.

"But enough about me," she said. "What about you?"

It had been a while since anyone had asked. Maybe because I knew her writing, I felt like I knew *her* and could confide. At the Sorbonne, fellow students used the informal "*tu*," like we were already friends. Mary Louise and I had met up with them for readings and art shows. After graduation, a few of our classmates got married and had kids. They needed bigger apartments and could no longer afford Paris. They bequeathed us cast-off belongings—that's how I'd inherited the wonky bookcase. Now, the people I met used the formal "*vous*," and try as I might, we never made it to the warmth of "*tu*." I explained to Wendy that though I had a dream job of organizing literary events, I wasn't writing.

"So you're an author," she said.

"I'm not published."

"You'll get there."

"Would you consider giving a talk at the ALP?" I handed her

my business card. Wendy would be my first acceptance, my first choice.

Silence.

"What's wrong?" I asked.

"Nothing." She traced the ALP lettering. "I'm just surprised. It's been a year since anyone's invited me to give a reading."

"But you're so good. You brought Jessie Carson back to life!"

"When I got here, I considered buying an ALP membership for my research, but decided it was too expensive."

"Lots of us can relate to being broke," I reassured her.

She looked like she wanted to say something more.

"What is it?"

Wendy gave a shake of the head, and I didn't press any further. "Nothing . . . Thanks for the invitation! I'm honored."

We agreed on a date. I was stoked.

"Are you really not working on a new project?" I asked.

"Well . . ."

Recalling how I'd ruined lunch by cutting off Mary Louise, I waited for Wendy to speak.

"I'm usually superstitious about revealing anything," she said, "but I can confide in you, program manager to program manager."

She and her husband planned to shoot a documentary about Jessie Carson, who'd not only created libraries in Paris and war-torn Picardy but also laid the foundation for a library school to train Frenchwomen. (Before that, the profession was reserved for Frenchmen.) The school was housed in the ALP in the 1920s.

"She was at the library? Chills. I have chills." I held up my arm to show Wendy the goose bumps. "I can't wait to see your film!"

"The reason I came to France was to learn more about her. I spend my weekends at the Franco-American Museum in Blérancourt or the library she founded in Belleville. I'd love to check out the ALP archives."

"Why didn't you say so? Like the second we met?"

I was keen to help her but suspected that Hayes would nix the project ("No reason to bother with a no-name author!"). Thus, Wendy and I arranged to meet at the ALP at 7:00 a.m., two hours before opening, so we could examine the archives in peace.

"Just so you know," she said. "I've applied for funding, but I'm not a real filmmaker."

"You will be."

Chapter 9

MAY 1995

David Hassan—volunteer

The Afterlife is filled with the heavenly scent of musty books. Its walls are lined with tall bookshelves full of forgotten tomes—some slim, others stout. In this cozy mezzanine between worlds, there are neither windows nor clocks, though occasionally, a burst of children's laughter or whiff of a chocolate croissant wafts up from below.

Once you climb the clanky metal steps, you'll find yourself shrugging off your jacket and making yourself at home. On the shelves, gold-embossed titles glint in the glow of the table lamp. At first, the sheer number of books overwhelms, but somehow, the eye is drawn to just the right one. If you're like me, you'll choose a novel by Irène Cohen. Curling up on the couch, you'll decide to read just one chapter, but find yourself still reading at three in the morning, racing toward the end.

As you might expect, the Afterlife is located in the poshest district of Paris. About an hour before sunset, the shadow of the Eiffel Tower becomes an arrow. Follow its silhouette to the pointed end, down a *rue* named for a *général,* to a nondescript building. During the day, not just anyone is allowed in—you're required to present a membership card. However, the greeter has a soft spot for misfits. And like Saint Peter, she knows who to let through the pearly revolving door.

Most evenings, there is an open-door policy—you merely sign in to enjoy the fellowship of Brie, baguettes, and Bordeaux. You can eat and drink to your lonely heart's content. The toady director might pester you to pay for a membership. Just scratch your chin with gravitas until he is called away. Events start at 7:00 and feature an array of art historians, journalists, and authors. You'll be on the edge of your folding chair.

Once inside the Afterlife, you can come and go as you please. Having bunked here awhile now, I find that the best place to store belongings (a toothbrush, a pair of pajamas, a few francs, letters from friends) is in the narrow space behind the set of 1972 encyclopedias—no one thinks of looking there.

These days, few find the Afterlife—the Faithful, Cohen scholars, lost readers, and folks like me. But don't worry, after hours in the Afterlife, there's no librarian to shush you, no security guard on nightly rounds, no police ordering you to move on. You're safe. I've been homeless for two years now. During the day, I roam the city, but nights you'll find me at the American Library in Paris.

Chapter 10

MAY 1995

Lily Jacobsen—program manager

Dear Mademoiselle Jacobsen,

Thank you for your interest in having Pat O'Malley speak at the library. We are finalizing the touring schedule for him to promote the French translation of his new book in October and will get back to you when we know more.

Sincerely,
Colette Levy
Editor in Chief

At my desk, I held the letter to my heart. This reply wasn't exactly a yes, but it wasn't another nameless no. Things were looking up. It was Friday, and I couldn't stop thinking about my date with Chris. During my lunch "hour," a mere fifteen minutes, I jotted down the banter from our meet-cute. Putting the pen to my journal felt good. For some reason, I'd hesitated to add the scene to my work in progress, *French Kisses.* The roar of Jennifer de Narp's vintage gold Mercedes broke my train of thought. In the courtyard, she slammed the car door, and even though I wasn't doing anything wrong, I hastily tucked my journal into my pocket.

Unfortunately, she spent the afternoon at the desk beside

mine, working on the layout of the newsletter. She peered at me every so often, probably trying to figure out how she knew me. I squirmed in my chair and pulled my hair from my ponytail to shroud my face.

She beckoned me. I approached skittishly. She asked my opinion on the pages, which were laid out next to her Louis Vuitton purse.

"I like the font?" She made me jumpy, so my comment came out a question, though I knew Georgia to be safe territory.

"Is the paper too pink? I wanted cream."

"I tried to tell you," Mr. Hayes crowed as he approached.

Ms. de Narp glared at him.

I was relieved that he took the attention from me. I returned to my workspace and considered how I would describe a character like her—seething. That was the word that came to mind, even before beautiful or smart. And him? Hapless or overconfident. And the two of them together? Power struggle.

~

After work, I found Chris waiting for me in the foyer. He'd brushed his hair, which was too bad—I preferred the book-head look. For our date, I'd put my best foot forward, too, in high heels and a crushed velvet dress.

He regarded me like I was an intriguing work of art. "You're gorgeous."

"Thanks," I replied as I breathed in his scent of sandalwood soap.

When he touched the small of my back to accompany me out the door, I felt the same anticipation I did at the beginning of a book, when I liked the first line but didn't know what the rest of the story would hold.

He asked how Italian food sounded. When I said delicious, we strolled to a restaurant that I'd been longing to try. There were only six tables, all pressed together. We chose one near the window.

The space was so small that our knees knocked. I felt a spark, a longing. It had been months since my last date. I felt too much. Anticipation. Desire. Hope. Wild hope. I didn't know him, but God, I liked him, and not just his adorable book head and gray eyes. He seemed like a good person, unlike the city planner I'd dated for four months, who "forgot" to tell me he was married, or the Ph.D. candidate who dumped me because I didn't share his devotion to Ayn Rand. Then there was the volunteer at S.O.S. Help who answered the hotline when I felt depressed about my writing "career," and the Australian co-worker with whom the only thing I shared was a hatred of business English. I'd begun writing my novel with optimism, but it only served to record my abysmal dating record: a liar, a snob with bad taste, a good listener but no chemistry, a terrible listener but great chemistry. Maybe with Chris, I'd break my losing streak.

After we ordered our pizza, talk turned to books—one of the benefits of meeting your date in a library. I didn't believe in soul mates, but I definitely believed in book mates. Would we have the same taste?

"I took your recommendation—*The Liars' Club* is like nothing I've ever read," Chris said. "The author painted East Texas, and even her family, with words."

I was psyched that he'd read it. "I feel that way about *My Ántonia*. Willa Cather makes me nostalgic for the plains."

"Is it hard to be far from Montana?"

The truth is, it was complicated. In my hometown of Froid, I'd felt restrained, even bolted down. After my mother's death, my father remarried quickly and had two sons. I'd felt like a third wheel, convinced that my stepmother, Ellie, would be glad to see me go. But more than anyone, she called and wrote; she became a bridge between my dad and me. I missed my family *and* Montana.

The whole state was empty—a fact I didn't appreciate until I lived in a city where every centimeter was filled with noise and people. Even now, inside the restaurant, we could hear police sirens and the vrooms of scooters racing up the boulevard. Our waiter held the phone receiver to his ear and yelled, "We do not deliver. We will never deliver!" The owner complained to no one in particular that Chianti was becoming as expensive as champagne. A busboy tossed handfuls of silverware into the drawer with careless clangs. At the table two inches from ours, a couple argued over whose turn it was to pay. It was like a scene in a movie whose soundtrack is so loud you could barely hear the dialogue. In Paris, much of my energy went to blocking out the clamor so I could concentrate on the essential.

I felt a pang of wistfulness and longed to take Chris to the Linden Marsh so we could watch the birds call to each other, listen to their quiet symphony. I'd bring the binoculars, he a thermos of hot chocolate. We'd hold hands. We'd be alone.

"I wasn't homesick at first," I explained. "My best friend used to be my roommate here in Paris. She and I came from the same place; having her nearby was like holding a piece of home. The best piece."

"And now?"

I thought of the studio, where I felt Mary Louise's absence with every breath. No whiff of coffee to wake me up. No oily pastels to color the day. No scent of lavender lotion as I drifted off to sleep.

I shrugged. "She moved out, and I have the place to myself. More room for books."

"Books are the best roommates. They're quiet, they don't hog the bathroom, and they rarely pass judgment."

I laughed. He was fluent in English, and just as I was about to ask him if he'd studied abroad, he said, "Speaking of books, what do you do at the library? I rarely see you up front."

"You seek me out?"

"Of course," he replied, holding my gaze.

"I look for you, too."

He grinned. So did I. A happy silence ensued. We'd been talking about something, but for the life of me, I couldn't remember what.

"You were going to tell me about your job," he prompted.

Sitting up a little straighter, I couldn't help but preen. "I'm in charge of programs."

"That must be fun."

"It can be, when good opportunities come up," I explained. "Wendy Peterson is my favorite author, and now I get to share her writing with Parisian book lovers. I hope that you'll attend."

"I'll try—it depends on my work schedule."

"What do you do?"

"I'm a cop."

"Wow." Nothing could have surprised me more—I'd assumed he was a scholar. "I thought you were studying—maybe architecture or law."

He explained that he was at the ALP to prepare for the *culture générale* section of the detective exam.

I had questions—Had he always wanted to be a policeman? Was it a family tradition? Why did detectives need to take a test on general knowledge? Chris replied that he'd wanted to be a cop for as long as he could remember. It was a family tradition that had skipped a generation—his grandpa was a policeman, but his dad, a businessman, was horrified by Chris's decision. Suddenly, I felt lucky that though my dad and stepmom didn't understand my choices, they accepted them.

"It must be tough not to have his support."

"Making money has always been his goal. After my mother died, I barely saw him—my grandfather raised me. In fact, I barely see my father now. He's a member of Air France's million miles club."

My heart went out to him. "My mother died when I was young, too."

He squeezed my hand. "I'm sorry."

As Chris and I ate, I asked again why he had to take a general knowledge exam. He thought it might be because the French considered it important to have a well-rounded education.

"There'll be questions like 'What is the highest peak in France?' or 'How many nuclear power plants are there in France?'" he explained. "The French love giving exams."

"They love to test people, all right," I muttered, and he laughed.

Chris changed the subject to movies. His favorite was *Pulp Fiction*; mine was *To Kill a Mockingbird*. He said he loved the book, which endeared him to me.

When we finished pizza we ordered a slice of tiramisu to share. As he ate, flecks of cocoa dotted his lower lip. I couldn't stop staring. It took all my willpower to not kiss his cocoa-y mouth.

After we finished our dessert, he paid the bill and walked me home. On the Alexander III Bridge, we paused to watch the silver waves of the Seine. We continued along winding streets, and as we made our way closer to my studio, I wondered if Chris would kiss me. At the front door of my building, I opened my mouth, maybe to invite him up, maybe to say goodbye. He tugged gently on my scarf to bring me closer and leaned down to brush his lips against mine. He tasted like coffee and cream. When the kiss ended, I stood with my eyes closed and felt his hand caress my cheek.

"See you Monday?" he said.

"Monday?" I was dazed from our kiss.

"I'll be studying in the reading room. Unless I get called in to work."

Unwilling to wait that long for another kiss, I stood on tiptoes to touch my mouth to his.

~

On Monday, I awoke at the crack of six o'clock in an excellent mood, still jazzed by my date with Chris and psyched to help my favorite writer. It would be a long day, but worth it.

When I arrived at the front door of the ALP, Wendy grabbed my shoulders. "Lily, you'll never believe it. Remember how I said my dad has never visited me? He's flying in for our event!" She hugged me.

"That's amazing." I hugged her back.

"To be honest, my research and writing had stalled. Maybe I was too tired from teaching. Anyway, I was on the cusp of giving up for good. I'd told myself that I needed a sign. Well, not a sign, but some encouragement. And then came your invitation. How can I ever thank you?"

"By continuing to write."

"It's about time you got here," David teased as he ushered us inside.

To carry the hefty boxes for Wendy's research, I'd enlisted my favorite bookworms, and introduced Wendy to David and Tolstoy, the reserved Gulf War vet who was the ALP's inaugural writer in residence. Like me, they were excited to help a novelist with research. In the dank basement, the four of us played a kind of Tetris, stacking and restacking dust-covered boxes. I wiped at my white blouse, hoping Jennifer de Narp and Mr. Hayes wouldn't notice the smudges at tonight's event.

We spread our findings on the conference room table, and I soon forgot my worries. It was fascinating to go back to the 1920s. Thanks to Odile, I knew about the ALP's World War II history, but I had no knowledge of its founding, or the fact that it had housed an international school, which the French establishment sneeringly dubbed "The Wild West Library School." The archives contained a gorgeous photo of the class with the instructors. Wendy pointed out Jessie Carson, who sat serenely in the middle of the young women, her hair braided in a crown.

Wendy told us that there were only two other known photos of Carson, so this was an incredible find.

"This means everything!" She contemplated the photo. "Look at that pensive expression. For a documentary, images are indispensable."

Wearing white gloves provided by Marius, we photographed each document since the photocopier would damage these fragile papers.

While Wendy jotted down notes, I asked David how his French classes were going.

"My teacher said that if I keep up the progress, I can enroll in college classes next autumn. She even helped me fill out scholarship applications. I'm torn between library science and law."

"It'd be cool to be a librarian," Tolstoy said.

"Maybe with the G.I. Bill, you could take some classes," I replied.

"Do you like working here?" he asked me.

It was a tough question. I was thankful for my all-consuming job: Hayes, newsletter in hand, covered in his Sharpie criticism, circling my desk like a persnickety shark; trustees with their "You, there!" demands and designer lives; ten minutes of bliss as I headed to the photocopier in the hope of talking to Chris; and finally, armed with cleaning supplies at the threshold of the men's room, I hollered, "Anyone in there?" only to hear the response from within, a frantic "Don't come in!" before I moved to the ladies' to wipe down the sinks and fill the paper towel dispensers then darted back to the men's. I loved featuring authors from our community but worried I'd never become published myself. On Saturday, one of my short stories had been returned with a not-what-we're-looking-for-at-this-time rejection from the *Harvard Review*.

I gestured to Wendy, who grinned from ear to ear as she deciphered a handwritten letter from Jessie Carson. "Authors like her make the job worth it."

~

After an incredible morning with Wendy, I needed to share the good news. At my desk, I wrote:

Dear Odile,

I know how you must have felt working at the library. It's gratifying to fortify writers, to get the pen moving, to keep the dream alive. . . . And I know that you loved seeing your beau in the stacks, as well. And speaking of beaux, guess what! I had dinner with Book Head! How are you? How is everyone there? Did you attend the high school winter concert? I wish I could have gone. I miss you.

Love,
Lily

Just as I signed my name, Mr. Hayes approached, in his hand a copy of the latest ALP events calendar. He gestured for me to follow him to his office, where we sat at the table near the impenetrable safe.

He pointed to the upcoming month. "No big names here."

"I'm waiting for confirmation from a French editor. Until then, I thought it would be good to invite local talent."

"You should have discussed it with me."

"But I'm the program manager."

"Yes, your job is to order snacks and booze."

Ouch. I placed my palm against the cool gray safe to help absorb the burn.

"And to make sure we have the speaker's books," he added.

"I made that mistake months ago."

"You haven't earned any points since." He smacked the calendar with the back of his hand. "Poor choice of authors."

"Most of them were invited before I started here! And I think audience members would disagree."

"What audience? There's barely anyone in attendance."

"You want better attendance? Budget so we can place ads in the newspaper."

I opened my mouth to apologize for my lippy tone, but he held up his hand. "I told you that the program manager needs to be diplomatic. Maybe think before you speak? Especially to your boss."

He paused to let that sink into my thick skull.

"We've gotten off topic." He glanced at the events calendar. "What's this Wendy Peterson written?"

"A book called *The Library Card*. It's about a librarian who—"

"Never heard of her. The title sounds dry. I've organized another event that evening, so you need to cancel her reading."

This would break Wendy's heart. It would break my heart, not that he'd care.

"The information about her event is already on the calendar," I argued, hoping he'd see set in print as set in stone.

"Tell the author it's off."

I swallowed. "But her dad is flying in to attend."

"Nothing I can do about that—this is why you should have gotten my permission. She's low-hanging fruit."

"Stop referring to writers as fruit! Just because they're not famous yet doesn't mean they're not interesting. We're here to nurture them. Without authors, we wouldn't have a library."

"Without money, we won't have a library! I'm here to ensure the ALP doesn't go bankrupt."

Bankrupt? Could that really happen? I wondered.

"I have to make tough choices," he continued. "Believe it or not, I don't like it any better than you."

I tried to put myself in the director's shoes, or in his skin, as Odile would say. I knew firsthand it wasn't easy to constantly worry about finances.

"I've booked Philippe Lester," he continued. "He's a big name, and his aunt Mazie is a millionaire. Inviting him will ensure her attendance, so I can encourage her to donate."

"But—"

"From now on, I will approve your list of speakers."

I needed to change his mind. "You're right. I should have checked with you first, and will from now on." My voice broke. "About Wendy . . ."

"I'm sure she'll understand." He gestured to the door. "That will be all."

As I rose, I clung to the gray safe to steady myself. "Please don't make me cancel."

"There's nothing else I can do."

Fleeing to the stacks, I found myself in 170, ethics. Usually, perusing titles cheered me up, but now my eyes, bleary with tears, wouldn't focus. I felt sick to my stomach. I needed privacy and slid up the steps to an abandoned section of the library. I plopped onto the plush gray couch and brooded over how I would tell Wendy the bad news. No, I couldn't, I just couldn't. My tears fell. Why did Hayes have to be so callous? Why hadn't I been more articulate? Why hadn't I fought harder for Wendy? I wiped my eyes.

On the far bookcase, I spied rows of navy-blue manuscript boxes. The identical exteriors did not allow for preconceived notions—impossible to judge a book by its cover. There were no titles. There was ceremony and respect in wrapping the works this way. I chose a box on the top shelf and untied the bow. I wanted to lose myself in a story. To stay inside it forever, so I wouldn't have to disappoint Wendy. I would forget my boss, my job, myself.

Memoir of subscriber Margaret Bauer, submitted in 1985

War.

You don't know what lengths you will go to until you're handed a rope. Nowadays, people assume they're experts—on strife and suffering, deprivation and depravity—because they gave up chocolate at Lent, or watched a documentary on *Résistants*, or played soldier in a video game.

I should start at the beginning. But what is my beginning? Perhaps the way I engineered the meeting with my first husband, Lawrence. Our marriage altered the trajectory of my life, moving me from London to Paris. He was attracted to my bosoms and blond hair, I to his tuxedo and social class. England is a ladder, each person on a rung.

With titled parents, Lawrence was near the top. Mum told me that education was the best way to move up, but as a girl, I'd never enjoyed studying. My gran, who was hard-working but illiterate, convinced me that I could barter my beauty and virginity. Lawrence's mother viewed me as a social climber who belonged on the bottom rung. She wasn't wrong. With all my might, I reached above my station and tugged at Lawrence's pant leg to pull myself up to his level.

On our dates, a handful of dinners at chic restaurants engulfed in cigarette smoke, I didn't say much. Women were conditioned to be vases, whilst men were fountains. Lawrence's words flowed, and I was there to catch them, even the ones I didn't understand. He boasted about his work, making it seem as if he were the English ambassador to France, rather than a clerk. When he asked if I spoke French, I said that I'd taken classes, but didn't admit to failing them. Lawrence proffered bouquets and perfume. Too inexperienced to know that these were generic gifts, I treasured each.

Over the years, I've met many an English girl engaged to a dashing Frenchman. I always advised living together before marriage. In my day, courtships were short and people married far too fast and too young. After our hasty wedding came the wedding night. I expected him to be romantic, like he'd been on our dates, but in bed, there was no tenderness, no connection.

Soon after, at a posh dinner party with diplomats, Lawrence saw I didn't understand French, and worse, was ignorant of the political situation. Enraged that I'd deceived him, he considered divorce, but his mother, who abhorred scandal, threatened to disinherit him. Thus, he and I remained tied together. We moved to Paris for his work. Eventually, I mastered French, but he never did become a gentleman. I'm making excuses for myself. I knew when we married that I was a selfish fraud. I could not see past the wedding, to the marriage and the wife he would need.

From the one time we had sex, I fell pregnant. During my pregnancy, he was quite attentive. After a peck on the cheek, he asked how I was "getting on." Naïvely, I hoped our relationship was improving, though he often "worked late," while I dined alone. Lawrence surely convinced himself that taking a mistress was a kindness to me, that he would not disturb me with his "needs."

Even with all the museums and monuments, I didn't know what to do with myself. I paced the parquet of the flat, pausing at the long windows of the reception room to admire the view of the Eiffel Tower. Once my pregnancy began to show, my confinement started, as society matrons dictated. My gran would have snickered. She worked in the cannery nearly up until she gave birth. But she and my mum had both passed, so there was no one to help me when Christina was born. Lawrence did not view a daughter as an heir; he saw her as another failure on my part. Even when she was a child, I suspected she could sense his coldness on his rare visits to the nursery.

Lawrence hired a French nanny for our daughter, but I wanted Christina to learn her mother's tongue. On the advice of the consulate's wife, I went to the American Library, though I viewed books with skepticism. I remember my first visit. Cowed by the book lovers crowing about their favorite novels, I felt like a peasant entering the palace. I nearly walked out; then a librarian welcomed me into the fold. I began volunteering with that aim—to ensure that everyone who entered felt at home.

Now, it's amusing to recall that I was afraid to enter. But at the time, I was timid and felt out of place. Soon, thanks to my new friend Odile, the ALP was the one place I felt at ease. Isn't it odd that I didn't feel at home in my flat?

And then the war. The American ambassador urged foreigners to leave, yet the librarians remained. Christina and I should have left like Lawrence did, but I did not want to leave Odile.

Odile? Had I stumbled onto her long-lost friend Margaret Saint James? I flipped to the title page. Margaret Bauer. Was that her married name? And now I find a trace of her here? Would Bauer be in the phone book? Had I finally found a lead? I continued to read, hoping for more clues.

During the Occupation, the Nazis tightened the noose. More and more barricades were built each day. People were arrested for no reason. As an Englishwoman, I was considered an enemy alien. Young and naïve, I was convinced that I could evade the German soldiers. Of course, I was wrong. Still, I helped Odile and her family as much as I could by bartering my jewels and clothing for food. Eventually, I was jailed and slated to be sent to an internment camp for women in eastern France. Of course, I'd heard from others what happened there. From behind the bars, I convinced the German guard to release me and the other ladies from our cell. He agreed on one condition.

The first time he and I met, at the bus stop near the Panthéon, I could see that he'd been beaten. I touched his swollen cheek, the gash above his brow.

"Because of me?"

"Just read," he responded.

We continued each week, in his off-duty hours, two strangers sitting at a bus stop. I read; Felix listened. His neck was long and slim; he resembled a man in a Modigliani portrait. Instead of his uniform, he wore a white dress shirt and gray flannel trousers. He no longer resembled "one of them." Eventually, we exchanged a few words. "I was an English teacher, before," he said. I told him, "My daughter's name is Christina." Eventually, there was a spark of electricity when his arm brushed mine. Eventually, we fell in love. Which made us both traitors.

After a year, he proposed a trip to Deauville. I mulled over what I knew of him. He'd been aware that his superior would beat him for releasing us ladies, and he freed us anyway. I admired his courage and his acceptance of consequences—characteristics that Lawrence lacked. I accepted Felix's invitation. In the hotel room, though I desired him, I was stiff with apprehension. I didn't know where to put my hands, didn't know what to say. I would disappoint him, just as I'd disappointed my husband. After what Lawrence had put me through, I just couldn't. At night, in the bed, Felix and I stayed fully dressed. He held me until I fell asleep in his arms.

During the days of August 1944, rebellion was in the air. News was not printed in the papers, only propaganda. Rumors swirled—the Allies were on the way; they were retreating; no, it was the Germans who were retreating. In the tug-of-war, I knew that I needed to rope Felix in. On the top floor of my building, each grand flat possessed servants' quarters. My maids had returned to England, so their small bedroom was empty. Inside, I filled a cupboard with enough food and water to last a week.

On a rainy afternoon, with the pretext of an indoor picnic, I lured Felix up the servants' stairs to the *chambre de bonne*. After lunch, he stood to leave; I unbuttoned my blouse. He swallowed. I swallowed. He asked if I was certain. I wasn't, but I nodded. My fingers gripped his upper arms as he gently grazed my neck with his lips. My heart heaved in my chest. With each minute, I expected him to throw me down and use me. But he held me gently, kissing my cheeks, the hollow of my clavicle, my throat. I tilted back my head, and surprised myself by letting out a contented groan. We undressed each other and moved to the bed. Together, our legs and arms enlaced and entwined. Together, we tickled each other and giggled, we whispered and writhed. I pulled him on top of me with sure hands, but still he met my gaze and asked again if I was certain.

"Yes." The word was a sigh. We rocked together, my hands on his shoulders, his back, his bum. Was I doing it right? Could I make him feel as cherished as he made me feel? And then I couldn't think any longer. All I could do was let go and let sensations pour over me.

I'd never felt so marvelous. And yet, I knew he had to leave. While Felix dozed, I locked him in. I would not lose him. He'd freed me, but I imprisoned him.

Over the next week, Paris fought, and in the battle to free herself, civilians as well as Allied and German soldiers were killed. But Felix was safe. I worried he would be punished again on my behalf, this time for desertion; however, the German army was in such chaos that I doubt his superiors were able to perform roll call. Then, the city went silent, except for the joyous peal of church bells. Paris was Liberated. I could release Felix, but hesitated, afraid of his reaction. If I'd dared lock Lawrence up, he'd have slapped me across the face.

My hand trembled as I stuck the skeleton key in the lock. "Please don't be mad," I pleaded.

Felix opened the door and pulled me into his arms. "Thank God you're safe."

He was trembling, too. He said he'd heard the staccato of machine-gun fire, the rumble of explosions. He wasn't angry, only relieved that I was unharmed. Together, we decided he should stay hidden away until the situation was more stable.

All over France, the Allies were making progress. Foolishly, I thought that life would soon return to normal, to happy times, like before the war, when the library's biggest problem was where to find more shelf space for the weighty translations of Dostoevsky. Odile seemed tense in those days, but so did everyone. I never expected her to just disappear.

After the war, everything was shattered. The city itself—gratings that protected the trees had been tossed together as makeshift barricades, cobblestones pulled up from the streets lay in piles, charred automobiles smelled of smoke and violence. Lines were drawn between neighbors and within families. Ration cards remained in use. In winter, we were all hungry, all cold. We all aged. I wasn't even thirty, but felt worn, weary. That period was, in many ways, more complicated and difficult than the Occupation.

At the library, staff expected that Odile would return. We expected her to write, or at least contact her parents, but a year, then two slipped away with no word. I was angry with her, then worried, then bewildered. My self-righteous fury subsided, helium seeping from a balloon.

And now, with the blink of bloodshot eyes, decades have gone by. Why hasn't she reached out? Where is she? I would go to her anywhere. Sometimes, I revisit the places we spent time. In the corner of a thrumming café, arm in arm under the oaks of Parc Monceau, in the Afterlife. When we were together, it was not so much places as a feeling. When I was with her, my best friend, I was my best self.

Until I met Odile, I hadn't liked Paris. I was alone in that cavernous flat, or with standoffish neighbors in the elevator. Unable to communicate with modistes, the baker's wife who sold baguettes, the flower girl proffering petunias on the street corner, I'd never felt so lonely. Odile was laughter, and long walks, and tea and biscuits, and heart-to-hearts. Without her, when I passed before a mirror, I found myself staring at my reflection, asking who I was, who I wanted to be. I could be less critical of others. I could and would be a better friend. I vowed to volunteer at the library until she returned.

With each passing year, each white hair, each birthday spent without her, I feel the hands of time grip my shoulders and try to shake sense into me. *She's gone*, the voice cautions. I refuse to believe it, and would give anything for us to be reunited. But how? Time is running out.

"Oh, I didn't expect to find anyone else up here," I heard a woman say.

Her words—the sore disappointment at not being alone—brought me back to the Afterlife. Trying to get my bearings, I blinked. I was on the couch; the faintly typed manuscript rested on my lap. A few pages had fallen to the floor and lay on a puddle at my feet; I'd sped through them, unable to read fast enough. I'd finally found the footprint of Margaret Saint James.

The memoir was written in 1985. Was she still alive? How could I find her?

In the doorjamb, Jennifer de Narp frowned, and I didn't know if she was unhappy with me or unhappy in general.

"What are you doing up here?" she demanded.

How long had I been away—ten minutes, twenty? How much trouble was I in?

"We don't pay you to sneak off," she added.

These days, I worked through my lunch "hour," scarfing down a sandwich at my desk while researching possible speakers. Now, I took one lousy break, and she pounced.

I remembered why I'd fled to the Afterlife in the first place—Hayes had ordered me to cancel Wendy's event, even though doing so would break her spirit. I glanced at the pages in my lap. Odile and Margaret had faced actual Nazis, I merely had to call a friend to say there'd been an unfortunate change in plans. And yet . . .

"Well?" Ms. de Narp crossed her arms.

"Mr. Hayes said—"

"Hayes," she scoffed. "What's he done now?"

I still felt raw from his criticism, and the story poured out. "I invited Wendy Peterson, an author I adore, to speak, and he's making me cancel. Only her dad is flying in from Canada for the event, and I don't know how to break it to her that she can't come." My voice became squeaky. I hated sounding unprofessional, especially in front of Ms. de Narp, with her sleek updo and manicured life.

"Rescinding an invitation is the height of rudeness! Did Hayes explain why?"

"He booked Philippe Lester to speak that night instead."

Ms. de Narp's eyes narrowed. "That far-right wing nut shouldn't be given any podium, most certainly not ours."

"Mr. Hayes said I didn't have a choice."

"I don't care what he told you, he's not in charge here. Hayes answers to the trustees."

She glanced up at the ceiling like she was attempting a difficult math equation. Adding up the concerns. Subtracting the bottom line. Dividing, devising. I wondered what her takeaway was.

"The solution is obvious," Ms. de Narp finally said.

"It is?"

"There's more than one date on the calendar. Book your novelist the evening after Mazie's nephew. If you don't mind 'helping out' at the event, that is."

"Helping out" was library speak for working for free. Honestly, I'd volunteer for the rest of my life if it meant that I could keep my word to Wendy.

"Oh, Ms. de Narp, thank you!" I felt like an idiot for not finding the solution on my own. If she were the hugging type, I'd have thrown my arms around her neck. "You're a genius!"

"There's no need to exaggerate."

Still, she seemed pleased.

Thrilled to have a solution, I gathered Margaret's manuscript pages to Xerox them before moving toward the entry. Ms. de Narp didn't budge from the doorjamb. We stood inches apart. I waited for her to step aside, but she didn't. I felt trapped in her calculating gaze and cigarette stench.

"Put that manuscript back." She pointed to the box. "These stories are priceless!"

Ms. de Narp was right, I should be more careful. I needed to think on whether or not to send the story to Odile. Normally, I'd talk it over with Mary Louise, but what if she told me to mind my own business and leave Margaret Bauer in peace? After all, Mary Louise was mad at me in part because I didn't know when to keep my mouth shut and consider other people's feelings. I pondered the fifty-year rift between Odile and Margaret. What if that happened to Mary Louise and me?

As I put the box on the shelf, I asked, "Should I tell Mr. Hayes about the added event?"

"You needn't worry about that. I'll take care of him." Ms. de Narp turned on her Louboutin heel.

I'd misjudged Jennifer de Narp—first on the street, then on the job. Clearly, she had the ALP's best interest at heart.

On my way back to my desk, I peeked into the reading room, hoping to see Chris. But there was still no sign of him. Maybe tomorrow.

The back office staff had already left for the day. It was blissfully quiet when I rang Wendy, who agreed to the date change. Everything had come together. I felt like a pool player whose shot had landed all the balls in the pockets.

I got home about eight and slipped into my long johns and favorite flannel pajamas. I poured myself a glass of merlot, dregs from a recent ALP event's bottle. It felt strange to have a drink without Mary Louise. I called her, hoping to talk about Book

Head; about Jennifer de Narp, friend or foe; about sending a copy of Margaret's memoir to Odile. There was no answer.

After a few days of reflection, I made the decision to photocopy the pages. Just having the war memoir in my possession soothed me. Should I send it to Odile, even though she'd specifically said she had turned the page on her past? Would the memoir dredge up hurt feelings or spark a reconciliation? Odile was a private person. The one time I'd delved into her privacy, she'd felt it was a betrayal.

Meg greeted me and started to copyedit the newsletter at the desk across the aisle. I longed to ask if she was Odile's friend Margaret. But why did she change her name to Meg? For a fresh start? To leave the past behind, like Odile had chosen to do? I watched while she added corrections in the margins, as if I could gauge her mindset from the flick of her pen. If she were an employee, I'd dig around payroll to learn her last name. Why hadn't I asked when we first met?

"Hayes flew to Washington," Meg said. "He'll be gone a week."

Good riddance. I was thankful that for a week, no one would bother me.

"He's there to meet the ALP advisory board," she added.

I kept staring at her.

"What is it, Lily? Is there something you want to tell me?"

The martini of my mind was one part reticent to delve, two parts insatiably curious. I'd ask a question, and she could confide as much or as little as she wanted. I resorted to the most common icebreaker in Paris: "I was just wondering—what brought you to France?"

"My first husband's job."

The tone clearly stated *End of subject*. She didn't want to discuss the past. We worked in a rare silence until eleven on the dot, when Lorenzo stomped through the office (muttering about how easy we had it back here) and into the courtyard for a cigarette break.

He never lit up, he just held one between his fingers. While he was away from his post, I grabbed the updated events calendar and hightailed it to "his" photocopier. As always, I kept an eye out for Chris. He wasn't in his usual spot. Again. I felt a sting of disappointment. I hadn't seen him since our date. Over a week, an eternity. Maybe he felt awkward after our kiss and decided not to return. Or maybe he was seeing someone else. I never should have gone out with him. What was that expression about not dating people from work? Don't check out guys where you check out books?

I fired up the photocopier. To keep from staring at his empty chair, I focused my attention on the warm pages that slid onto the tray. I shouldn't have let myself get my hopes up, but Chris was the first guy I'd liked in ages. I didn't know why my eyes had sought his out. There were other attractive, single guys at the library, like Tolstoy, who parked himself in the corner and read *All Quiet on the Western Front* like it would save his soul. Or David, whose demeanor was stoic, almost sad, yet when he told a child a joke ("What's the tallest building in the world? The library, because it has so many stories."), his smile lit his whole face.

So why Chris? I didn't understand chemistry any more than I understood Greek. I only knew that I liked him. Even though I told myself that we barely knew each other, the ache I felt at not seeing him was akin to homesickness, as if he were already my country.

~

The next evening, with the director away, it fell to me to introduce our speaker—my first solo event! Lena Kaufman, a correspondent with the *Los Angeles Times*, had two children with her French husband and had recently published a book on education. As a tutor working with kids, the subject was dear to my heart.

At the entrance, I welcomed Lena, who wore a green jumpsuit and matching heels. She was on time and sober, unlike last week's author, a buddy of Mr. Hayes's, who'd penned a roman à clef set during their prep school days. (No surprise: cheating on exams and chronic masturbation ensue. Mr. Hayes snuck out during the reading the same way he'd ditched class.) At the end of the talk, no attendees bought the author's novel. Feeling bad for the bookseller, who'd bicycled across the city for nothing, I bought a copy and asked him to sign it *To Lily*. He didn't write my name, just scribbled his own. Afterward, I helped the bookseller lug the box to her bicycle and tie it onto the rack.

"What a jerk," she said.

"What did you think of his book?" I asked.

"*Dick and Jane Go on a Bender.*"

I couldn't disagree.

On the other hand, I hadn't been able to put down Lena Kaufman's treatise on education. Now, when I asked if she wanted anything to drink, she replied that tap water was fine. I liked her immediately because of her simple tastes. We went to the director's office, where she could leave her coat and briefcase. Having an author to myself was heaven. I asked how she'd found her agent, the challenges of researching her books, how long it had taken to write her first draft. She nodded at my questions, like maybe she'd had the same ones. She gave me tips on writing a killer query letter and said that research takes a certain relentlessness. She'd had false starts, too.

When I escorted Lena to the podium, we saw all fifty chairs were filled. Success! I wished Hayes were here to see it. As I recited my introduction, I gazed at the audience, readers like me, spellbound by writers who brought us unexpected worlds. We adults weren't any different from children at story hour. I finished the intro with the catchphrase I'd begun hearing in my sleep: "If you appreciate fine events like these, please consider supporting the ALP by purchasing a membership. If you're already a member, consider donating."

"It's lovely to see so many friends and colleagues. Thank you for coming," Lena began. "Studies show that French schoolchildren are more anxious in class and more afraid of speaking up than their peers in the States. They feel unaided by teachers, and overall have a less warm relationship with their schools. Sixty-three percent of French students suffer bouts of nervousness. Forty percent have difficulty sleeping. Why does France discourage children for what they cannot do, rather than encouraging them for what they can do?"

"My kids went through the French system," the bookseller whispered to me. "It's a miracle that we all survived."

I nodded. School was tough for the teens I tutored.

Lena went on to explain that French students had strong scores on international comparative tests, but when asked about their results, they insisted that they did poorly. On the other hand, many American students had mediocre scores yet felt confident about their abilities.

"American students need less coddling, and French students could use some praise," she finished to a hearty round of applause.

I asked the audience if they had questions. Several attendees raised their hands, but Mike Roth spoke before I could choose one. "I've been a professor in France," he said. "Students here are fine. Kids just need to quit being babies."

The Faithful tsked. No one appreciated Roth's commentaries.

Lena raised her brow. "Did you have a question, or are you just the kind of man who feels the need to contradict a woman?"

"He feels the need to contradict everyone," David said quietly, and those of us who heard laughed appreciatively.

Before Roth could respond, I called on an audience member. She explained that her son had been kicked out of the lycée his senior year because administrators suspected he would fail the exit exam and ruin their 100 percent success rate. How could schools treat children like this? Bewildered parents shared stories and asked questions. Expat parents were as traumatized by the French school system as their children.

Beside me, David gestured to the room full of readers talking animatedly. "You did this. You created this camaraderie."

"*We* did," I told him and Meg, who was right alongside us.

Once the Q and A portion wrapped up, I escorted Lena to the circ desk, and the audience besieged the bookseller. The author spent an hour signing books and chatting with parents. The bookseller and I exchanged thrilled glances. For the first time, she'd sold her entire stock—tonight, there'd be no precarious pile of books to balance in her basket as she bicycled away.

Attendees took their leave; David stacked chairs, and Meg cleared the aperitif table. I escorted Lena to Hayes's office to pick up her belongings, then back to the main entrance. My eyes swept the stacks, on the lookout for book lovers who'd lost track of time. I gestured for them to follow us out.

Meg congratulated me on a successful event and kissed me on each cheek before grabbing the garbage to take out. I thanked the author, who said a cheery *à bientôt* as the last of the Faithful departed.

I turned off the lights, and then, I heard something: the flick of a page. Like antennae, the hair on my arms went up. Even as my brain argued that I was being silly, my body knew something was wrong. In the reading room, near the window, was the silhouette of a man. He must have hidden in the children's section—a place I never checked for stragglers.

He flicked another page. I froze, every nerve in my body on high alert, as I remembered Meg's warning: *Watch out for Mike Roth.* I was on my own in a three-story building with no alarm system. It wasn't a coincidence that he'd stayed behind on a night when Hayes was absent. Roth knew I'd be alone.

"I didn't see you there." I heard the tremor in my voice. "The library is closed. Time for you to leave."

"I'll go when I'm ready." He bowed his head to peruse the magazine, but I still saw his smirk.

He knew there was nothing I could do. "Please leave," I said, trying to sound more confident than I was.

"Make me." He leered at me. Clearly, he was enjoying this.

I was scared. Did he just want to lord his power over me, or would he pounce? He was between me and the front door, the closest exit. I didn't know what to do. Could I make a run to the door before he attacked?

I thought of my grandma Pearl, who'd chaperoned our high school choir at the state competition. There were four girls to a hotel room. Mary Louise had brought a cowboy back to our room to mess around. "Don't tell," she warned. It was late, and three of us girls huddled in the hall. Grandma Pearl approached. With just a scowl, she had us confessing. Grandma Pearl strode into the room, grabbed the cowboy's boots at the foot of the bed, and beat the man until he yelped for mercy and fled in his stockinged feet.

But that hotel had been full of people. Here, I was completely on my own.

Roth stepped toward me. "Time to get better acquainted."

I glanced around the library, full of potential weapons, and grabbed a book to heave at him. Maybe the surprise of it would throw him off and buy me enough time to get to the back office. I could lock the door behind me and call the cops.

I steeled myself to launch the book and run.

From above, I heard a voice say, "Go home, Roth."

David descended the staircase. He turned on the light and moved to my side. His expression was grim, like that of a boxer stepping into the ring. His worn tee emphasized his broad chest. No one in their right mind would spar with him. And anyway, Roth only picked on women.

When he didn't budge, I stepped toward the circ desk. "Maybe I should call the cops."

Roth threw the magazine to the floor and strode to the exit. He cast a glance at me before he slammed the door. The look said, *This isn't over.*

David locked the door behind him.

My body was tensed. My jaw, my shoulders, my legs hurt.

"Are you okay?" he asked.

I could see the concern in his eyes. I nodded.

"He's gone," David said. "You're safe."

I exhaled shakily and felt a last tremor of fear run through me.

"I don't know about you," he said, "but I could use a drink."

In the kitchen, he pulled a seat from the table, and I sank onto the stiff chair. He poured us each a glass of red. He sipped his. I gulped mine.

"How did you know what was happening?" I asked.

"I heard."

"You heard?"

He regarded me gravely as he made up his mind about what to tell me. Finally, he said, "I live here."

"You live here?"

"In the Afterlife." He pointed up, as if to heaven.

The Afterlife, upstairs, a better place. Now I understood why he just disappeared after events—you can't say goodbye if you don't leave. Thank God he'd been here. I didn't want to think about what might have happened.

My whole life, libraries had been my safe havens. I'd never expected to be in danger in one. I reached across the table and squeezed his hand. "Thank you."

"Are you sure you're okay?"

"I will be. Let's talk about something else. Anything else. How long have you lived here?"

"For two years, since I arrived in Paris."

He said he was from a country in East Africa called Eritrea. I was ashamed that I'd never heard of it. He explained that it had a one-party government, a dictatorship. There, mandatory military service could last for years. David was scared to be drafted for life, so with the goal of getting to London, he crossed the Sahara, mostly on foot, and had nearly died of heatstroke. He then found his way across the Mediterranean. In Toulon, a trafficker arranged for him to travel in the back of a semitruck with twenty others.

There were more and more checkpoints along the way, so the driver chucked everyone out forty miles south of Paris.

I shook my head, both at the situation and at the fact that I had no idea about the world outside my bubble. "Lily-land," Mary Louise had called it.

"How did you end up here?"

"At first," he continued, "I lived on the street and in the parks, never staying long. The police get after you—the city doesn't want the homeless tainting tourist spots. One day, I was shuffling along—depressed, really—and I saw the ALP banner. Meg invited me in for a spot of tea. When I started sneaking in regularly, she turned a blind eye—she's been through hard times, too, so she's less judgmental than most."

I took in all that he recounted. "What will you do next? Can your family help?"

"No one there has the money, and I can't go back. I'd like to apply for a French visa, to be able get a paying job and send money to my parents."

"Maybe Jennifer de Narp could help—she's a lawyer."

He held up his hand. "No trustees. I'm happy for now. I have my books. I enjoy our events, meeting folks, giving back to the community. Everyone here has been kind."

David outlined the system in place to support him: Meg had contributed clothes and bedding. Marius had brought the gray couch from home. Odessa, the secretary, put extra food in the fridge. Lorenzo siphoned the cash from library fines so David could buy toiletries, use the laundromat, and shower at the municipal bath.

"Get out!" I said. "Lorenzo?"

"A man of many surprises."

When the old custodian retired, Marius and Odessa had proposed an exchange: the job for room and board. It was the best they could do since David didn't have working papers.

"Does Hayes know you live here?"

David shook his head. "He doesn't know most things. In his office, the garbage can is always empty. I don't think he actually does any work."

It was nearly midnight. My legs were wobbly, and I didn't want to go home, where I'd be alone.

"What's it like to sleep here?" I asked, fishing for an invitation to stay.

"Cozy," he said as he put our wineglasses in the sink. "You should stay."

In the Afterlife, he put a few beanbag chairs together and covered them with a blanket for my bed.

"You were brave tonight." He lay down on the couch.

"I was scared."

"Understandable."

I settled onto my makeshift bed. The light rubbing sound of the beanbag's stuffing beads made me feel like a kid again. "I like it here, surrounded by books."

"It's nice to have someone to talk to," he said as he fought a yawn. "I hate sneaking around. I'm glad I could confide in you."

"I promise I won't tell anyone you live here."

"I know."

~

The next morning, while David vacuumed and returned the tables to the reading room, I updated the Entre Nous literary series statistics. Forty books sold! Fifty attendees!

I should've been proud of myself, but then I thought about other statistics:

Hours a week I tutored: **20**
Hours a week I was paid to work at the ALP: **20**
Hours I actually worked at the ALP: **40**
Amount I was paid for those extra hours: **zero**
Times I've been threatened at the ALP: **1**

"David told me what happened," I heard Meg say. "Are you all right?"

I nodded. She hugged me.

"Roth's lucky I wasn't there." She pulled a canister of pepper spray from her pocket. "Don't let the white hair fool you. He would have got a face full."

"Isn't pepper spray illegal here?"

"Accosting women is illegal, but it happens," she said bitterly. "You never want to be at a man's mercy." She put the spray in my hand and closed my fingers around it. "The library may not be able to ban Roth, but we can be prepared. Keep the spray on you at all times. Danger often comes from the people you know."

Her words made me wonder who'd hurt her. Was she Odile's Margaret? How could I broach the subject? Did I have the right to bring up painful memories?

"On my way in, I spied a certain young man with book head," she said, her voice restored to its chipper tone.

"Really?"

"I noticed the newsletter slot was empty. Do you want to make more copies or should I?" she added with a knowing grin. Meg really did know everything.

Chris studied at his usual spot. Should I go over, or stride by as if I hadn't seen him? A coward, I made a beeline for the circ desk, keeping my back to the reading room for good measure. I checked the paper tray and programmed thirty copies, then let the gentle whir of the Xerox machine lull me.

I heard Chris say, "Hey, I'm glad to see you out here."

I forced myself to concentrate on the number pad, 19-18-17, so I wouldn't turn around and gush that I was glad to see him, too.

"I figured you wouldn't want me to bother you at your desk," he said.

8-7-6. I composed myself.

"Sorry I wasn't able to come earlier," Chris continued. "A sick co-worker needed me to take his shifts."

3-2-1. I turned. "Hope he's okay now."

"He is. I wish I'd asked for your number, though."

"Me, too."

"Do you want to go out tonight?"

Piccadilly Books had decorated their entire window with a catchy book on dating called *The Rules*. I'd skimmed through it and found thirty-five directives to achieve wedded bliss. Don't call a man. Don't ask a man to dance. Don't accept a Saturday night date after Wednesday. *The Rules* gals would want me to say that I was busy. They'd insist on not accepting any last-minute invitations. Their motto: *Pretend to have a life, even if you don't.* But I was tired of playing games. I wanted a boyfriend. I wanted Chris.

"I'd love to. How about couscous for dinner?"

"Perfect. I'll pick you up after your shift."

At seven, I straightened the newsletters and event flyers on the information wall near the entrance.

"Going out with Chris?" asked Lorenzo from the circ desk.

I frowned. "How'd you know?"

"My dumb little dumpling. I know everything."

"Doubtful!"

"Do you want the Dewey Decimal number for serial killers? That way you can look him up."

"If anyone's on that list, it's you."

"Only one way to find out," he said with a sly grin.

Chris approached. "Hey," he said, giving me a peck on the cheek and a nod to Lorenzo.

Lord, he was handsome in his duffel coat. I longed to snuggle close, but with Lorenzo looking on, I threw open the door and said, "Let's get out of here."

"It's 364-1523," Lorenzo shouted after us.

"Was that his phone number?" Chris said.

"It's the call number for murderers."

"He has it memorized? That's intense."

"Lorenzo's a time bomb in a sweater vest," I said.

"I can't tell if you're joking."

"I'm not. He's tired of dealing with the public."

"Maybe he needs a vacation where he doesn't have to talk to humans."

"He needs a change," I agreed. I explained that the ALP had over two thousand members and only eleven employees, most of us part-timers.

"How is that even possible? You'd never guess. Everything runs so smoothly."

"I'm glad it appears that way. We have an army of volunteers, and staff put their hearts and free time into the place."

At the restaurant, the lights were dimmed. Our table was set with a votive candle and two small colored glasses. After taking our order, the waiter brought a clear teapot of peppermint leaves steeping in water. With great flourish, he held it at his shoulder level and poured a stream of tea into each glass.

Chris reached out and took my hand in his. It felt right. I could hold on to him my whole life and wanted to know everything about him. I wondered why he was studying for a French exam at the American Library.

"How did you first discover the ALP?" I asked.

"My grandpa used to take me when I was a kid. He said he wanted me to learn English, but I think he wanted to chat up the children's librarian."

"So flirting with staff is a family tradition?" I teased.

"Not until now." His thumb grazed the inside of my wrist and I thought I would melt.

"He and Bitsi were just friends," he continued. "I think they'd both been through a lot during the war, though neither would ever talk about it. She taught me English. I spent more time at the library and at the precinct than I did at home. My dad worked nonstop."

The waiter set a feast before us—a stew of root vegetables, a platter of chicken thighs and merguez sausage, and heaping plates of golden couscous. Though I was starving, I reluctantly let go of Chris's hand and grabbed a fork and knife.

A tender carrot melted in my mouth. I asked him how the studying was going. He told me he felt confident about the police stuff but was struggling with the *culture générale* section. "'Name the site of the nuclear plant in Alsace-Lorraine,'" he said, "Or 'What year was Julius Caesar assassinated?'"

"That sounds hard, but I bet you'll ace it."

"I wish I had your optimism. Most people don't pass on the first try. What about you? How long have you worked at the library?"

"Five months." It felt like longer. "Before that I taught English."

"It's hard to become a teacher here."

To teach languages in the public school system, university students had to pass a difficult competitive exam and master translation. They also had to have French nationality.

"Not when you're working with adults," I explained. "My former boss hired any native English speaker with a pulse."

We heaped more couscous onto our plates. I didn't want to talk about my jobs—past or present—and changed the subject. "Why do you want to go to Texas?"

"When I was little, my grandpa and I watched a documentary on NASA. The astronauts said, 'Houston, we have a problem,' and this steady voice guided them. As a kid, I always wanted my own Houston to help solve problems—when my mom passed, I also lost my dad, in a way. He became a workaholic."

I knew all about fraught relationships and tilted my head in sympathy.

"Now that I'm an adult, I'd love to see the NASA Space Center." He shrugged. "A dream trip if I pass the exam."

"Was your grandpa a detective, too?"

"He didn't make that rank, but he was good at understanding people."

I knew it was my turn to offer something about my life. I

wished I could talk to Chris about Mary Louise. He seemed really understanding. But the hurt was too fresh to discuss.

Instead, I brought up something else that weighed on me: Odile, and the quandary of whether to share what I'd learned by reading Margaret's memoir. Should I mail a copy to Odile or stay out of it?

"If it were me, I'd want to hear about an old friend," he replied.

It felt good to talk to Chris, and I took his advice seriously. I thought maybe I'd send the copy, and Odile could decide if she wanted to read it.

He and I finished our tea, and the waiter brought the check. I offered to pay, but Chris wouldn't accept. "You can treat for ice cream."

I held a hand to my stomach. "But not tonight."

"Definitely not."

Good. Another date in the near future.

"Do you want to switch over to French?" I asked as we walked down rue de l'Université, toward my apartment.

"I prefer English. It's more direct, and there are fewer decisions to make."

"Like the formal and informal," I said with a groan. "It's always hard for me to know if or when to switch."

"In the library," he said, "when you first came to say hello, would you have used '*tu*' or '*vous*'?"

"I would have wanted to use '*tu*,' but to be on the safe side, I would have used '*vous*.'"

"Same for me. We're not students any longer—so, the formal. But it adds a barrier, when I only want to get close to you."

We stopped walking. Somehow, we were already at the door of my building. I didn't remember which streets we'd meandered down, didn't remember waiting at stoplights to cross. I could only focus on him. We faced each other. He took my hand and placed my palm over his heart. It pounded as hard as mine.

I brushed my lips against his. He kissed me back. I ran a hand through his hair, something I'd wanted to do from the first moment I saw him. Soft and warm, it caressed my fingers. I felt a thrum of desire, of happiness, of fear. It felt too good, it felt too right, which meant it was too good to be true. I pulled away.

"I should get going," I said. "See you at the library?" Before he could say a word, I slipped inside and closed the door behind me.

Usually, the best part of a date was afterward, when Mary Louise and I curled up on the futon with cocoa and conducted the postmortem: what he wore, what he said, how he kissed, would there be another date, did he like me as much as I liked him? In our jammies, we pondered what we'd wear the next time we went out and if it was too soon to meet his friends. Sometimes, when I described a date, she didn't like what she heard and cautioned me. *Make sure he doesn't have a girlfriend back home.* Or, *Go slow. You have time.* Other times, when I doubted, even for a minute, she would say, *He likes you, he definitely likes you. How could he not?* Her optimism was the sweetest of lullabies, and I fell asleep to the sound of her certainty. But now, here was a beginning that could really go somewhere, and Mary Louise wasn't around to share my joy. I entered the dark, stale-smelling studio. I was alone, and desperate for her company.

Chris was right, who wouldn't want to hear from an old friend? I'd slipped a copy of Margaret's memoir into a manila envelope and addressed it to Odile. At the post office, I stood on the threshold, unable to mail the pages. Margaret had painted a different picture of the past, of Odile's memories. What if the contradictory perspective upset Odile? What if it gave false hope for a reconciliation? I didn't want to cause her any pain, knowing she'd already been through so much. So the envelope sat on the corner of my nightstand. Where I stared at it, or it stared at me.

On Mr. Hayes's first morning back from Washington, he approached my desk. From the scowl on his face, I feared the worst.

"Something disturbing took place in my absence. Let's talk in my office."

Maybe he'd heard about Mike Roth's threat and wanted to check on me. I was touched, since he'd never uttered a kind word or shown any concern. Mr. Hayes closed the door behind us.

"You complained about me to a *trustee*?" he shouted.

"What? No!"

"The second I leave town, you go crying to Jennifer de Narp?"

It took me a moment to process this—my conversation with her was the furthest thing from my mind.

"She saw I was upset and asked what was wrong. I didn't think—"

"Damn straight you didn't think. Next time, keep your mouth shut."

Mr. Hayes didn't give me time to respond before he flung open his office door. I slunk back to my desk. This job was supposed to be a low-stress way to cover my rent so I could write, but it was all-consuming. Had I made all the arrangements for the authors? Contacted the bookseller? Ordered taxis for the trustees? Would Mr. Hayes fire me because I hadn't booked a big name? Would my end-of-the-year statistics be good enough? Would I even last that long? I'd made so many mistakes. . . . I felt like a loser. Sometimes, I wanted to go back home to Montana. I missed Odile and my family. But I'd vowed not to return until I was a published author. I just had to try harder.

Statistics:

Times a day I wonder if Meg is really Margaret: **5**

Times a day I pick up the phone to call Mary Louise: **5**

Times I daydream about Chris: **5**

Times I worry that my boss hates me: **17**

Chapter 11

JUNE 1995

Quentin Hayes III—director

The *Wall Street Journal* was all my father ever read; the Dow was his Tao. Though he insisted fiction is a waste of time, *Herzog* remains my favorite book. *With one long breath, caught and held in his chest, he fought his sadness over his solitary life. Don't cry, you idiot! Live or die, but don't poison everything* . . . If only I had Saul Bellow's gravitas, his way with words. He once lived in Paris; I used to walk by his building as my Sunday pilgrimage.

I used to devour a book a week, too, but to my great regret, since I started at the ALP, over a year ago now, there's simply no time for necessities like novels or sleep. I don't get more than four hours of rest per night. With the exception of a short fundraising trip to Washington, I haven't had a weekend away, let alone off. If it's not the ancient boiler threatening to blow, it's the burst pipes that flooded the children's room. If it's not the cataloger calling in sick *for ten weeks in a row*, it's lazy French artisans—a repair that should have taken a fortnight has taken six months . . . so far. Then the sculptor squatting in the neighboring building got drunk and fell from a third-floor window onto the plexiglass roof of our mezzanine. He's fine—it was a four-foot drop. Unfortunately, journalists continue to call for quotes about the semifamous *artiste* who tried to end his days at the ALP. "Not *at* the library *on* the library!" I end up shouting. His fans, none of whom are members, now sneak in to admire the crack he caused as if it were another of his deranged oeuvres. On their way out, I've seen more than one stuff a book down his trousers.

The title "library director" had a regal ring to it. Of course, acquisitions editor, financial planner, and diplomatic outreach coordinator hadn't sounded bad, either. But those jobs didn't last. I excel at first impressions; follow-through is where I fail. I got through school by identifying the smart kids and looking over their shoulders during tests. That's harder to do in work situations.

My interview for the position of director took place over a three-course lunch at Le Bristol with the ALP chairman of the board of trustees, Moe Mandelbaum, and board member Jennifer de Narp. I don't know what her problem was—she barely acknowledged me. When I excused myself, ostensibly to use the men's room, but really to let them come to the conclusion that they should hire me, I overheard Moe say, "He's the right sort."

"You forced my candidate to come up with a yearly budget on the spot, yet the only question you ask Hayes is 'You understand money, right?'"

Moe waved away her objection like it was a pesky wasp. "His prep school contacts will come in handy. We're seeking spheres of influence, something what's-her-name didn't have."

"Joan Graham. Yale graduate. Master's in library science," she said between clenched teeth.

"Do you know who Hayes's father is?" he riposted.

"Was."

Touché.

I returned to the table confident as ever.

"I won't lie," Moe warned me. "In this role, you'll have to do a hell of a lot with very little."

"I was a financial planner." I didn't mention that I'd lost my clients (that is to say, my father's friends) *and* their money. If Moe didn't check my references, he deserved what he got.

"We need someone who can bring the library into the twenty-first century." Jennifer de Narp didn't glance up from her Filofax.

Clearly, in her mind, this meeting was already over. I turned to Moe, since he was the one who mattered. "Yes, I'm familiar with *message boards*." I repeated the peculiar phrase I'd heard my son use. "Computers are the future."

The truth is that these days, I'm more concerned with the past. Since he died, I think of my father more and more. His contacts got me into Choate, the prep school that was to pave my way to the Ivy League. But with my mediocre grades in math and science, even his alma mater passed. Only Notre Dame accepted me—certainly hoping to cultivate a connection of their own to my father. In four years, he never visited or even wrote. We spoke only when I returned home on break. Well, he spoke, always complaining that I was reading instead of playing polo. I responded "Yes, sir," or "No, sir." I enrolled in the classes he ordered me to take and got my bachelor's in business. Don't ask me to tell you the difference between macro- and microeconomics. I don't know and I don't care.

After graduation, I went on to fail the LSAT as well as the foreign service exam. I never mentioned the tests to him, so they couldn't be counted in his tally against me. Father found me a job at Merrill Lynch, and I married one of the secretaries. Stuck in the office with such long hours, where else was I supposed to meet someone?

The marriage ended on the day I was ousted from the firm. "No money, no wife," my father liked to say. But I told him that wasn't fair; the divorce was my fault. Of course, he assumed I cheated. In fact, I pursued her until we wed, then stopped making an effort. I disappointed her—once again, a case of first impressions not lasting.

I met my second wife on the rebound. After she'd borne two sons, my father shifted from severe misgivings about her to lukewarm approval via gifts—a Cartier watch on Mother's Day, a Kelly bag at Christmas—all of which delivered the subtext I'd never be able to match such presents myself.

She and I spend more time apart than together, which keeps us from divorcing but makes the marriage feel like a failure anyway. We both failed at parenting. Our sons, one in China, the other in Italy, only contact us when they want something. Perhaps I shouldn't complain. I'm as good at keeping in touch as my father was.

In my career, I advanced from job to job, resigning just before they'd have fired me. Each press release made it appear that parting ways was my choice. "Deciding to spend more time with family" or "In order to pursue other goals." Job eulogies.

This role as director was the last lead my father gave me before he died. Of course, he knew the chairman personally. I'd considered my father a safety net, always there when I landed with a thump. It was only recently that I viewed him as a trampoline—an impetus to rebound that propelled me into another career, another romantic relationship, another life. I was never grateful. At the time, I couldn't see that he risked his reputation and friendships to recommend me. I didn't care. I brushed off the angry clients and my boss, telling myself that they had time to make more money. My father surely lost his friends when I lost their savings. I'd been careless, callous. I didn't want to live like that anymore.

This job was to be a fresh start. Recalling my interview, I see that I was naïve. I thought I was pulling a fast one on Chairman Moe. Now, I understand that *he* duped *me*—the bastard never mentioned the pain-in-the-ass trustees who'd fired the previous director (lawsuit pending). At the time, I figured, *I like to read. I can certainly referee shouting matches between testy patrons. Really, how hard can running a library be?*

Very hard, as it turns out. I don't have a lot to work with. Since I've been here, the only thing the assistant director has done is the writer in residence. The head librarian is a kleptomaniac who pockets the fines. Old-timers like Marius and Nutmeg latch on to me and yammer about how the library used to be run. Jennifer de Narp is out to get me, and I have no idea why. At monthly board meetings, the trustees demand to know why I haven't reached the fundraising goal. Unlike the program manager, I can't fudge the statistics. And don't get me started about the pretentious "cultural curator" of Piccadilly Books—that battle-ax loves to rub her event calendar of Booker winners in my face.

In the role of director, my mistakes have lost the ALP hundreds of patrons—and membership fees. When I opened the library on Sundays, Tamara Jones, a wealthy Catholic donor, ripped up her library card and convinced dozens in her parish to do the same. Marcus Midboe, president of Neo-Cons Abroad, complained about *The Joy of Gay Sex*. I abhor censorship and refused to remove the book from circulation. He retaliated by canceling the corporate membership of his five hundred employees, which cost the ALP $50,000 in annual fees. Now, every time the phone rings, I fear Moe Mandelbaum is calling to fire me.

The library has an illustrious past. In 1914, Alan Seeger, a bohemian Harvard grad, enlisted in the French Foreign Legion just days after war was declared. He wrote sonnets in mud-soaked trenches. His poem "I Have a Rendezvous with Death" was a favorite of John F. Kennedy's. During the Battle of the Somme, Seeger was killed, a bayonet in his hands, on the Fourth of July. His father, Charles Seeger, helped found the library, a living monument to his son. Fifty thousand francs, royalties from the war poet's books, published posthumously, was the seed money. Sometimes I ask myself if my father would have loved me if I'd died young.

At the outset of World War II, Ambassador William Bullitt advised Americans to leave France. The ALP librarians remained. Directress Dorothy Reeder and her staff defied the Nazis in order to hand-deliver books to Jewish readers. At the height of the Red Scare, director Ian Forbes Fraser stared down Joseph McCarthy's government-sanctioned goons and barred them from entering. Today, the ALP has members from sixty countries. Nearly 25 percent of our members are French. It is a United Nations of readers.

In my life, I've failed at everything—school, career, marriage, parenthood—but was able to keep up appearances. If I fail this time, and the library closes for good, everyone will know I'm a failure.

Chapter 12

JULY 1995

Lily Jacobsen—program manager

Dear Odile,

Sorry it's been ages since I've written—work has been hectic. To be honest, I'm struggling. My boss hasn't liked any of the authors I've booked. (Mr. Hayes is no Miss Reeder!) Trustees are hypercritical. When Jennifer de Narp barrels toward me to demand why I didn't order the kind of cheese she prefers, the left side of my face twitches.

*Despite coming from Dallas or New York, the wealthy all seem to know each other—they ski at Aspen, summer on Martha's Vineyard, or their brothers attended Exeter the same year. Sometimes, the library is fertile ground for meetings of the mind. At others, it's a reminder that people can be divided into two categories—*tu *and* vous, *plastic cups and wineglasses, crumbling studios and palatial apartments. I'm at the bottom of an invisible hierarchy. Maybe Mary Louise felt that way growing up in our small town. Maybe I never thought about hierarchy before because until now, I was at the top. Maybe I'm finally starting to understand her.*

When you worked at the library, was it nonstop chaos? Today, our fire alarm went off again (another teen smoking in the john), and Tolstoy, a Gulf War vet, dove under the circ desk and covered his head with his hands. Lorenzo and I didn't know what to do, so like penguins, we huddled with him for an hour, till his storm passed.

I long for your leek-and-potato soup. I wish you were with me. I miss your wisdom. I miss you.

Love,
Lily

At 7:00 p.m., just as I was leaving work for the day, Mary Louise phoned and asked if I could meet for dinner to celebrate our French-iversary. It had been months since I'd seen her, and in that time, we'd barely spoken. Every time I'd called—even at 9:00 p.m., she was "on her way out the door."

Dying to see her, I rushed over. In the métro on the way to the restaurant, I wondered if I would finally meet her boyfriend, Antoine. I wondered if she was happy, if they celebrated little things, like their one-month anniversary. I had a hundred questions, but after our last lunch, I knew I needed to let her do the talking.

Upon arriving at l'Hexagone, I glanced at the menu, encased in a large silver frame on the side of the building. The restaurant had two Michelin stars, and I felt a thrill at dining in a hallowed sanctum of French gastronomy, until I realized that main courses started at 350 francs, a whole day's salary. The waitstaff probably expected diners to order starters and desserts and drinks besides. The price of seeing Mary Louise was a week's wages. Aware that my work "uniform," bland khaki pants and a boatneck top, was not fancy enough, I dawdled at the door. The maître d'—elegant in a gray suit—ushered me in. When I gave him Mary Louise's name, he gestured for me to follow. As we passed through the haze of cigarette smoke, six waiters chirped, "Bonsoir, mademoiselle. Welcome, mademoiselle." This was the friendliest Parisians had ever been to me. At the table, the maître d' pulled out my chair, and I slid onto the green silk seat across from Mary Louise.

At first, I thought she'd pulled her red curls into a chignon, but it was more than that—she'd bleached her hair. Beige foundation covered her constellation of freckles. The style sapped her vitality, and she looked all used up.

"A new do," I said in the even tone my stepmother had used when I'd dyed my bangs pink.

Mary Louise reached up to pat her hair. "What do you think?"

You're beautiful and unique, why would you want to change? I longed to say. *Now you resemble every other blasé Parisienne, just like Jennifer de Narp.*

"It's always fun to experiment," I said.

We were in one of the city's chicest restaurants, the kind we'd strolled past in amazement when we first arrived in Paris. In our studio, we'd spent hours discussing what we'd order in a place like this (bouillabaisse for Mary Louise, scallops for me); who we'd wear (Chanel for Mary Louise, Jean Paul Gaultier for me); and which idol we'd invite (Marc Chagall for Mary Louise, Simone de Beauvoir for me). Now, I wasn't sure what to say, so I tried "Have you been here before?"

"Oh, yes, Antoine and I dine here several times a week with friends."

I didn't know what stung more, that she chose a spot I couldn't afford or that she'd already been here *with friends*. I scanned the menu for the cheapest thing—cassoulet—and marveled at how the French could make "beans and sausage cooked in duck fat" sound delicious.

"It is heavenly," Mary Louise said approvingly. "What about a starter?"

"I'm not sure . . . I'm not really hungry."

"You? Not hungry?"

She knew me so well. I glanced at the menu. Sea scallops

perched on a bed of rocket, seasoned with lemons from Sicily; foie gras on a slice of brioche, served with a bundle of green beans wrapped in bacon . . . the list went on. I chose the cheapest—*velouté d'asperge,* a bowl of asparagus soup with a fancy name.

When the waiter arrived, he addressed Mary Louise in French, "And how is monsieur?"

"Busy with work."

"And you? What takes your time? You did not come for three whole days, we missed you terribly!"

"Flirt!" she admonished with a pleased chuckle. "Since I quit my job—"

She quit her job? Since when?

"I've been going to movies and doing a little shopping," she continued in French, "things I haven't had time for since I first arrived."

Movies and shopping? Why didn't she invite me to go with her? And what about her art? Wasn't that why she got her own place—to paint? How could she afford that humongous apartment on her own with no income, when I barely made rent? Was Antoine paying for her apartment? Or was she living with him? Or worse, was he married?

"Amusez-vous!" the waiter said. "I'm happy you can enjoy our charming city."

"Life is short, and the to-do list in Paris is long," she replied.

Her French had become fluent. When Mary Louise and I used to go out, she stuttered, mixing up the masculine and feminine. She got verb conjugations all wrong, so I often took over, dealing with cashiers, writing out her résumé, informing the concierge that our heat went out again. I'd thought she needed me, but she was fine on her own.

As she recited our order, first course—velouté, second—cassoulet, I was reassured—she and I still had the same taste, still wanted the same things.

"Which wine?" he asked, like it was obvious we would order a bottle.

Without a glance at the wine list, she ordered a bottle—Domaine du Château de Something-or-other—that sounded insanely expensive. I felt a flash of jealousy. I'd never bought something without considering the price.

"Et le dessert?" the waiter continued.

I glanced at the menu. At fourteen dollars, *tarte tatin*—a slice of upside-down apple pie—was the cheapest.

"I can't afford dessert, too," I whispered, angry that she made me admit that I was broke.

"It's my treat."

"Let's split the *tarte tatin*." That's what we used to do. We'd shared everything.

"No need," she replied.

"I know mademoiselle prefers *les profiteroles*," the waiter told her with an indulgent wink.

She handed him our menus. *"Les profiteroles et la tarte tatin."*

"Thanks," I said to her, feeling more resentful than grateful, and couldn't help but wonder if it was Antoine's money or her own. I hoped it was hers, because maybe that meant she'd sold some paintings. "How are your landscapes? Or are you working on portraits?"

"It's slow going." She took a gulp of water. "Your writing?"

I leaned back as the waiter placed porcelain soup bowls before us.

"I got a few rejections, but that's good, because it means I'm putting myself out there." I didn't mention that those stories had been sent out before I started at the library. These days, I didn't have the energy to write.

"You never give up." She pointed her soupspoon at me. "I've always admired your gusto."

Gusto? She sounded like a completely different person.

"Will I get to meet Antoine tonight?"

"He's on a business trip." Mary Louise pulled her purse from her lap. "But as a consolation for missing tonight, he got me a Louis Vuitton handbag."

As if I didn't recognize the famed checkerboard.

She held it out to me. "Feel it, isn't it superb?"

Superb?

I ran my hand over the cold leather. Since when did she need something snooty to feel good about herself? I'd promised myself that I was going to hold my tongue but couldn't help myself. "Remember those gold bracelets Rhonda wore to church? We hate gaudy displays of wealth."

Mary Louise stuck her chin out. "Well, now that I have one, I like it."

I regarded the blonde before me and did not recognize any part of my childhood friend.

She raised her glass. "Happy French-iversary."

I touched my rim to hers. "Happy French-iversary," I echoed quietly.

"The soup is organic," she said to fill the silence.

"Healthy!" I replied with *gusto*.

I was dying to ask her about quitting her job but was afraid to say anything that would make her retreat again. I used to dream of eating in a restaurant like this, but now . . . I realized Mary Louise and I had more fun at a crepe stand—chatting with students and tourists as we waited in line, teasing the burly cook, licking the Nutella from the corners of our mouths. More money did not mean more fun.

Oven mitts on, waiters came with our cassoulet. The gold-brown sauce bubbled in each individual Le Creuset cast-iron pot. I took a bite. Honestly, Campbell's bean with bacon soup tasted almost as good, and a can only cost a buck.

"Mmmmm." Mary Louise closed her eyes as if it was the best thing she'd ever eaten. "This dish is from the southwest, where Antoine's family has a château. We went last week, and it was divine!"

I waited for her to say, *Maybe you could come next time*, but she didn't. Like a speaker at the library, she lectured giddily on her pet topic, Antoine; like an audience member, I listened, biding my time until the Q and A.

"Antoine sounds wonderful, but let's talk about you," I said. "What's going on with you?"

She set down her fork. Her expression became stony. "The French don't ask prying questions. *They* know when to hold their tongues."

"Now you're lecturing me on the French?"

"Me lecture you?" Mary Louise said. "That's rich. You rarely let me get a word in."

The waiter placed our desserts before us. Her cream puffs were drizzled with chocolate, my pie glistened with butter and sugar.

"Wait until you try it," she said.

"I've had *tarte tatin* before." Annoyance crept into my voice. We'd been in France the same amount of time; we'd eaten the same food.

"Not here. It's the best."

As a caramelized apple melted in my mouth, I stifled a groan of pleasure. "You're right."

"I guess there's a first time for everything."

"What?"

"You admitting I know something."

"You know things," I sputtered. "Lots of things."

"Never as much as you."

We finished the meal in silence. When the check came, I pulled out my wallet to pay my share, but she waved my hand away. Without even verifying the tab, she thrust a gold card at the waiter. Mary Louise had entered the next phase of life without me.

I thanked her for dinner as we made our way toward her apartment. She and I used to love evening strolls together, exploring neighborhoods, peering through windows into other people's lives. Now, we passed blond Haussmannian buildings. On the first floor, I spied a woman in a pink blouse opening a bottle of wine for three girlfriends.

I gestured at them. "Do you think they're celebrating an engagement? Or a book deal?"

"Probably just having a chat."

On the second floor, I glimpsed a man scowling at the mirror above his fireplace mantel.

"Did his girlfriend dump him, or is he having problems with co-workers?" I asked.

"You don't have to accompany me home."

I wanted to. "It's on my way to the métro station."

She shrugged. "Okay, then."

Had she forgotten our walks? I pointed to the dusky sky. "Our favorite time of day."

She nodded. *L'heure bleue,* the time between day and night, when the sky turned a dreamy shade of blue.

In front of Mary Louise's building, the concierge had set out the trash. Five canvases were propped against the green bin. The one on top depicted a pastel Eiffel Tower, and I realized these were Mary Louise's paintings. I was stunned. How could she discard her life's work like it was garbage?

"Why would you throw these out?" I demanded.

"They're puerile."

Where'd she get that word? It wasn't one of hers. Neither was "gusto" or "superb." She didn't talk like that. She didn't think like that.

"They're not childish," I replied. "They're evocative and original. No one else can do what you do!"

"You're the only one who thinks so."

In her petulant tone, I heard a world of hurt.

"That's not true." Trying to console her, I reached out to squeeze her shoulder, but she stepped away.

"No one here wants pictures of Paris."

"Sell them to folks back home."

"People there don't pay for art. It would be self-indulgent."

She had a point. In our small town, pleasure was foreign, even suspicious. No one there got massages or used aromatherapy. A vacation was a weeklong trip you took once a decade, not a yearly monthlong certainty, like for many French families.

"Sell your paintings to tourists here," I argued.

"Don't you think I've tried?" she shouted.

A Parisienne walking her corgi looked down her nose at us as she passed.

"The constant rejection is too hard," Mary Louise continued in a whisper. "I can't cope with it."

"Just because the paintings haven't sold yet doesn't mean they won't. Plenty of tourists want souvenirs. Let's go to Montmartre." I gestured north.

"Don't be naïve! Artists need to buy a permit to sell there."

"Tomorrow morning. We'll stand on a street corner and hawk your paintings—"

"Quit suffocating me!"

We used the word to describe our parents, our small town, our life before. It was the worst insult I could think of. All I'd ever done was to support her.

I crossed my arms to stop myself from shaking some sense into her. "Suffocating you?" Now I was the one shouting.

She shrugged. "Anyway, my paintings are just clutter."

"Is that your opinion? Or Antoine's?"

She exhaled sharply. "It's my opinion. I don't want them anymore. They suck."

"Don't say that. Don't think that."

"Quit telling me what to think! I have a mind of my own." She spoke in a low, fierce tone, the same one she'd used to defend me to my dad, to the principal, to my stepmother years ago. Mary Louise had always been on my side, and I was on hers, now and always. How could she not see that?

"I didn't mean to tell you what to think. I just meant I love your work. And once they have the chance, other people will, too." I moved to take the paintings.

"Don't touch them."

Her voice was so hard that I froze midstep.

"I never want to see them again."

She regarded me in a way that made me afraid she'd add *I never want to see you again.*

I quickly thanked her for dinner again and took off. When I rounded the corner, I listened for the jingle of her keys and the click of the door, then peeked past the black wrought-iron fence to see if she'd left the paintings. They were still there. Between our argument and seeing her life's work thrown out like junk, I felt queasy. I wished I could curl up in a ball at home, but I needed to keep an eye out to ensure no one nabbed her work. When the lights went out in Mary Louise's apartment, I crept back and hugged the paintings to my chest like long-lost friends.

Negotiating the métro turnstiles was hard with the unwieldy canvases, but we all made it home safely. I propped the paintings against the wall. The *l'heure bleue* pastel of the Eiffel Tower with Mary Louise's loopy signature in the bottom left-hand corner. It was one of her first. The yellow sunrise Eiffel Tower she completed a year later; a hair from the brush was stuck in the foot of the tower. Each morning, I'd touched it for good luck. Her hydrangea-purple Cubist version, the signature just a scrawl, was the last of the series. How I'd missed them.

I was dumbfounded by Mary Louise's transformation, her quitting her job without a word to me, and her decision to throw away her paintings. Then there was the assertion that I suffocated her. That was the hardest to swallow.

Sinking onto the futon, I wondered how she could say such a thing. I thought she liked following my lead. All through junior high and high school, she sat behind me in class. She didn't know where to apply for college, so I helped her find art schools—granted, they were in Paris, but still, I'd helped. After graduation, when she'd wanted to move back home, I insisted that real artists live in Paris. And so we stayed.

When I was a girl, Grandma Pearl had given me a plaque that read, "Some people call it 'bossy,' but I call it 'leadership'!" I saw myself as a leader, but maybe I was just overbearing. Tonight was the angriest I'd ever seen Mary Louise. How long had this been simmering?

Looking back, from college graduation to now, events took on a different interpretation for me. For example, she'd wanted to return to the States, but I'd stopped her. I thought I'd pushed her in the right direction, encouraging her to focus on her art. But if I was honest, I'd lacked the courage to stay in Paris on my own. Mary Louise had remained in an expensive city and worked a secretarial job that she had no affinity for—for me. And now, not only had she given up painting but she'd rejected it completely.

She'd declared her independence when she moved out. I'd assumed she wanted space to paint, but really, she'd needed space from me. There was a reason Mary Louise hadn't come to the ALP—she hadn't wanted to get sucked into my orbit once again.

I had acted like we were still kids, when I was the banker's daughter and she grew up wearing her sister's stained hand-me-downs. Finally, Mary Louise owned an elegant purse that belonged only to her. A real friend would have been happy for her.

She was my best friend. She was *the* best friend. She'd supported my dreams, she'd known—even if I hadn't—that I'd needed her moral support to survive here. She'd put her plans on hold for me. I'd used Mary Louise as a crutch, and she'd bowed under the weight of my demands.

I'd screwed up, but had no idea how to make it right. If Mary Louise even wanted me to. I pondered her paintings—the soft optimism of their colors, the bold confidence of the lines—and wished they could give me an answer. Should I respect Mary Louise's wishes—perhaps for the first time in our twenty-year friendship—and dispose of her paintings? Or should I protect her art? What was selfish and what was selfless?

I wondered what Odile would do. At a crossroad in her relationship with Margaret, she'd fled Paris. She'd always regretted giving up and letting go.

"*She told you to go,*" I'd reminded Odile.

"*Sometimes that's when you should stay,*" she replied.

I was ready to fight to keep Mary Louise in my life. But how, when she only seemed to crave time away from me?

Chapter 13

JULY 1995

Felicity Jenner—volunteer

As usual, I arose at six, did three sun salutations, and fixed my hair and makeup before frying bacon and eggs for Franklin, which he ate while perusing the business section. I poured myself a tea and joined him at the dining room table, where I read the culture pages. At seven, he gave me a distracted peck on the cheek and left. He hadn't looked at me in a long time. Given his long hours at the office, one might suspect an affair, but I knew he preferred pursuing accounts to chasing women. To him, I was a steady client he no longer had to woo.

Ellen got up, and over grapefruit, she recounted the plot of the book she was reading and its funny French vocabulary like the word *pamplemousse*. I held these moments close to my heart.

Tokyo, Toronto, Manchester, and now Paris. Every few years, we started over in a new home in a different country. Struggling—with culture shock, with making friends, with French—had brought Ellen and me even closer.

Three years ago, after ten years abroad, our family had returned to England. Franklin promised that we'd stay until Ellen's graduation. Yet the minute he got a plum job offer, we moved countries again. She and I both felt foolish for having believed him.

This morning, when she left to meet up with friends, the flat became unbearably quiet. I cranked "Walking on Sunshine" by

Katrina and the Waves before assembling my portfolio of PR campaigns and changing into a pantsuit for my appointment at the ALP.

At the library entrance, Meg greeted me with a cheery hello and asked after Ellen. So often in Paris, I felt invisible; Meg's kindness made all the difference and was certainly why I'd chosen to volunteer here. She escorted me to the director's office, where Quentin Hayes III and Jennifer de Narp sat side by side, heads bowed over their work. She verified numbers in a ledger, while the director copyedited the newsletter. He struck a sentence with his Sharpie; I was impressed by this diligence—no task was too small. However, the pair resembled opposing counsel who refused to acknowledge each other until the judge arrived.

"Nice to see a young woman in the role of trustee," I whispered to Meg.

With one last comment in the margins, Mr. Hayes set aside the newsletter. "There's so much to do that every second counts," he said apologetically.

"Lovely to meet you." Ms. de Narp closed the ledger. "We're thankful that Meg encouraged you to share your expertise. She has a nose for talent."

Meg blushed. "I think you'll find you have a lot in common," she told us before taking her leave. "You're both lawyers."

Ms. de Narp gave a nod of respect, and I saw that I rose in her esteem; Mr. Hayes stiffened as if I were about to serve him with divorce papers.

"No one's perfect," he joked. At least, I hope he was joking.

He scanned my volunteer information sheet. "Why don't you work in your field, then?"

I explained that when my family relocated for my husband's job, Franklin was awarded a work visa; as a trailing spouse, I was not. Jennifer de Narp nodded sympathetically, which made me think she understood how painful it had been to give up my career.

I slid my portfolio across the table and outlined my experience in publicity and fundraising. "It's volunteer work, but I've become quite good at convincing people to donate."

Mr. Hayes pored over the images and wording I'd used to convey the work of a nature conservancy as well as the vital role of individual donors.

"You've highlighted the history," he said. "That's something we don't do enough."

"Tasteful." Ms. de Narp perused the brochure for a theater that included a range of recommended giving and a rundown of how donations were used—everything from playbills to costumes.

"Your interview with the director there was very insightful. Wonderful photo." Mr. Hayes straightened his retro tie. "I'd like to see the same spotlight on staff here."

Easy to see that he imagined a glossy eight-by-ten of himself in the ALP fundraising packet. Ms. de Narp and I exchanged knowing glances.

She explained that members' fees barely covered payroll, insurance, the heating bill, utilities, and taxes. Suddenly, she and the director resembled lawyers with an unwinnable case. I couldn't believe the situation was so dire.

"How has the library lasted this long?" I asked.

"Constant begging," Mr. Hayes replied.

"Prayers and sporadic donations," Ms. de Narp said. "We'd love your help, if you have any ideas."

Off the top of my head, I suggested presenting gems from the archives to journalists in order to raise awareness; creating promotional items to distribute at school fairs and to publish in *Paris Parents* magazine and *The Expat's Guide to Education in France*; or even a gala with a silent auction.

Ms. de Narp raised her brows. "Interesting. Tell me more about the gala."

"It would never work." Hayes rolled his eyes. "We don't have the budget for a venue."

"The library *is* the venue," I continued, as if I hadn't heard his outburst, and focused my attention on Ms. de Narp. "Every week, you throw a literary party. Why not organize something a little more festive? Champagne instead of wine, canapés instead of baguette. Choose a date at the beginning of December, when people are feeling generous and need to organize their tax-deductible, end-of-year donations. Decorative touches such as holly are elegant—and inexpensive. Of course, the fundraising campaign would start immediately, as would the outreach for items featured in the silent auction."

Their defeated expressions were replaced with cautious enthusiasm. We were on our way. "We"—what a lovely word.

After the meeting, to check out photo ops, Ms. de Narp and I nipped into the children's room. It was so homey—perfect for pictures and brochures. What a treat to see toddlers enjoy story hour just as Ellen once had. And with her long chestnut hair and rosy cheeks, the librarian was so photogenic! In the back office, Ms. de Narp introduced me to Lily, the program manager, who signed me up for the Better Off Read book club and WE, the Wives of Executives, a trailing spouses' support group.

"Do you have time for a bite?" Ms. de Narp asked me.

Lily stilled and regarded us hopefully. She wanted in on lunch. I waited for the trustee to extend an invitation, but she seemed to look right through the girl. Next time, I'd find a way to include Lily.

At the bistro, Jennifer insisted that I use her first name, since we'd be working together. She even ordered champagne. We raised our glasses. "To you," she said. "Thank you for your time and expertise."

When I heard her praise, a lump formed in my throat, and I guzzled the bubbly to conceal the unexpected emotion at being complimented. Of course, I appreciated her confidence in my abilities, but more than that, this was the first champagne I'd had in Paris. I'd expected to share a toast with Franklin. Like many things— gratitude for how I steered our household, date nights at romantic restaurants, weekend getaways—it never happened.

Over a salade niçoise, Jennifer and I discussed everything from books (*The Joy Luck Club* was her favorite, *Excellent Women* mine) to complaints about judges ("She snored during my closing argument." "He hit on me after every trial.") to workaholic husbands (hers spent more time tromping around their vineyard than at home, they now lived separate lives).

"At least the vines have roots," she said. "I can't imagine how challenging it is to pick up and move on the whim of a husband or his company."

"It's been hard on my daughter. Five schools in fifteen years."

"She has you. That's stability."

"Still, I'd have liked her to spend time with our family in England. I wish I could make Franklin understand."

"Speaking of trying to get through to a man . . ." Jennifer frowned. "Sometimes I think Hayes's ears don't register women's voices."

I gave a bitter laugh. "I'm used to it."

When the check came, Jennifer grabbed it. I argued, but she said, "You can treat next time."

I flushed with happiness, and maybe champagne. "Yes, let's make a habit of this."

In the ALP conference room, we pored over boxes of archives to find photos for the fundraising campaign. I arrived home at 7:30, just after Franklin, who was inching out of his too-tight blazer in the foyer.

"Hello, parentals," Ellen said from the couch.

"Why don't I smell dinner?" Franklin demanded.

The raw pork roast was in the refrigerator. I'd expected today's meeting to take no more than an hour. All day, I'd felt important, listened to, exhilarated—until now.

"Hello, dear," I said pointedly.

"What time are we eating?" he replied.

"Geez, Dad," Ellen said. "You sound like a caveman. 'Me want food.' You know they sell pizza in Paris, right? When you're away on business, Mom and I order in."

"But I'm home," he pouted.

If it had been just Franklin and me, I'd have skipped his heaping plateful of guilt and gone straight to bed, but with Ellen there, I said, "Pizza sounds lovely, I'll place an order now."

Chapter 14

AUGUST 1995

Lily Jacobsen—program manager

Dearest Lily,

Thank you for your last letter. It's always a joy to hear from you. While it's always interesting to hear about the goings on at the library, I can't help but wonder what you aren't telling me. I sense that something is wrong. I'm worried about you.

All my love,
Odile

After the disastrous dinner with Mary Louise, I'd thought long and hard about our relationship. I acknowledged that I put too much pressure on her. In Paris, she'd been my everything—best friend, roommate, cherished piece of home, book mate, psychologist, short-term lending bank, cheerleader, and crutch. Filling all these roles was a lot to ask of anyone. To save our friendship, I needed to lift some weight from Mary Louise's shoulders and expand my social circle. I phoned Wendy and invited her to tonight's lecture. She accepted, which made me feel a bit better.

I stared at the receiver. Maybe instead of writing to these publishers, I should just call. I rummaged through my drawer to find publishers' catalogs of their forthcoming publications. The phone numbers were listed inside. Hayes had cited National Book Award winner Pat O'Malley. I'd written to his French publisher, and received a response. Maybe it was up to me to follow up. I called them now and asked to speak to his editor. I was shocked when the receptionist put me through.

"Yes, this is Colette Levy," she said in French. With her deep voice, I imagined her as a chain-smoking brunette surrounded by piles of manuscripts.

"Allo?" she said.

After a brief pause, I gathered my wits and introduced myself. I asked if Pat O'Malley could speak at the ALP when he was in France to promote his forthcoming book.

"Yes, I received your request," she said briskly. "I warn you, he's very busy that week. Today alone, you're the third person who's requested him. Everyone wants Pat."

I should have realized. My heart fell. Maybe it was better to get the rejection on paper.

"Oh, okay," I stuttered. "Sorry to bother you."

I was about to hang up when she added, "I understand you might be under pressure. That is the book life." As she spoke, I could hear the flicking of pages and imagined her scanning the schedule in her Filofax. "Tell me about your little library. What is its capacity? Can you sell Pat's books in English and French? Pat would come straight from the TV studio, with no time to eat a proper meal. A long, tiring day of promotion, starting with an early morning radio show. Will you fete and feed him?"

"Counting folding chairs and standing room, we can cram in two hundred attendees, the bookseller will order his work in both languages, and I'll ask my boss about food."

"Well, Lily." She pronounced my name Lee-lee. "We could perhaps fit in a reading on Thursday the seventeenth, after Pat's appearance on *La Grande Librairie* at 5:00 p.m. You get back to me with the information about hosting a dinner in his honor."

"Merciii, oh merciiii!" I gushed, then recited my work and home phone numbers and told her she could contact me day or night. She laughed at my eagerness.

Finally, I'd received a maybe. These days, everything felt fragile, so I remained cautious. Hayes was in a meeting with the board. When he and a handful of trustees exited his office, I discreetly asked him about hosting a dinner for Pat O'Malley.

"*The* Pat O'Malley?" he boomed. He bounced from one leg to the other, so excited I thought he might pee his pants.

Jennifer de Narp was speechless.

Pam de Laney said, "Of course, we'll honor him. He's a national treasure!"

"A *National Book Award–winning treasure*!" Moe Mandelbaum, the chairman, corrected. "Powwow now."

They all returned to Hayes's office to scheme.

While they worked out which wealthy donor would pay the tab, I called Colette Levy. Unfortunately, she was out. I'd fulfilled her requirements, and now had to pray she'd keep her end of the bargain. At lunchtime, I got out my journal to edit a scene in my novel, *French Kisses*. When I'd recounted the real-life versions of my dates to Mary Louise, we'd laughed our heads off. But now, skimming the pages alone at my desk, I found nothing funny about being stood up and let down.

And speaking of a letdown, unfortunately, tonight's speaker showed up drunk. I dragged him to my desk before Hayes could notice and somehow blame me for the mess. I served the guy a trough of coffee and assured him he had nothing to worry about—our audience was the kindest in all of Paris. As Hayes delivered the introduction, I feared it would be a rocky reading, but the art historian gripped the podium to steady himself and recounted the fascinating life of Élisabeth Vigée Le Brun, portraitist of Marie Antoinette and Catherine the Great. At the back of the room, I leaned against the wall to steady myself, and didn't realize how nervous I was until Wendy put her hands on my stiff shoulders, which were almost to my ears, and lowered them gently.

"It's a nerve-racking job," she whispered. "On any given night, you never know what will happen. Will the author get stuck in traffic, or show up high? Will they go off on an anti-Semitic rant? Will audience members get in a shouting match? Or worse, no attendees, and you're an audience of one for the author, who is equal parts pissed and humiliated."

I looked at her gratefully, glad that she got how I felt. "That's my biggest fear."

"Which scenario?"

I exhaled nervously. "All of them. This job is killing me. Shouldn't working in a library be more . . ." What was the right word? "More peaceful?"

"As long as you're working with humans, you'll never find peace. Maybe that's why we love writing. We're out of the rat race and on the page."

Afterward, she and I lounged in the cozy kitchen of the ALP, noshing on leftover Brie and baguette. Most events nights, these leftovers were my dinner.

"It's so cool that you have the keys to this place," she told me. "When I was program manager at the NYPL, I'd have loved to come and go as I pleased."

As we sipped our wine, she asked about my writing. I couldn't bear to admit that the queries I'd sent recently weren't for my own stories. They were to French editors in the hope of scoring a coup by booking a "big-name" speaker.

Instead, I confided that I'd become unsure about my work in progress. She told me that I shouldn't feel bad, that the first book is practice. She didn't publish hers, but writing it gave her confidence and honed her skills. She advised me not to put so much pressure on myself.

"Is there a goal you can manage, even a small one?" she asked. "Maybe writing a paragraph each workday?"

"There you go. A strong paragraph." Then she added, "Could it be that writing about failed relationships isn't where your passion lies? Is there a bigger story you want to tell?"

I told her I loved how she'd recounted the story of Jessie and the Cards, bringing in themes of class and cultural differences, and that I couldn't wait until her presentation next week.

~

I half-expected Hayes to boycott Wendy's Entre Nous event, given the way Jennifer de Narp had used it to stir up trouble; however, when Wendy arrived with her father and husband, he gave them a tour in magnanimous director mode ("This is a photo of Dorothy Reeder, the sexy directress who defied the Nazis." "And here's trustee Clara de Chambrun, the old broad who capitalized on family ties to the French prime minister in order to protect the ALP during the Occupation"). Though there was nothing to be gained, Hayes treated them with the same respect he gave to rich donors.

Promptly at 7:00 p.m., he ushered the trio to front-row seats next to Jennifer de Narp. From across the reading room, my gaze met his, and I put my hand to my heart in thanks. He nodded in acknowledgment before welcoming the crowd. A thrill ran up my spine at seeing all seventy chairs taken. Proof that you didn't need a big name to bring in big audiences.

I kept an eye out for Chris, but it appeared he hadn't been able to get off work. We'd exchanged numbers, but our chaotic work schedules kept us from chatting on the phone. Wendy was my first real guest speaker, and I wanted Chris to admire her work as much as I did, wanted him to be impressed by my discerning taste.

After Hayes's warm introduction and appeal for donations, Wendy took her place at the podium and greeted the audience, many of whom pulled out pads of paper to take notes. Meanwhile, Hayes headed toward his office and presumably slipped out the back door.

"Whether you're reading novels or writing them," Wendy told us, "you never know where books will take you. This one began at my job in the basement of the New York Public Library. Under the flickering fluorescent lights, I discovered my predecessor, Jessie Carson. Though my colleagues and I had never heard of her, she quickly became one of the great loves of my life. I'm inspired by her, and in awe of the road we've traveled together, albeit seventy-five years apart. I never dreamed I'd be standing in the hallowed reading room of the American Library in Paris like she once did. It's an honor and a privilege to be here.

"Heiress Anne Morgan, founder of the American Committee for Devastated France, hired this destitute children's librarian to head up the library section. In French, this aid organization was called Le Comité Américain pour les Régions Dévastées, and known by its acronym CARD. The women called themselves Cards, which is apropos because there is a calling card, a recipe card, a report card, and of course, my library card. She brought something to France that French people did not yet have, yet desperately needed. In sharing the Cards' story, I hope to shed light on the incredible women who left behind the comforts of home to care for French civilians who'd lost everything during World War One."

Wendy reminded us that France was the United States's oldest ally, beginning with their support of the American Revolution. Lafayette lobbied his government to support the American cause. He joined the Continental Army led by George Washington. Later, when France was in need, the Cards answered the call. Most accounts of war featured men, but it was important to remember women were there, too.

She then read from her book, the one I'd loved so dearly when I first discovered it.

"In times of difficulty," she finished, "it's heartening to remember the way total strangers rallied around folks who'd lost everything, heartening to see what one stubborn librarian can achieve.

I don't need to tell you that books change lives, inform, comfort, and bring us together."

Wendy had us remembering these incredible women forgotten by history as well as the power of the written word. A rousing round of applause ensued.

"Any questions?" I asked the audience, and felt a jolt of happiness when I spied Chris near the entrance with his hand raised.

"Jessie Carson sounds amazing," he said. "Did any of her letters survive?"

"I've only found one letter, from Jessie to her mother. It underlined how broke Jessie was. She wanted to visit her mother before leaving for France but couldn't afford the ticket from New York to Pennsylvania. It was heart wrenching to read that. In the same correspondence, Jessie wrote 'I never knew Miss Morgan could be such a fairy godmother.'"

After a few more questions and another round of applause, I escorted Wendy and her father to the circ desk. While she signed copies of *The Library Card*, her father beamed with pride.

"Now I understand why you write," he told her. "And why you came to Paris."

As she hugged him, Wendy's eyes met mine. "Thank you," she mouthed.

Surrounded by her fans, she sparkled as if a light had been switched on inside her, such a change from the first time we'd met. I had a feeling that tonight would give her the energy to keep writing and finish her documentary.

At the refreshment table, where David and I served drinks and nibbles, Chris was first in line. "Great choice of speaker," he said.

It was the best compliment I could have received. We grinned at each other like idiots until the Faithful elbowed him out of the way as they grabbed slices of Camembert.

"Catch up with you later," he said ruefully.

"Your young man asked a good question," Mrs. Coolidge told me.

Was it obvious how much I liked him? Could people tell just by observing us that Chris and I were together? I blushed. *Your young man.* I liked that. Yes, he was mine.

"Lovely to see so many students."

"Another wonderful event!"

I basked in the Faithfuls' praise, certain that this was how Odile felt with her habitués, M. de Nerciat, Mr. Pryce-Jones, and Professor Cohen. I loved how this job made me feel close to her.

Ms. de Narp sidled up to me. In one hand, she clutched her Louis Vuitton purse; in the other, a wineglass wanting a refill. Since she never acknowledged me at events, I steeled myself for a critical remark à la "The cheese is chalky."

Instead, she merely gestured to the line of attendees in front of Wendy. "We do good work. *You* do good work."

I teared up at the acknowledgment. Until now, neither she nor Hayes had ever said a kind word to me. Most of the time, she looked right through me, while he picked at my flyers, my choice of speakers, my self-worth.

"We want to focus on library history," Ms. de Narp continued. "Maybe you could write a column in the newsletter."

Still stunned by her unexpected compliment, I looked closer and noticed the faint crow's-feet. I couldn't know if the lines came from afternoons spent suntanning in Nice or from worrying about faraway family members. She was fifteen, maybe twenty years older than me. At my age, she already had a law degree, a husband, an apartment, and a vacation house. And me? I rented a room with a bathroom down the hall. I had a manuscript that had gone nowhere.

I realized that I was jealous; she seemed so together, while I was falling apart. On the street, the day of my job interview, I'd kicked her because of my insecurities—Mary Louise moving out, my not making headway as a writer. My belligerence had more to do with my feeling that I was a failure than with one more smoker tossing a cigarette butt on the sidewalk.

Mary Louise was right. I was selfish. I needed to start thinking about others, needed to stop lashing out and be accountable for my actions.

Plastic cup of wine in hand, I took one last glance around. Wendy continued to sign books. Chris waited in line to buy one from the bookseller, and when his gray eyes met mine, I felt my heart flutter. His "book head" was mostly tamed tonight, but a tuft still stood up straight. It reassured me somehow. Thanks to the library, I'd gotten to know my favorite author in the whole world; as well as the bookseller, who shone a light on books and women forgotten by history; and Chris, the first decent guy I'd dated. The wide-eyed Yearlings chatted with the grunge poets in ripped jeans, while the on-a-budget Faithful mingled with the wealthy Select Few—the ALP was the only place I knew of that could bring together such disparate groups. In his sweater vest and checkered pants, Lorenzo took a swig of Burgundy as he debated with David about whether *Cairo Now* or *London Then* was Professor Cohen's best novel. Tolstoy chimed in, asking what had become of her lost Paris novel. Since I'd been here, both David and Tolstoy had opened up—the library had given us all the confidence to talk to people from all walks of life.

I relished the cozy camaraderie of Entre Nous events. A dozen empty bottles were tucked under the refreshment table. On the cheese tray, only a few crumbles of Roquefort remained. Bellies were full, the laughter warm. The evening was a success. Man, I loved this community. I wasn't ready to say goodbye, but I had to make things right. I owed Jennifer de Narp an apology. I would give her one, even if it meant she fired me.

While she rambled on about the newsletter, I worked up the courage to confess. After I'd kicked her, maybe she'd felt shaken. Because of the late-night encounter with that creep Mike Roth, I now knew how she felt. I opened my mouth, and was finding the words, when she snapped her fingers in front of my face. "Are you listening?" she demanded. "Honestly, girl!"

"Sorry. I need to tell you something. You see, that day on the street, I was the one who—"

A splash of liquid hit my chin and cheeks. "What the—?" I gasped as I breathed in the pungent bouquet of bargain Burgundy. Rivulets of red flowed down my neck and soaked my blouse, my bra, my skin. Stunned by the attack, I scanned the vicinity to find the culprit. Lorenzo held up an empty cup.

"Oops," he said with a beurre-wouldn't-melt-in-my-mouth smile, certainly for the benefit of Ms. de Narp. "How clumsy of me to trip."

"Accidents happen," I replied in a measured tone, refusing to make a stink on Wendy's big night. I shot Lorenzo a look to let him know there would be retribution.

"We better get you cleaned up." Grabbing my elbow, he shoved me past the stacks, into the kitchen.

I yanked my arm free. "I wish you'd go back to the 001.9 section, where you belong!"

He grinned. "You see me as an unexplained phenomenon?"

"In the same league as Bigfoot," I confirmed.

"I'm flattered." Lorenzo dabbed at my neck with a tea towel.

I pulled it from his grasp and ran it over my chest. Then I closed the door so patrons wouldn't hear me hiss, "What were you thinking?"

"What were *you* thinking? Do you want to get yourself fired?"

"I need to be honest."

"You need to keep your job. To the trustees, staff are replaceable. Don't give her an excuse to get rid of you."

"I'm taking responsibility for my actions."

He threw his hands up. "In public? With a vindictive trustee who's had too much to drink? My slow-witted snickerdoodle, you need to watch your step. The previous library director dared to disagree with her. Once. De Narp had him fired. Now she's gunning for Hayes. It's a good thing you're dating a cop. If you cross de Narp, you'll need police protection."

"You're joking."

"She's been known to go off the rails. And the last thing any of us wants is for her to steamroll you."

What was he saying? It sounded like . . . "So does that mean you're fond of me?"

He crossed his arms. "I don't hate you."

"You like me!"

"Breaking in yet another program manager would just be a hassle."

It was as close as I'd get to an admission that he was partial to me, so I didn't press for more. I lifted the damp polyester from my skin. I only had three evening event blouses. "You ruined my best shirt."

"I saved your job."

"I want to tell her."

"And you will. On your last day here. Which might be sooner than you think."

"What?"

"This place is nearly bankrupt."

He let that tidbit sink in. I knew money was tight, but didn't realize things were *that* bad.

"What about the trustees?" I asked.

He let out a snort, the kind a bull makes before goring a matador. "For most of them, the library is a do-gooder line on their CV. They'll move on."

"And Hayes?"

"I peeked at his résumé. The guy never lasted more than two years in a job. Ever." He took a deep breath. "If anyone is going to save our community, it's us."

"Us?" My salary barely covered rent. Even if I wanted to, I couldn't contribute. "How?"

"The new volunteer has ideas. Have you met her? Felicity seems savvy."

This scene was surreal. I smelled like a wino. Lorenzo had revealed that he was an idealist. He was the last person I thought would be vested in saving our community. Since when did he care about staff and patrons? Narrowing my eyes, I looked at him askance. "Don't you hate people?"

His head shot back, as if he couldn't believe the absurdity of my question. "Of course, I hate people. People are the worst. But folks like David and Tolstoy and Meg need a place to call home. And I need the library—under French law, with my seniority, I'm practically 'unfireable.' Not to mention, everyone here is used to me."

"There you are!" Meg said as she and David squeezed into the kitchen. Arms akimbo, she turned to Lorenzo. "What on earth were you thinking?"

He pointed at me. "Lily was about to confess."

"I should've known you had your reasons," she told Lorenzo. "But you didn't have to look like you were having so much fun!"

"Have you ever thrown your drink in someone's face? It *is* fun."

"You could've taken Lily aside, you lunatic," David said.

"A lovable lunatic," he replied with a goofy grin.

Weirdly, after hearing Lorenzo's concern for the library, that's how I began to see him—a lovable librarian invested in the patrons and staff. In his own flamboyant way, he'd done what he thought best.

"Lily, dear, go home and get out of that wet top," Meg ordered.

The hum of voices emanating from the reading room reminded us that we had a full house.

"How can I? I need to lock up after the event."

She glowered at Lorenzo. "This one will be happy to do that for you." She sounded like a high school principal meting out punishment.

Back in the reading room, I glanced around, relieved to see Chris waiting in the newspaper section. We cut through the crowd and met near the entry.

His expression brimmed with concern. "What happened to your blouse?"

"My co-worker happened."

"The time bomb in the sweater vest?"

"How'd you guess? Anyway, the good news is that I get to leave early."

"Shall I accompany you home?"

I wanted to invite him over, wanted to be with him. But I had to think: what was the state of my studio? I hadn't washed the dishes in a week, which meant my mugs, plates, and glasses were strewn all over the place. Which would win out—decorum or lust? I had the walk home to decide.

The night air was cool. I started to shiver in my damp blouse. Chris took off his sweater and wrapped it around my shoulders.

"It'll get dirty," I protested.

"Who cares? Let's get you warm."

He wrapped his arm around my waist. His heat seeped into my skin; suddenly, I was grateful to Lorenzo.

"I'm glad you could come," I told Chris.

"Fortunately, a colleague was okay with swapping shifts—it's not always the case."

I gestured to the stain. "Believe me, I know about difficult co-workers."

"Still, you must enjoy your job. Bringing in authors every week, watching people connect."

Another reason I liked Chris so much—he understood what the library meant to me.

"Students gorged on the Brie," he continued. "I had the impression that they didn't eat regularly. David pushed the cheese plate toward them and encouraged them to finish it off."

"It's not easy being poor in Paris." On event nights, that cheese was my dinner, too. Tonight, I'd been so busy, I hadn't had a bite.

"You're feeding the mind and the body."

When we crossed the Seine, the wind picked up, and he pulled me closer. The *lampadaires* of the bridge bathed his face in a soft, warm light. For once, there was no traffic, and I liked to think I could hear the lap, lap, lap of the river coursing beneath us. It had been a long time since I'd felt so happy. Turning onto the boulevard, we caught a glimpse of the Sacré Coeur basilica, bright and silvery as the moon, before we turned onto a side street and ambled along—slowly, slowly—as if neither of us wanted the evening to end.

Upon arriving at my building, we stood inches apart. I stared at his chest. It had been ages since I'd brought a man home, ages since I'd felt this thrum of desire and trepidation. I wanted to be with him. I wanted him. But what did he want?

"My studio's a mess," I said, a little worried that he'd judge me.

His lips curled into a gentle smile. "No worse than mine."

"Do you want to come up?"

He took my clammy hands in his. "More than anything."

He followed me up the steep servants' stairs. Knowing that he was watching, I swayed my hips. My heart pounded, in part from the six flights, in part from the anticipation of being alone with Chris.

I unlocked three dead bolts and ushered him inside. "Let me slip into something a little more comfortable," I joked as I slid his sweater from my shoulders.

He turned away so I could change. Rummaging about, I found a mostly clean tee. It would have to do. To salvage my bra and blouse, I doused them with seltzer and set them in the hamper. Chris peered past the dirty dishes, straight to the painting on the wall. In it, Mary Louise had extended le Champ de Mars, the stately lawn, to the base of la Tour Eiffel. She'd planted poppies and let the grass grow wild. Her Eiffel Tower was awash in prairie.

"I've never seen it depicted like that," he said. "It's evocative, lyrical like a poem."

On the upside, Chris wasn't horrified by the mess. On the downside, he seemed to have lost interest in me. I couldn't be upset about being upstaged by the painting, though; I so wanted people to appreciate Mary Louise's art.

"There's more where that came from." I pointed to the canvases stacked against the wall.

"May I?" Squatting on his haunches, he thumbed through them. I could sense his admiration, and I liked him even more.

"These are incredible," he said.

I knelt beside him. "If only we could convince the artist."

"Where did you get them?"

"The garbage."

He searched my face to see if I was joking.

"Je ne comprends pas." He slipped into French, as if the situation would become clear if only we spoke his native language.

"I don't understand, either." I ran my finger along Mary Louise's signature on the hyacinth-blue tableau. "The artist is my best friend. Well, former best friend. She threw out these paintings. Told me if I touched them, she'd never speak to me again."

"Was she serious?"

I nodded. "And if she finds out . . ."

He stood and held out his hand to pull me up.

"You don't know how she'll react," he finished.

"Exactly."

"Did you ever read *Metamorphosis*?"

I nodded. Kafka, 833.912.

"Franz Kafka doubted his talent," Chris said, "and he asked his friend Max Brod to burn his manuscripts after his death."

I remembered the story. "If Kafka had wanted his manuscripts gone, he could have burned them himself."

"Exactly. I don't blame Brod for refusing."

We contemplated the canvases. I told Chris that part of me was thrilled that they'd come home; the other part worried that Mary Louise would be irate. How could I confess that I'd saved—or stolen—them without destroying our friendship? And maybe more important: Could I let her give up? Her paintings were powerful, her talent immense. I'd assured her that the fact those gallery owners craved bland canvases didn't mean her work wasn't excellent. Should I continue to push her, even if she ended up hating me?

"Do you think she really meant to throw them away?" he asked. "Or was it an impulse that she'll regret? Perhaps in a few months or years, she'll thank you."

I couldn't be sure.

"Do you know why she threw them out?" Chris asked.

"She said she couldn't take the rejection."

"These days, gallerists prefer blobs of paint to beautiful paintings. She shouldn't take it personally."

I winced, thinking of the rejections I'd accumulated. "It's hard not to take personally."

"Maybe it's tough to go from art classes, where classmates praise your work, to the hard, cold world."

I'd received plenty of rejections for my short stories. Maybe rejection was easier to take from faraway magazines than it was face-to-face from an art-world professional.

"Is she in a rut?" he asked.

"It's more than that. She didn't just quit painting. She moved out and quit talking to me."

"Who would ever quit talking to you?" He gazed at my mouth. Self-conscious, I gnawed on my lip. Suddenly, paintings were the furthest things from my mind. All I could think of was Chris.

He closed the distance between us. Staring into his eyes, I ran my fingers through his hair. Tentatively, his lips grazed mine. He held me tight; our tongues entwined. He tasted of sweet white wine. I wanted him. I wanted more. We moved to the futon, where he lay down and eased me on top of him. Our legs became entangled. I reveled in the heat of his hands exploring my back. My whole body came alive. Wanting more, I straddled him. His hips rose to meet mine. Being with him felt so damn good. I worked his shirt off and sank my teeth gently into his shoulder.

"Yes," he groaned.

He tugged off the shirt I'd donned just minutes before. Our torsos met, and this time it was me who moaned. I ran my hands through his hair, over his back as he kissed my cheek, my neck, my chest.

He sat up. "We should stop," he said, his breathing ragged.

"What?" I responded, though I knew he was right. We were moving too fast.

"I don't have any protection."

The condoms in my medicine cabinet had been there so long, they were surely wizened fossils.

"And I don't want to rush this," he said.

I remembered the last relationship I'd rushed. It was with the guy who didn't take the time to tell me he was married. Still dizzy with desire, I sat up. Chris put his arm around me.

"I like you," he said. "I want you. It's just . . . I don't want to screw this up."

"I like you, too."

"Maybe we can just talk?"

Tonight was too much. The shock of wine thrown in my face. The thrum of desire doused with the cold shower of restraint. I was light-headed from lack of dinner and lust. Hungry for Chris and for Brie and baguette. Thirsty for tenderness and connection.

What I needed was a cup of Swiss Miss. The cocoa was my comfort food, something I couldn't find in France. When my stepmom asked what I wanted for Christmas or my birthday, I requested a box, the kind with marshmallows. Dad grumbled about the exorbitant cost of airmail, but twice a year, I received a Swiss Miss care package. With my birthday several months away, I had to ration my dwindling stash.

Once, Mary Louise and I had invited our friend Aurélie to share our coveted hot chocolate. "Beurk! I can taste the chemicals," she complained after one sip. For months, the ritual was ruined. I switched to French cocoa, but it didn't taste like home.

Then one day, Mary Louise mimicked, "Ew, the chemicals!" and the judgment became our in-joke.

I couldn't drink a cup without offering Chris one and only hoped my singular pleasure wouldn't be ruined again. "A cup of coffee, or Swiss Miss?" I asked.

His brow furrowed. "*Une Suissesse?* What does a Swiss woman have to do with anything?"

"It's a brand of hot chocolate."

"Sounds perfect."

I heated the water in a pan and washed two mugs. When the water boiled, he poured it. We watched the mini marshmallows float. He took a sip, and I waited for his verdict.

"Delicious," he said.

"The marshmallows make it special."

"Indeed, they do."

English sounded better coming from his lips. He enunciated clearly, as if each word was special and deserved attention.

We sat, shoulder to shoulder, hip to hip, knee to knee on the futon. I told him about how much I'd loved sharing a cup with my two little brothers after an afternoon of sledding. How much I missed them, even though we talked twice a month. How when I'd lived at home, the significance of Swiss Miss hadn't registered because I could always pick up a box, but now . . .

"Proust had his madeleine, you your Swiss Miss. Reminders of childhood that offer solace and make us nostalgic."

"What's yours?" I asked.

"My grandfather's dear friend Bitsi makes quince jam. I smear it on everything—my afternoon tartine, even my pork roast. Sometimes a spoonful in my tea."

I spread my calico quilt over us, and we burrowed underneath. It was two in the morning, then three. Neither of us wanted to say goodbye. The electricity of desire had transformed into a desire to know everything about each other. Did he have siblings? No, he was an only child. How long had he been a cop? Seven years. The last time he'd been in love? A year ago, when he and his girlfriend had broken up. She hadn't been ready to commit. He was ready for a serious relationship.

"Do you think you'll stay in France?" he asked.

I explained that at first, Paris was a puzzle that Mary Louise and I wanted to solve. The city was all-consuming—French slang to decipher, art galleries to explore, readings at bookstores every night of the week, jazz concerts in the basements of bars for the price of a watered-down drink.

"In those days," I told Chris, "I was having too much fun to worry about family or be homesick."

"And now?"

"Paris will always be a mystery. You could live here two hundred years and still not see everything." I swallowed. "But I miss loved ones. I'm starting to pine for the quiet of Montana. I never thought I'd say that."

It was nearly 5:00 a.m. We didn't want to sleep, didn't want to say good night. We regarded the squares of my quilt, the box of Swiss Miss on the counter, the paintings leaning against the wall. Thinking of Mary Louise, I sighed.

"It's hard to lose a friend," Chris said.

As hard as losing a lover, I wanted to say. Many movies and novels focus on the pain of divorces and breakups, but few seem to acknowledge how painful it is to lose a dear friend.

"Maybe she followed you to Paris, and now she's figuring out what she wants? Don't lose hope." He glanced at his watch and jumped up. "I don't want to leave, but I'm working the six a.m. shift."

He leaned down to kiss me. He tasted of chocolate.

"Get some rest," he murmured.

His sandalwood scent imbued my quilt. I fell asleep upright on the futon. Happy. Sated. With much to think about.

Chapter 15

SEPTEMBER 1995

Meg Bauer—volunteer

Jennifer and Pam treated me to high tea for what would have been my fiftieth wedding anniversary. On rue Royale, in the pastel pasture of Ladurée, we sipped Earl Grey from gold-rimmed cups and savored finger sandwiches. Each girl wore a brooch I'd designed; Jennifer sported a mosaic on the lapel of her ivory Chanel blazer, Pam affixed a tree-of-life square to her mandarin collar. It gave me great satisfaction.

We three unwound in plush velvet chairs; beside each was a matching stool for a handbag and/or a lapdog. Pam had fed her shih tzu Melvin a sliver of *rosbif,* and now he snored contentedly in her Birkin. I'd encouraged her to volunteer at the animal shelter, and he was one of the first dogs she worked with. She adopted him after just three days. At first, he cowered in her handbag, refusing to peek his head out. He soon became the star of story hour and pranced from lap to lap, cheering up any child having a down day. Pam was brittle, but when she petted Melvin, there was tenderness in her touch. She was terrible with most people, but good to animals and books.

I'd met Jennifer on her first week in Paris, when she was as sweet as Lily—still at uni, ready to right wrongs as a lawyer. Her parents wanted her to marry French nobility and had even found her a suitor; Frédéric's parents, *le baron* and *la baronne,* wanted him to marry money. During the short courtship, he did the predictable, the stereotypical—weekend getaways to Nice, red roses, flowery poems he probably plagiarized, and flattery. *Tu es belle. Tu es magnifique.* Compared to staid Texans, he seemed dashing.

Frenchmen are masters of staging. Now, a flurry of waiters in starched suits brought a chocolate cake and champagne. One set the dessert before me with a flourish. Another opened the bottle. The cork popped. I loved the sound, which promised celebration. Even after all these years, I recalled the way the bubbles tickled my nose on my wedding day. Or maybe I was just tickled to marry Felix. I took his surname and shortened my name to Meg, hoping to leave everything that happened during the war behind, to become another person. It wasn't possible—we are our experiences and choices. Thus, professionally, I remained Margaret Saint James. After Felix died, I went to Johannesburg to spend time with my daughter. I'd intended to move there, but after only a month, Paris called me back. The city wasn't done with me. So I made my peace with the past.

"You girls are spoiling me!" I took a sip of champagne. Ah, those lovely bubbles. "This is too much."

"Nonsense!" Pam replied. "You deserve the best."

"She and I rarely see eye to eye," Jennifer added, "but on this we do agree."

She squeezed my hand. I knew this splurge was her idea, and it meant a lot that she'd made a fuss. As Felix used to say, spending a special occasion alone was "heartacheful."

He'd been devoted. One couldn't say the same for Jennifer's husband. She'd thought marriage meant fidelity. Frédéric thought it meant free financing to restore the family château and vineyard. Jennifer could seem harsh to others. She was harsh. But I'd known her when she was green. I'd seen her heart break, seen how his callousness changed her. Not just changed her. Warped her.

Jennifer raised her glass. "To Meg!"

We three clinked rims.

What a relief to see these two move from hatred, to uneasy truce, to actually getting along. I suspected that they could be the best of friends, if only they could overcome the past. Wasn't it odd how people who were so similar could rub each other the wrong way? Of course, the girls did have one thing too many in common—Jennifer's husband. I didn't blame Pam for sleeping with him. Frédéric was a suave liar, and when he began romancing Pam, he'd neglected to mention that he was married.

Suspecting him of cheating, Jennifer returned home early from a law conference and found them in bed. She confided that his infidelity hadn't been the most painful shock. No, it was the way he'd erased any sign of her: their wedding portrait above the mantel, a photo from their honeymoon on her nightstand, the collection of perfume bottles on her vanity, the beloved childhood classics she'd hoped to read to their children—all in a heap in her walk-in closet.

To her credit, Pam ended the relationship immediately. She blackened his name in every social circle, from wine enthusiasts to the Franco-American Chamber of Commerce. He retreated to his château.

She apologized to Jennifer, which I thought showed character. After all, it had hurt Pam's pride to be conned by that "Don Jean." Unfortunately, the damage had been done. Jennifer was unable to forgive or forget. It was why I didn't tell her that Lily was the one who'd kicked her—even after all these years, I never knew how Jennifer might react. Lily had a good head on her shoulders and smart instincts—she was right to avoid Jennifer. For someone else, the encounter on the street could be a quirky story to chuckle over, but not for Jennifer.

I closed my eyes as I tasted the cake. "Delicious!"

"Love like yours and Felix's deserves to be honored." Pam hugged me. "And *you* deserve to be feted. What would we do without you? What would the ALP do without you?"

"I can't tell you how many mothers have confided that they

maintain their memberships because of you," Jennifer added. "They're touched that you remember their children's names and the books their little ones have read."

"We do have lovely members and staff," I said.

"We must do something about the program manager, though," Jennifer said. "At a recent event, she was sloshed, her blouse was drenched with red wine."

"Lily only had one cup," I said sternly. "It wasn't her fault someone spilled a drink on her."

"You always give people the benefit of the doubt," Jennifer chided. "She was glassy-eyed and could barely finish a sentence."

Pam's eyes widened. "Do you think she's on drugs?"

"Most certainly not!" I said. "You two make her nervous. What's my rule?"

"If you don't have anything nice to say—" Jennifer began.

"Shut the hell up," Pam finished.

"I wish you'd be kinder to staff. The younger ones make minimum wage. I'll remind you that Lily *worked for free* so Hayes wouldn't cancel Wendy Peterson's event. That shows dedication."

"Sorry, Meg," they said in sync.

That was more like it.

Talk moved to fundraising.

"Felicity suggested hosting a gala," Jennifer said.

"A gala?" I asked. "Are you sure the library can afford a venue?"

"We absolutely can't," Jennifer said.

"The ALP will host a cheese-and-wine evening in the reading room," Pam explained. "And not the same swill we serve on event nights."

"My in-laws are donating their winery's very best bottles," Jennifer said.

I'm sure Jennifer gave them no choice, probably by threatening to turn them in for tax evasion.

"It will be a lot of hard work," I cautioned. "Creating a guest list, designing and sending out invitations, tracking down addresses for the mailing list, creating budget-friendly centerpieces and decorations."

"Deciding how to style my hair," Jennifer said dreamily.

"A chignon, definitely a chignon. And that little Dior number you wore to the Musée d'Orsay fundraiser would be perfect," Pam told her.

"*J'adore,*" Jennifer answered with a grin.

Despite myself, I gave thought to which outfit to wear and the friends I would treat to tickets.

"We're also hosting a silent auction," Pam said, giving Jennifer a nudge.

"A literary evening with select items to bid on." Jennifer leaned closer to me. "We know there's something every Parisienne wants." She pointed to her lapel. "An original Margaret Saint James brooch."

Fifteen years ago, I'd closed my atelier, in part to retire, in part to care for my husband, who had Alzheimer's. But every so often—on the street, in line at the bakery—I spied a woman wearing my colorful porcelain and felt a jolt of joy. In recent years, jewelers rang to inquire if I had pieces that I'd be willing to sell—the brooches were now vintage. In fact, I'd created three pieces specifically for Odile—covers of her favorite books, *Jane Eyre, Their Eyes Were Watching God,* and *The Priory*—intending to give them to her when she came back. Though she never returned, I didn't have the heart to sell them.

"Would you consider coming out of retirement, Meg?" Pam asked.

"Oh, you girls." I could feel my cheeks flush with pleasure. "It's kind of you to ask."

Jennifer insisted kindness had nothing to do with it. Pam added that my pieces were "all the rage" and would go for "beaucoup bucks."

I knew how much my jewelry was worth. Over the years, burglars had broken into my atelier and flat. But I'd made sure there was nothing to steal. In order to protect my remaining brooches, I stole into the library, opened the safe in the director's office, laid my porcelain pieces on Professor Cohen's manuscript, and locked the door.

I'm the only one left with a key. Years ago, Boris, the Franco-Russian head librarian, had entrusted it to me. We didn't share it with any of the directors, suspecting they'd be tempted to sell the "long-lost" Irène Cohen manuscript to fund the ALP. In accordance with Irène's last will and testament, that novel belonged to Odile.

When Hayes first arrived, I offered my assistance—decades of institutional knowledge and familiarity with each patron. For example, I could have informed him that though he courted her as if she were a wealthy debutante, the woman he referred to as "Crazy Mazie" had no money—the only inheritance from her husband was his gambling debt.

Aside from my daughter and husband, the library was my greatest happiness—staff and volunteers had become my family. However, for me, the ALP was also a source of pain. With each successive year, I became more disillusioned. The worst was two years ago, when the outgoing director promised me the program manager position. For decades, I'd done the work for free, and now my dedication would finally be recognized with a job title. The money would come in handy, and the acknowledgment meant everything to me. Then Hayes arrived and hired a voluptuous undergrad. When pressed on why he didn't follow through, he joked, "Why hire the old cow when we get the crème de la crème for free?" That girl didn't even last six months. Neither did the next. He was smitten by pretty girls, then became enraged because they didn't have the experience to do the job. Behind my back, he referred to me as Nutmeg.

I'd begged Hayes to highlight the ALP's illustrious literary past—a peek in the archives would tell you that the Lost Generation found themselves at the library; Ernest Hemingway and

Gertrude Stein published their articles in our newsletter—but my suggestions fell on deaf ears. Yet when Felicity, an attractive *young* woman, suggested underlining ALP history, he decided it was a brilliant idea.

"What do you think?" Jennifer grasped my hand. "A silent auction featuring an original brooch by *the* Margaret Saint James."

The girls regarded me with pleading puppy eyes. I didn't want to tell them no, but I couldn't say yes. Most of me would do anything to help the library. But a small part said, *Not while Hayes is in charge.*

Chapter 16

SEPTEMBER 1995

Lily Jacobsen—program manager

Dear Odile,

You're right—there's a lot I haven't told you. First, I've put aside my novel French Kisses. *In rereading, I realize that I put the "man" in "manuscript"—it's chapter upon chapter of lousy boyfriends. My friend Wendy suggested that I should find a more meaningful topic. You mean so much to me. I'd love to write about your experience as a war bride. I know your story by heart and feel readers would love it as much as I do. Mary Louise accused me of living in Lily-land. She's not wrong, and I want to change.*

Speaking of Mary Louise, she moved out several months ago and isn't talking to me. I can't say I blame her. Here in Paris, I expected her to follow my lead like we were still in junior high. I didn't realize how overbearing I'd become. She never told me. Well, she probably tried, but I didn't listen. I didn't confide in you because I was embarrassed and thought I could fix things on my own, but now I'm not so sure. I miss her, but I don't think she misses me.

Most important of all, I've been sitting on some information, partly unsure you would want it, partly not wanting to hurt you. In the ALP manuscript collection, I found

*Margaret's war memoir. She doesn't describe events the same way you do. I hesitate about sending it, and hope that I'm doing the right thing in sharing it with you now. I *might* have a lead on where to find her, and am not sure if I should press on. I'll do as you ask.*

Love,
Lily

Dearest Lily,

Thank you for sending me Margaret's pages. They were the best gift I could have ever received. I know now that I judged her wrongly. Sometimes I want to see her more than anything, other times I'm so ashamed of how I treated her that I'm afraid to face her. And anyway, why would she want to see me? She went on to become an artist, and what was I? A part-time secretary in a dying town. I wish I could encourage you to follow the lead that you mentioned, but honestly, the past is better in the past.

You're a wonderful, true friend, and have a gift for bringing people together. I got used to keeping my back to everyone in Froid, but you turned me around. You have a good heart. That's why I am certain Mary Louise will understand. Take the first step. Go to her and ask forgiveness. Friendships, like romantic relationships, go through trials and tribulations. The important thing is not to run. The biggest mistake I ever made was leaving Paris and abandoning my friend. If I could go back in time and talk things through, I would. It's too late for me, but not for you.

Nowadays, psychologists call this point of stress "fight or flight." I always chose "flight." It's daunting to stay and fight.

Don't be like me. Give everything you've got to Mary Louise, just like she has always given her all to you.

Love,
Odile

At my desk, I read the letter over and over. She was right about giving my all to Mary Louise. But how to take the first step when Mary Louise accused me of suffocating her?

And then, as if I'd conjured her, she peeked into the back office. Mary Louise? I rose from my desk as though my veins were infused with happiness and helium. How I'd dreamed of this moment, of showing her around—in the foyer, this ink splotch on the carpet is where I stand while waiting for speakers to arrive; in the reading room, this seat at the oak table is where I first spied Chris; and in the stacks, here's my favorite nonfiction section, 808 (writing and getting published). I'd dreamed of Mary Louise attending my events and being struck by the wisdom of each speaker. Now that she was here, I felt awkward and tongue-tied, as if we were on a blind date.

She looked like her old self. She'd dyed the washed-out blond back to her original red. I wished our friendship could be put to rights as easily.

"Hi," I said. The word came out a question.

"The jerk at the front desk charged me twenty-five francs just to enter," she started.

"Sorry about that. It's a day fee for folks who aren't members."

"I told him I was here to see you, and he wouldn't believe me."

"Lorenzo isn't so bad, once you get to know him. Dealing with the public isn't easy."

"The front-desk Doberman is a great way to scare people off."

"Doberman?" Had she come here just to judge us? "Did you forget what working with the public is like? It's hard!"

"Sorry, he got my back up."

Arms akimbo, I demanded, "Are you seriously complaining

about donating five bucks to a good cause? Also: please don't insult my co-workers." Man, my voice had gotten loud. I wanted so badly to repair our relationship, but I couldn't help it: I had to defend the library. "Why are you even here?"

"Today's the fourteenth."

Suddenly our French-iversary mattered to her?

"And . . ." she continued, "I didn't like the way we left things the other night."

"The other night?" I snarled. It had been two months.

Across from me, Marius cleared his throat, his way of saying *Pipe down, girl!* Holy crap, I'd taken him and Meg hostage and made them witnesses to our fight. Worse, patrons had likely heard.

"Sorry, guys," I said softly. "That was unprofessional of me." Turning back to Mary Louise, I continued: "I'm sorry I yelled at you. Maybe we should talk another time."

"Can't we go outside?"

To my surprise, fighting had felt good. In the past, when we were mad at each other, we retreated to separate corners—friendship time-outs—never discussing why we were upset. Then, when we were over it, we resumed as if no harm had been done, no pain inflicted, and there was no acknowledgment that those wounds added up over time.

I opened the door and gestured for her to step into the courtyard. Maybe having it out would help.

"I came to say I was sorry. And that I miss you." She reached into her Louis Vuitton purse and pulled out an oblong present.

I unwrapped the paper and found a bookmark and stationery set in the shape of the Eiffel Tower. She understood how much I adored these pieces of Paris. Back in Montana, la tour Eiffel had been my beacon, the promise of an exciting writerly life. I hugged her gifts to my chest. "I'm sorry, too. I've missed you."

"I know."

"You withdrew," I said, still hurt. "Why couldn't you tell me how you felt?"

"Why couldn't you listen? My whole life, I've been stuck in your shadow. God forbid I make other friends or follow my own path. You don't need to know everything about me."

"I don't want us to grow apart."

"It's not growing apart. It's growing up. We each need to do our own thing. I know you have my best interests at heart, and that you love my paintings, probably even more than I do."

"I can't believe you threw them away." It was years of hard work. Of imagination and dedication. Of honing her craft. I had to tell her I'd scooped up her paintings. Now that time had passed, she'd thank me for protecting them. But just as I was about to admit the truth, Jennifer de Narp pulled up in her Mercedes and exited into a fog of black exhaust.

"Why aren't you at your desk?" She poked her Virginia Slim in my direction.

My mouth went dry. It was funny—I could defend Lorenzo, but couldn't defend myself.

It turned out I didn't have to. Scowling at her, Mary Louise let out a low whistle. It sounded a lot like *How dare you, lady?*

"Don't dally," Ms. de Narp told me. Nodding approvingly at Mary Louise, she said, "Nice handbag," before swishing into the back office.

"Who was that?" Mary Louise asked. "Or what was that?"

"The reason I deserve hazard pay."

"Rich Parisians are weird," she said.

"Tell me about it."

It felt like we were *us* again.

"Thanks for defending me," I said.

"She's a real piece of work."

"No, I'm the piece of work."

"What do you mean?"

I recounted that I'd accidentally kicked Ms. de Narp in the shin before my job interview.

Mary Louise snorted a laugh. "'Accidentally,'" she repeated in a knowing tone, clearly unconvinced. "Lucky for you, Ms. Mercedes wasn't on the hiring panel. But why would you do that? Not that she didn't deserve it."

Because I was mad at you, mad at the world, I thought. "In my mind, it was because she littered."

"Good ol' Lil, fighting for what she thinks is right."

I shrugged. "It was impetuous and dumb. More than anyone, you know I don't always think before I act. I'm working on that, I really am."

"I can see that. Thanks for listening that evening, and for walking away. I know leaving my paintings behind was hard for you, but it made me feel like there was hope that we could be friends again. I finally got through to you."

"I'm glad," I said weakly.

"Maybe I could swing by for dinner sometime? I miss the old place."

If she did that, she would see her paintings, see what I'd done. I began to sweat.

"Or you could come to one of our evening events here."

She said she'd think about it and left through the courtyard. I returned to my desk. Mortified about having made a scene, I avoided eye contact with Marius or Meg. Even though Mary Louise and I had finished on good terms, the unexpected argument left me on edge. My body had become a pressure cooker, the vapor of fear and anger stuck inside me. Writing eased that pressure. Putting a pen to paper released the steam of thought. At my desk, I reached out to the one person who always understood.

Dear Odile,

I wish you were here, I wish I were there. Mary Louise and I came to Paris to become artistes, and now she wants to give up. How can she quit being a painter when that is who she is? Even though my writing career isn't going anywhere, I'll never stop trying—I've vowed to write a paragraph a day. I did what you said—I apologized. Shouldn't that be enough?

Love,
Lily

Actually, I hadn't followed Odile's advice, which was to take the first step. Mary Louise had come to me. And I'd yelled at her. I tossed the letter in the bin and started over.

Dear Odile,
Please come. I need you.

"Tough day?" Meg set a mug of Earl Grey on my coaster. "I heard you fighting. We all did. And I wanted to say that I lost my best friend and would hate for you to lose yours. Try to be gentler with yourself and with her. I became angry with mine when she . . . betrayed my trust. She said she was sorry, but I refused to accept her apology. I told her to go, and she disappeared. I did everything I could to find her, but Odile left Paris without a trace. I've regretted my stubbornness for five decades."

This was the opening I'd been waiting for. "Your friend's name is Odile?"

I dug in my purse and proffered Odile's latest letter.

Meg skimmed the missive, her gaze flittering between me and the page. "You know her? She writes to you?"

I heard a universe of hurt in that last question. *Why you and not me?*

I explained that Odile was a war bride and had ended up in my small Montana town.

"Finally, after all these years, there are answers." Meg sank onto the corner of my desk, as if her legs could no longer hold her. "You have no idea of the horror when a person you love goes missing.

We—her parents and her friends—didn't know what happened to her. When she didn't return, we feared she'd perished in the war. We never knew if she was dead or alive." Meg gulped down some air. "Each one of us—her father, mother, and I—was convinced we were to blame."

I was startled by the intensity of her words, of her guilt.

"She's really all right?" Meg's voice was shaky, incredulous.

I nodded, feeling protective of Odile. I knew she had her reasons for leaving, so I measured my words. "She was my neighbor. It's thanks to her that I fell in love with French, that I'm here. So you're her Margaret?"

"She told you about me? About . . . what happened?"

"Yes." I now found myself feeling for Margaret and had to hug her. She held me tight, and I felt hot tears melt into the collar of my blouse. Hers or mine, I could not say.

"Tell me what you can."

I explained that from what Odile had confided, leaving Paris had been painful. It took years to adapt to life in Froid, Montana. Folks hadn't always been kind. Though she'd been withdrawn, she was now active in the church and had friends. She'd kept up with Paris news through the *Herald,* and knew that Margaret had become an artist. I showed her a photo of me and Odile, with her hennaed hair and bright red belt.

Meg traced Odile's belt with her finger. "My last gift to her."

"She wore it every single day."

"Really?"

I nodded. "For high school graduation, she bought me a plane ticket to Paris. I found your atelier, but it had closed."

"Why didn't she come herself?"

"Odile said that Paris held dark memories. But I'd been trying to find you. The man at your atelier said you'd moved to South Africa."

"I'd intended to, but came back after two months. I thought I could leave everything that happened behind me, but learned it's better to make peace with the past." Meg pointed to my letter begging Odile to return. "If you send it, will she come?"

"I think so. Do you want to write a note to her?"

"If I started writing, I might never stop," Meg said shakily. "She won't want to hear from me. Send the letter yourself."

Chapter 17

OCTOBER 1995

Tolstoy—Writer in Residence

Sometimes, I feel more dead than alive.

That's what I first told Bill Delaney when I was admitted to the VA in DC without my foot. He visited me in the hospital every day; sometimes his wife, Pam, came, too. He'd served in Vietnam. That's why he understood what I was going through. He promised the memories would fade. That life would get better. That someday, I would feel like myself again.

My name used to be Rick Lager. I'm from a dying town in eastern Kentucky. You've never heard of it. When I was eighteen, I wanted to study journalism but couldn't afford college. After graduating, I got a nine-to-five stocking produce at the grocery store. Rent and food ate up my salary, so I couldn't save. My pastor advised me to join the National Guard to earn money.

As a "weekend warrior," I saw myself running drills on base, driving Humvees down the highway at a mind-numbingly dull fifty-five miles per hour, and evacuating families during natural disasters like hurricanes. Like the other guys in my unit, I never expected to be sent to Kuwait. We'd signed up for the National Guard and found ourselves in an international war in a country none of us could have picked out on a map.

We guardsmen were unpopular overseas. The enemy hated us, of course. But some of the career army guys did, too. Who could blame them? They'd had years of training; my unit had a few weekends. One sergeant resented the hell out of me. Complained that he always had to save my ass. Twice, when missiles screeched through the air, I froze. Wouldn't you? Scuds were erratic and dangerous, the five-hundred-pound warheads known to hold chemical weapons. Sarge had to shove my gas mask over my face and drag me to shelter. The seconds of delay could have killed us both.

During downtime, my nose was always firmly planted in a book. He started calling me Tolstoy. To him, the moniker was an insult. Though most of America had moved on from the Cold War and found new people to hate, Sarge still had a sore spot for Russia.

When I started taking notes in my journal, he taunted me about keeping a *diary*. He said the word in a high-pitched voice, imitating a girl. I didn't let him stop me. Active duty was overwhelming. Recording what happened helped me comprehend it, not that anything could make sense of the deaths by friendly fire.

Okay, my own sergeant didn't like me. That stung, especially since I'd gotten along with teachers and troop leaders back home. Later, I noticed Sarge kept his distance from all the guys, and figured he didn't like anyone. Later still, I saw that he couldn't like us. Sentiment was dangerous. His job was to stay rational and composed in order to keep us alive.

When a group of us got in the rig and went on patrol, I was okay. Maybe because I trusted Sarge. I'll say one thing about him: He protected his own. After a while, thanks to his steadfastness, I got used to the sound of shells, got used to facing danger. When the attack came, the last thing I remember before losing consciousness was grabbing him by the scruff of the neck and covering his body with mine.

In the makeshift hospital, when I came to, I was lying on my belly. The first thing I saw was Sarge's ruddy face. He was sitting in a chair, leaning forward, hands folded together. "Hell, Rick . . ."

I had no idea he knew my first name. That's how I knew my

injuries were bad. I understood the next words out of his mouth would be an apology. I didn't want it. None of this was his fault.

"The name's Tolstoy," I barked.

That shut him up.

He stood and saluted me.

~

When the lacerations on my back healed some, I was sent stateside with a medal. At the VA, I got fitted for a prosthetic foot and started physical therapy. In hindsight, I probably should have got some regular therapy, too. From outward appearances, I seemed okay. But I could no longer stand loud noises. Could no longer go to action movies or concerts. Could no longer go out of the house. Even an ordinary walk down the street was out of the question—a wailing ambulance siren had me diving for the gutter. The Fourth of July about did me in.

But it was more than that. Back in my hometown, I just wasn't comfortable. At church, the whole congregation tilted their heads in pity when they saw me. They brought me baked goods. They shook my hand or patted my shoulder. Bill said that when he got back from Vietnam, folks treated him like shit, spitting on him and calling him a baby killer. With this war, the nation repented and behaved better toward returning soldiers.

Bill never forgot how it felt to go back to a place that didn't understand. Now, he and his wife, Pam, run an organization to help "wounded warriors," whether it's with a college scholarship or with a down payment for a house. They gave me the form, but I couldn't fill it out by myself. The phantom pain made it hard for me to think. Or maybe my brain was still scrambled. I couldn't make sense of anything. Bill asked what I would want, where I would go, if the sky were the limit.

"I don't know," I told him. "Away. I would go away."

Pam always lugged a blue granny purse around with her. I'm pretty sure she could have fit my whole life in there. Twenty years younger than Bill, she dressed matronly—high collars, quilted beige shoes—so the age gap wouldn't be obvious. I'm guessing that at some point in her life, she struggled, and he saved her. Like he was trying to save me now.

"What would you want to do, where would you go?" Bill repeated.

I glanced around the PT room, desperate for something to say to get them off my back. My eyes landed on Pam's purse. In the middle, near the top, embossed in small gold letters, was the word PARIS.

So that's what I said. They latched on.

It's liberating to live in a place where no one knows your past, Pam replied. The two of them spent part of the year in Paris. She'd just joined a library board. She and Bill would find a place for me.

With my writer in residence stipend, I signed a one-year lease on a small apartment in a fancy old building near the library. A volunteer named David and I became friends—we bonded over each of us almost dying in a desert. I told him I get mad for no reason. He said there's definitely a reason. He gets me. Since he crashes at the library, I gave him the spare key to my place so he can use the shower and washing machine, which is tucked in the corner of the bathroom, beside the bidet. Neither of us knew what that was. We peered into its basin, and when I turned the faucet, water squirted straight up like a fountain and soaked our faces. We laughed. How far we'd come. The world is so funny and foreign to us.

Most days, you'll find me at the ALP. When I arrive each morning, the program manager serves me a strong coffee. Sometimes, the assistant director helps me work out my aggression. The head librarian is wiry like my old basketball coach. He picks out books he thinks I might like. I do my best writing near the reading room window. The nicked wooden table reminds me of detention. The palmetto soothes me. If this southern transplant can thrive here, maybe I can, too. Touching its shiny new leaves makes me feel that everything, someday, will be fine.

Chapter 18

OCTOBER 1995

Lily Jacobsen—program manager

After work, Wendy and I met up in a booth at the Basement Brasserie. Talking to her made me feel like a real writer. She was so open, so bighearted that I couldn't help but ask for guidance concerning decisions I needed to make about my future—I wanted to write about something bigger than myself to get out of Lily-land. I explained that I longed to start a new project but was exhausted after working sixty-hour weeks as both program manager and English tutor.

"How did you decide when to move on from your job at the NYPL?" I asked. "Did you know it was time to quit? Or did you play it safe and take a leave of absence? Did you have a nest egg or did you leap into the void?"

I knew I might be overwhelming her, but I couldn't help it.

"First, stop doing unpaid labor," she ordered. "I'm sure you're pressured to 'help out' on a regular basis. Your boss counts on you to feel guilty and obligated to pitch in. I'm sure you work double the hours you're paid for."

It was true. I did.

"When was the last time you took a day off?"

"July." The library had closed for the Fourth, and I'd spent the day catching up on sleep. It had been my only day off since I'd started my job.

"Value your time and yourself," Wendy continued. "You need energy and mental space to create. Once you figure out your passion, what you *must* write about, the rest falls into place. I resigned once I had my book deal. There was no looking back. One program manager to another, I believe in you."

I mulled over Wendy's advice. *Write what you love.* As a child, I'd been obsessed with Odile. Before I got to know her, I'd composed her story in my head: *She was a spy in the Résistance. No, she was a collaboratrice. No, she was a hero.* My fascination with her had not waned. Maybe hers was the story I was meant to write. It couldn't hurt to give it a try. Over the weekend, I typed nonstop; it was a story I'd contemplated for a decade. Energy and words flowed.

NORMANDY, JANUARY 1945
ODILE

The U.S. Army did not know what to do with me. Or with Marceline or Lucienne or Huguette. Since the autumn, requests for permission to marry mademoiselles had cluttered commanding officers' desks. Some days, it seemed there were as many fiancées as soldiers, and as many awkward conversations. "You barely know the woman!" "You're shipping off tomorrow!" "You'll forget her!" "She'll forget you!" Nothing doing. The men wanted their brides with them in America.

Naturally, wounded soldiers like my husband, Buck, got sent home quickly, first-class mail. But the army brass thought it wouldn't hurt us ladies to sit in a depot in Normandy, waiting to be sent parcel post if our paperwork came through. While we were waiting at Camp Lucky Strike, Red Cross volunteers taught us to sew quilts. As we pieced patches of material together, we spoke of our darlings, of the country we would call home.

~

Meanwhile at the library, Colette Levy, Pat O'Malley's editor, still hadn't confirmed his visit. Each time I rang her, she was mysteriously out of the office. Was she avoiding me? Or could it simply be a question of "French time," whose hours moved more slowly than others', and Colette meant to confirm . . . eventually? Perhaps she'd received a better offer from Piccadilly Books. No, she seemed like a straight shooter; I suspected she was interested in having the author speak here. Too often, I'd jumped to conclusions and lashed out. This time, I would be patient.

Not everyone was willing to wait.

Today, Hayes strode into the back office, and I quickly closed my journal and slid it under a folder. He rapped his knuckles on my desk. "Any news?"

It was the fifth time he'd asked this week.

My chair squeaked as I swiveled to face him. "The second I hear, you will, too."

From the corner of my eye, I could see the color-coordinated events calendar, Pat O'Malley still penciled in.

Hayes's finger tapped the square over and over. "We need to fill the gaping hole in our schedule."

"Colette will come through."

"Face it, we've been stood up. It's humiliating!"

On his way out the door, he muttered, "This was the one thing you were hired for. And you can't even do it."

I hung my head in shame.

My first weeks at the ALP, I'd been carefree as I sent out letters to French publishers, hoping to book "big names." At evening events, I'd felt such joy in making a difference—authors sold books and connected with fans, while attendees learned something and were entertained, and friendships formed over wine and cheese and the written word.

I hadn't yet grasped the stakes—to survive, the library needed more members, more publicity, more donors. My role was to help secure the future. I'd underestimated how difficult it would be to reel in a literary star—since I loved the library, I figured authors and editors would, too. The ALP received as many rejections from editors as I did for my novel. I hadn't hit any of the targets I'd set for myself.

Now, the job felt like life or death, mainly death. No more ambling into the reading room to catch a glimpse of Chris. I ate lunch at my desk and barely strayed from my landline. Even when Marius's phone rang, I grabbed my receiver and squeaked "Allo?"—only to hear the dial tone. It sounded like a flatline, tolling the end of my time as the program manager.

Fortunately, there was very little downtime to dwell. Something was always happening—story hour, an Entre Nous event, a scuffle. The ALP seemed to be a calm, flowing river, but frustration bubbled beneath the current. We were all under pressure, homesick, and stressed by city life. For many, the library was a second home, and who never had arguments at home?

I supposed that every library had its problem patrons, but between him hitting on young girls and intimidating staff, Roth seemed worse than most. This afternoon, his voice filled the crowded reading room.

"The shelf I ordered has a scuff on it," he shouted into his Nokia. "I demand that you send a replacement."

From the circ desk, Meg, Lorenzo, and I watched Roth go red in the face as he continued to berate a customer service agent.

"Cellphones are man's worst invention since the atomic bomb," Lorenzo muttered.

"Mobiles make communication easy," Meg argued.

"Too easy," I responded.

Lorenzo told him to pipe down, which Roth did for two minutes before he forgot himself and started shouting again. At the table closest to him, three Yearlings covered their ears. Near the window, pen in hand, Tolstoy had turned pale.

"No, I'm not going to return it. Listen, you idiot, I'm not going to pay international shipping fees!" Roth kicked the terracotta pot.

Dirt spilled out, and the poor palmetto keeled over onto the floor.

Lorenzo moved to give Roth a talking-to, but Tolstoy got there lightning fast. "Take your call outside."

The Yearlings gazed at him gratefully.

Roth waved him away. He had a few pounds and a few years on Tolstoy and clearly didn't view the lanky writer in residence as a threat.

"You need to move outside." Tolstoy advanced, until the men were toe to toe.

Roth covered the microphone and hissed, "Mind your damn business."

Tolstoy motioned to the palmetto. "You've made it my business. Get out."

Roth glanced at the trio of young women, clearly getting off on acting like a tough guy. He poked Tolstoy's chest. "Make me."

Swiftly and elegantly, Tolstoy headbutted him. The cellphone hit the carpet with a thump. Blood flowed from Roth's nose, which appeared to be broken. For ten seconds, everyone froze, including Roth and Tolstoy, still just inches apart.

Tolstoy turned to us. "I'm sorry."

"It's not your fault," Lorenzo replied.

"The ALP should have rescinded Roth's membership long before this," Meg added.

"Man, I shouldn't have lost my temper," Tolstoy said.

I gently ushered him behind the circ desk, where Lorenzo poured him a cup of tea from his thermos.

Roth gesticulated in our direction. "You'll pay for this!"

Though his hand covered his nose, it did nothing to stop the gush of blood. No one, not even Meg, asked him if he was okay or handed him a tissue. I couldn't feel bad for Roth. Men like him only responded to violence.

The shouting brought Hayes from his office. "What is going on out here?" He took in the scene. "Not the carpet." He groaned as Roth's blood soaked into the nylon.

"He attacked me." Roth pointed to Tolstoy.

"I'm sure you provoked him," Hayes replied. "The way you provoke everyone."

"You need to ban that psycho," Roth replied.

"Psycho," Hayes repeated. "That's how you talk about a decorated veteran? He's not the one we'll be banning. We're done with you, Roth. I'll get the restraining order myself."

"You can't keep me out. I'll sue!"

"That sounds right," Hayes replied. "You hiding behind some lawyer."

"We have a lawyer of our own," Meg informed Roth. "Jennifer de Narp will kick your ass in court."

~

Back at my desk, I was so distracted that I didn't even hear the ringing of the phone. Marius shook my shoulder gently. "Are you going to answer that?"

I picked up the receiver. "Hello?"

Still fazed by the bloodshed, it took me a moment to realize who was talking to me and what she was saying.

"As you well know, Lee-lee," Colette said, "in the book life, there's never a moment of respite. I apologize for being slow in confirming the Pat O'Malley event."

I jumped from my chair and continued to jump up and down, gripping the phone cord for dear life. "He'll be speaking here? Truly?"

"Of course," she said indulgently, clearly used to program managers practically weeping in gratitude.

After a dozen rejections from editors, at last I'd accomplished what I'd been hired to do. *"Mon Dieu!"*

"If the evening goes well, who knows? Perhaps we could make it a regular occurrence . . ."

Oui! Oui! Oui! Meeting a real editor. Hosting top-notch events at the library—if I didn't screw it up.

"That would be great," I said, trying not to hyperventilate with excitement.

Since she'd been out of the office, I asked if she was okay. She explained that a beloved author had suffered a bout of writer's block and fled France. "I had to track him down. He flew to Las Vegas, of all places! Together, we talked through the plot. Not a moment of respite!"

She and I confirmed the run of show for Pat's event.

I clapped my hands, eager to share the news with my boss. Finally, Hayes would be impressed. I went to his office, where he hunched over his desk. I rapped on his open door.

"Yes?" He glanced up, saw it was me, and returned to his paperwork.

I remained in the doorjamb, waiting for him to invite me in.

"What is it?" he demanded.

"Pat O'Malley will be speaking here!"

I expected him to be as excited as I was and maybe even say, *Good job!* But all Hayes did was raise his eyes to the water-stained ceiling. "I needed this win," he said, sounding defeated.

Two weeks later, we were thrilled to welcome our first "big name." Lorenzo closed the reading room fifteen minutes early so David and Tolstoy had time to put out extra folding chairs. At the circ desk, the bookseller had outdone herself with the promised display of novels in English and French. I'd quadrupled the orders of cheese, bread, and wine to ensure I wouldn't run out and embarrass the ALP. Hayes had even rented real wineglasses for the masses. Usually, the only trustees to attend events were Jennifer de Narp and Pam de Laney, but tonight all hands were on deck to glad-hand Pat O'Malley. I couldn't wait to thank Colette Levy and imagined that she would greet me with a kiss on each cheek. We'd commiserate about the book life over a glass of wine.

At the refreshment table, over Brie and baguette, the talk was still of Roth.

Have you heard? He's gone.

No. Really?

The director booted him.

Good for Hayes. I didn't know he had it in him.

The Yearlings, the bookseller, and the Faithful all related their unsettling encounters with him and expressed relief that the director had kicked him out.

But there were at least fifty new faces, too, surely drawn by the siren call of a National Book Award winner. These visitors glanced around in wonder. Perhaps the scent of musty books was a reminder of warm childhood memories in their hometown libraries. Hayes had been spot-on—a big name had brought in prospective members and donors. Maybe a weekly diet of famous authors would raise our profile and bring in more donations to help save the library.

As always, the wine flowed quickly, so I went to grab a few more bottles. The kitchen door was cracked open; Hayes and Jennifer de Narp were inside.

"What's your problem?" I heard him demand. "Since day one, you've been out to get me."

"Senior year of college, semifinals. You really don't remember me?" Her voice was savage, as if whatever had happened between them was yesterday, not two decades ago.

"Semifinals?" He squinted at her, clearly trying to place her.

"Yes. You cheated!"

"I'm supposed to recall every time I cheat?"

What a thing to say. Yet I was not at all surprised.

"Impromptu Debate," she hissed. "Thanks to your prep school pals, you finagled the topic ahead of time. That's the only reason you beat me."

I saw the dawning in his eyes. "Boston. You had brown hair, and a different last name. You'd won every tournament that season. Our team called you the Terminator. How else was I supposed to beat you?"

"Well, you're not going to win here."

He smirked. "I already did. I'm the director, aren't I?"

Lorenzo had said that de Narp was gunning for Hayes. I hoped she would succeed, now more than ever.

Entranced by the quarrel, I'd lost track of time and was now late in greeting tonight's guests. I sped to the front door, where I spied Pat O'Malley. At his temples, silver strands threaded through his dark hair. In his denim shirt and jeans, he resembled a Ralph Lauren model. Beside him, his wife and Colette were chatting with Pam de Laney, her lapdog peeking out of her Birkin. I stopped to compose myself, straightening my blouse and sweeping my fingers under my eyes in case my mascara had run.

This moment had been nine months in the making. I would be meeting literary royalty.

Colette glanced from the sooty ceiling to the worn carpet. With her stiletto, she tapped my favorite ink splotch. "So this is the American Library. Apparently, grunge is all the rage here, too," she said in a crisp French accent.

When I approached, Pam de Laney's arthritic shih tzu barked at me. So did she. "We're out of wine. Please tell me there's more. At least you thought to order the author's books this time. And where were you? Thank God *I* was here to greet our esteemed guests."

I moved to introduce myself, but she cut me off. "The library is thrilled to *finally* have an illustrious author!" she cooed, scowling in my direction. "That will be all."

Colette shot me a sympathetic glance. "We'll talk later," she mouthed.

Though Pam had all but shooed me away, I stood frozen, my brain whirling with all I'd dreamed of saying to Colette, a real-life editor. *Thrilled to finally meet you,* I blinked in her direction, hoping she'd decipher my Morse code. And to Pat O'Malley. *It's been a nonstop day of promotion for you. Thank you for coming to the library.*

Luckily, Lorenzo swooped in to whisk me away. "What's wrong with you?" he demanded. "Didn't you notice damn Pam about to butcher you?"

We watched her usher the trio to Hayes's office.

"Fun fact," he whispered to me. "Our acerbic trustee is married to a salt-of-the-earth guy named Bill Delaney, an American with Irish roots. She changed Delaney to de Laney so people would assume they're French aristocracy." It was so outrageous, I accused him of making it up. He replied, "I'm not that creative." I stifled a chuckle. Lorenzo made me feel a little better about the botched introduction.

I moved to the refreshment table and was heartened to find Chris alongside David, serving wine. I loved how at home he was here.

He poured us each a glass. "To you," he toasted. When the rims of our glasses touched, so did our fingers. I felt a spark of happiness.

At the podium, pride radiated from Hayes's pores as he introduced Pat O'Malley. His hands shook slightly. Perhaps he was nervous. I could feel the frenzy of having a famous author in the house. It was standing room only, with at least seventy people packed tight along the walls of books and spilling into the foyer. Two hundred people total—my statistics for the month would be excellent. I was excited to see so many new faces and could barely wait for O'Malley to share his hard-gained wisdom. I wasn't the only writer to open a notebook to jot down every word he said. Around me, attendees readied their pens.

He grinned. "I'm glad to be here tonight. And for once I'm

telling the truth. You can't say you're happy to be in Detroit and mean it."

The Select Few chuckled. O'Malley looked gratified.

"Bah-dum-bah," the bookseller muttered. "Novelists are like stand-up comedians—they all have their shtick. I've heard that line ten times from other authors."

O'Malley read from his latest novel. Hayes nodded with gravitas at every line. Mrs. Coolidge, one of the Faithful, held her hands to her cheeks as she listened to his calm nasal tenor. I loved watching attendees—sated and happy—stare at O'Malley in wonder. It made all the stress worth it, the same way a sunny spring weekend wipes away the memory of winter's gloom. Still, in the short excerpt, I noticed he described his female characters with the words "bovine," "cow," and "bitch," and couldn't help but be disappointed—it was 1995, yet men were winning literary prizes for describing women this way.

After the reading, Hayes invited audience members to ask questions. For the first time, he'd stayed for an entire event.

"Pat, I've been a fan since your debut novel," Mrs. Coolidge gushed. "Who is your ideal reader?"

O'Malley explained that he wrote for blue-collar workers. Young men. Men who struggle. He recounted that he gave a reading in a mall bookstore where the audience was affluent, middle-aged women. Then, near the tail end, a guy in Wranglers and work boots strode in. Here was the man he described in his books, here was the man for whom he wrote. But then the guy zeroed in on the beverage bar, downed the jug of wine, and hightailed it back into the mall.

"Stupid wino," O'Malley muttered as an afterthought.

He pondered tonight's attendees, predominantly women. Despite the money, prizes, and status, what the novelist craved most was missing—his dream demographic. In his head-to-toe denim he saw himself as a rough-and-tumble man writing for ranch hands and mechanics. I could see he was disappointed.

He wasn't the only one. I slipped my empty notebook into my pocket. What was the lesson here? That we all had blind spots in our writing and in life? That no matter your career level, there were frustrations and a desire for more? Nothing is ever enough?

As O'Malley began to sign books, a line of attendees wrapped around the stacks to get their copies. Colette congratulated me. "Success! What a wonderful, warm atmosphere. We must collaborate on more events."

Oui!!!!!

"I'm publishing translations of Julia Alvarez and Isabel Allende next year."

"J'adore!" I told her *How the Garcia Girls Lost Their Accents* was my second favorite book, after *The Library Card* by Wendy Peterson.

"I do not believe Peterson's novel has been translated into French. Yet."

I recounted a bit of Jessie Carson's story of creating France's first children's libraries, which Wendy told so beautifully.

"You work in a library, so you are clearly biased!" Colette teased.

I stared at my favorite ink splotch, my starting block. Though writing was my life, aside from Mary Louise, Odile, and Wendy, I never discussed it. Maybe I needed to. "Actually, this isn't my real job. My real job is writing."

"The best American books are actually 'Made in France.' The best quality. When you're ready, show me your pages."

"Fantastique!"

Most attendees stayed for another drink. People from all walks of life came together here to celebrate the written word. Reading is a singular pleasure, but sharing a love of books at events big and small had brought me such joy.

"I didn't know this place existed," one attendee said to himself as he ran his finger along the spines of the nonfiction on the New Arrivals shelf.

"Incredible talk tonight," another told David as she wrote out a check for a family membership.

"Grab an events schedule for me, too," a woman told her friend.

I thanked attendees for coming and encouraged them to return; Meg pressed our newsletter into their hands.

After the signing, Hayes whisked the author, his wife (plump, affluent, middle-aged), and his editor (plump, affluent, middle-aged) off to dinner with select patrons (plump, affluent, middle-aged).

At 10:00 p.m., as the crowd ambled out into the night, the library seemed to heave a sigh of relief that it was just us again. Meg carried the empty cheese platters to the kitchen. Tolstoy stowed the podium. David stacked the folding chairs. I helped the bookseller box up the few remaining novels.

"So, Ahab." She clapped me on the back. "You finally harpooned your elusive white male."

"I did. Have you read his novels?"

"He has a rich vocabulary, except when it comes to describing women. To him, we're all the same."

I felt closer to her; it felt like we were the only two to notice.

"I couldn't agree more," I said as we tied the box on the rack of her bicycle. "Let's grab a drink sometime."

"It's a date," she replied as she pedaled off.

Back inside, Chris and I worked as quickly as we could to close, both wanting to be alone, wanting each other.

"My place or yours?" I asked as we stepped onto the boulevard. Clouds filled the sky. There had been a shower; the light of the streetlamps shimmered in the puddles. The air was cool and smelled of rain.

"Yours is closest."

Chris's hand on my waist felt like heaven. It felt like the future. I couldn't wait.

We hurried up the stairs. Once inside, we kissed. And kissed. I tugged off his shirt, he eased off my blouse. I ran my hands over his chest, he caressed my back, grazing my skin tenderly. It felt right.

It felt like love. When we fell onto the bed, our legs tangled, my thoughts tangled. What if he didn't love me back? It didn't matter. I had to say the words.

"I . . ."

"I love you." He kissed the palm of my hand.

"I love you, too. I want to be with you."

We shed the rest of our clothes, stripped ourselves of inhibitions. I pulled him on top of me. His tongue met mine, my hips met his. *You feel so good,* he said. I licked the salt of his skin. *You taste so good,* I replied. I breathed in the sandalwood scent of his aftershave, ran my nails down his back, listened to him groan my name. *You're beautiful,* he said. I closed my eyes. He kissed my temple, my breasts, my belly. *Yes,* I said. *Yes,* he said. Then words weren't enough.

Chapter 19

NOVEMBER 1995

Clara de Chambrun—founding trustee

You haven't heard of me. Though my memoir *Shadows Lengthen* was brought out by Scribner, the same publisher as Hemingway, I remain a footnote in other people's stories. Supportive wife of General Aldebert de Chambrun. Circumspect sister of Nicholas Longworth II, the Speaker of the House. Sage cousin of wild child Alice Roosevelt, whose father, Teddy, admitted, "I can be President of the United States, or I can control Alice. I cannot possibly do both." In-law of inglorious Pierre Laval, France's wartime traitor in chief, executed in a hail of machine-gun fire.

Aldebert and I are buried nearby in Paris, not that those ingrates at the library care. After all I did for them, would it kill them to bring me a bouquet? Only Margaret visits—on my birthday as well as August 25, the anniversary of the Liberation, when she herself lost so much. She reads me passages of my favorite books and keeps me abreast of ALP news. Apparently, today's staff blame every unexplained thump, every odd clink of the boiler on me, the disgruntled countess, making herself heard. As if I would waste my time haunting them.

Perhaps you'd like to stop by? I dwell in the Picpus Cemetery, behind Our Lady of Peace. In the chapel, on the wall near the altar, you'll see marble plaques with 1036 names, ages, and jobs. Jean Grand, 52, doctor. Leonard Antié, 36, hairstylist of the queen. Jean

Blaise Perret, 26, lemonade seller. Jude Massé, 48, haberdasher. Luc Bonneval, 22, valet. Louise Brisson, 26, scullery maid. These poor souls were guillotined during the Terror and tossed behind the church, into a ditch now covered by a long stretch of lawn. As you stroll over the grass, listen carefully—you might hear the hymns of the Carmelite nuns who sang up until the moment of their deaths. In Paris, pedestrians are always tramping over people's bones.

Walk down the tree-lined path, you'll find the cemetery. Aldebert and I reside one aisle away from our illustrious ancestor, the Marquis de Lafayette, the French hero of the American Revolution. In 1917, when American forces arrived in Paris to join World War I, they planted an American flag at his gravesite, where Colonel Charles Stanton declared, "Lafayette, we are here!" Old Glory has flown ever since, even during the Nazi Occupation.

People remain fascinated by World War II, when the City of Light went dark. Rations, danger, spies. *Résistants* risking their lives for others, *collaborateurs* in connivance with Nazis. Who remained in France? Who fled? Who got out while the getting was good? Who was trapped? From *Is Paris Burning?* to *The Last Metro,* people can't get enough.

I myself witnessed the Occupation, Liberation, *and* Retribution. Lie on the ebony granite of my tomb, marked IN ETERNAL LOVE, and I'll tell you how it really was, beginning in the summer of 1939, when the American embassy advised its citizens to leave France. The ALP staff and I chose to remain, while the other trustees—all men—returned to the safety of the States. Though I didn't judge them for leaving, these men were certainly quick to judge me upon their return.

During the Occupation, we Parisians carried on. My husband oversaw the American Hospital, raising pigs in the basement so patients would have more to eat than the meager rations. I oversaw the library, where we all hand-delivered books to Jewish readers. I fended off the beady-eyed Gestapo spies, who posed as patrons and tried to catch me out in lies. I slept on a pallet there, in case the Nazis tried to pilfer our collection. The library became my life.

Curiously, my husband receives full credit for keeping the hospital going, while in my case, it was written that I was able to protect the ALP thanks to family ties with Pierre Laval, prime minister in the Vichy government. Yes, I reached out to him—once—for a matter of life and death. Florence Frikart, the sister of my dear personal assistant, Hilda, was to be executed for copying and distributing *Résistance* tracts. Thanks to his intervention, her sentence was reduced to hard labor; when the war ended, she was released.

I, too, was "let go."

Dismissed, sacked, fired—despite my enduring affection for and affiliation with the library. I was one of the original trustees, along with my friends Edith Wharton and Anne Morgan. After the war, when Laval went on trial for betraying France, *the men* pondered the "de Chambrun question" and insisted that I was "an embarrassment." Because of my family ties, *the men* wanted to exclude, punish, and humiliate me. Future generations would call this being "voted off the island" or "canceled," but back then, there were no words. And without words, it is impossible to speak.

Yes, the trustees who'd fled France at the first rumblings of danger ousted me. They weren't in Paris during the war, and yet they're the first to tell you how it was. All they cared about was "appearances." You give your heart, and *the men* take it, wad it up, and throw it in the dumpster.

Even today, from what I hear, men keep fouling things up. One man in particular, according to Margaret. When she speaks of Hayes, she paces before my tomb, her ice-blue eyes narrowed. This new director is the worst of the lot—hiring pretty young girls with no experience, angering longtime volunteers, and repelling donors. I suspect he'll soon be gone, but who will take his place?

Chapter 20

NOVEMBER 1995

Lily Jacobsen—program manager

The whole library swirled with gala preparations. At the conference room table, staff, trustees, and volunteers gathered to discuss the guest list, menu, publicity, and items for the silent auction. The only person absent was Hayes.

Jennifer de Narp donated priceless bottles of wine and a weekend at her château. Pam and Bill de Laney proposed a week on their yacht, *Lucky Lady*. Marius offered several first editions. Lorenzo, David, and Tolstoy volunteered to "help out" as waitstaff. Tolstoy whispered to me that for the right price, he'd headbutt someone. With a grin, I elbowed him gently in the ribs. He'd felt mortified about the altercation, so I was relieved he could finally joke about it. I waited for Meg to offer an item, or at least a suggestion, but she remained silent. I wanted to contribute something typically Parisian that no one had yet suggested. When I didn't speak, Jennifer de Narp told me, "Contact the authors we've hosted. Surely they'll donate signed copies. Maybe one would be willing to offer a free manuscript critique to a budding writer."

"I brought something to donate," I whispered to her. "Could I ask you to evaluate it first?"

"After the meeting, but let's make it quick."

Table decorations were next on the agenda. Felicity explained that bouquets were costly and would wilt, so she proposed stacking antique books from the Afterlife to create elegant centerpieces.

"With sprigs of mistletoe, your centerpieces will be charming," Jennifer de Narp said.

Seeing everyone band together, I was cautiously hopeful that we could save the library.

Still, I wondered why Hayes missed such an important meeting. But then, as Pam de Laney rose to leave, her gaze met Jennifer de Narp's, and she nodded toward his office. Their dislike of him permeated the air like a rancid perfume. I suspected they gave him the wrong time. If they had their way, his days at the library were numbered.

~

Felicity and Jennifer had created an enticing invitation packet, underlining the ALP's history. Highlights included photos that Wendy had discovered in the archives; a World War II–era report marked "Confidential," in which the directress, Dorothy Reeder, chronicled life under the Nazis; as well as a letter on the importance of supporting the ALP. At my desk, Meg, Lorenzo, and I stuffed five hundred manila envelopes. My tongue felt like it had a hundred paper cuts.

I fingered the satin finish of the invitations. "How will people resist?"

Lorenzo pointed to the cost per ticket, in italics at the bottom. "The five-hundred-dollar price tag, that's how."

"Charging that much is a risk," I admitted.

"Life is a gamble," Meg said. "Life is a crapshoot. Life is just crap."

Lorenzo tucked his arm around her shoulders. "Such talk isn't like you. What's wrong?"

Her gaze met mine. I knew that it stung that we hadn't heard back from Odile. I'd wanted to offer some reassurance, but it had been two months since we'd sent the letter. I told myself to be patient. International mail service could be slow. Sometimes it took a whole month to get a letter from home. We'd hoped Odile would phone, but so far, there was no message on my machine. I told myself I should have called, at least then we'd have had an immediate answer. Now, I was afraid to reach out. While I was in high school, Odile had taught me the hardest lesson I ever learned: Silence is also a response.

But after everything she and I had been through, how could she not reach out? Maybe I expected too much, maybe I was too demanding. I felt the old anger rise in me, the resentment, the frustration. Feelings I thought I'd mastered, or at least been able to batten down, having become an adept on this ship of emotions. Then I heard Odile's voice in my head: *Put yourself in my skin,* the French metaphor for putting yourself in someone else's shoes. *I want to see Margaret more than anything, but I'm so ashamed of how I treated her that I'm afraid to face her.* Was this why Odile hadn't replied?

I wasn't a kid. I had to stop lashing out and believing that my feelings counted more than those of others. This was exactly why Mary Louise had stopped talking to me. Odile had her reasons, and I had to respect them. Though it hurt, I'd told Meg what I'd realized: Odile would not come.

"I'm just tired." Meg patted Lorenzo's hand. "Or tired of volunteering. After the gala, it might be time for me to retire."

Lorenzo blanched. "The library won't be the same without you."

"Let's not dwell on that now," she said, trying to sound chipper.

He told her that she was his lifeline, that without her reassurance, he never would have survived his divorce; that so many days, when he was fed up with the public, one knowing look from her was enough to sustain him. "Without you . . ."

Where did that sentence, that sentiment end? Would he move on, too? And if they left, where did that leave me?

I recalled my first day of work at the ALP. Lorenzo's disdainful regard, which insinuated I wouldn't be able to hack the job. I didn't want to be one of those girls who didn't last a year. But writing Odile's war bride journey had helped me understand that I wanted a career as a novelist. She'd chosen a new life, and I couldn't blame her, not when I'd done the same in leaving behind my family and small town. Mary Louise had also moved on—from me. For now or forever, who was to say? Should I accept that the Mary Louise–and–Lily era was over? And what was I to do with her paintings? Once again, I needed advice—and I knew just who to ask.

After a quiet evening event, Lorenzo, Meg, and I lolled at the kitchen table and finished off the last of the Brie, baguette, and wine. For courage, I took a gulp of red.

"I stole something," I admitted.

"You?" Lorenzo asked, sounding impressed.

I explained the situation. "If Mary Louise comes to my place and sees them . . . well, it'll end our friendship."

"Are you sure she'd be mad?" Meg asked.

"Yes. She said the only reason she's still talking to me was because I'd respected her decision."

"I have an idea." Meg left the kitchen.

Lorenzo and I followed her to the oversize book section, where she reached behind a row and grabbed what appeared to be an X-ray. She slid it between the door and the frame of Hayes's office. With a click, we were inside. Lorenzo and I exchanged glances. *Who knew that Meg was a cat burglar?*

"Don't act surprised," she said. "Hayes was always locking himself out. The locksmith got tired of trotting over here and showed me his trick." Meg continued to the gargantuan gray safe and inserted a skeleton key.

"The day of my job interview, you said no one had the key," I said.

"I'm sure I said *staff* didn't." Meg opened the safe.

Lorenzo and I peered inside as if we were players in a literary lottery with a possible winning ticket. What would we glimpse? A lost poem by Gertrude Stein? First editions by F. Scott Fitzgerald? Correspondence between Hemingway and one of his wives? Would we finally get to read Irène Cohen's long-lost novel?

The cavernous safe was nearly empty. There was a thick file that could have been deeds or banking documents or a yellowing manuscript. The top page read, *For my dear friend Odile.* I went to touch it.

Meg gently moved my hand away. "Before she died, Irène informed me that she had bequeathed the manuscript to Odile. That no one could read it before she did."

I raised my brows. "You weren't tempted?"

"Not without Odile. It didn't seem right."

Beside the file was a wooden jewelry box. Meg set it on Hayes's desk and opened it. Inside were three enamel brooches. They were iridescent; the light seemed to come from inside them. How? Such beauty, such magic. Peering closer, I spied a trio of miniature book covers. *Jane Eyre. Their Eyes Were Watching God. The Priory.*

"Those are Odile's favorite novels," I said.

"I know. I created them for her." Usually Meg's posture was Queen Elizabeth straight, but now, her shoulders slumped. "I miss her." She snapped the jewelry box shut and returned it to the safe. "It was silly of me to get my hopes up."

A snippet from Wendy's novel came to mind. "Jessie Carson once said: 'Sometimes our hopes are all we have.'"

"Bring the paintings here, where they'll be safe. Art deserves protecting," Meg said briskly. Though she had changed the subject, her wounded expression remained.

"Best to do it now," Lorenzo advised, "while no one else is around."

They offered to help, but I insisted that I could carry the canvases myself. I sped down the boulevard, across the bridge, along the pedestrian street to my building, and up the narrow servants' staircase to my empty studio. I stood there for a good long while, not ready to say goodbye.

My dear Lily, I imagined Odile saying as she selected a book from my shelf and opened to the first page. *What do you see here? Space between the words. Space is beautiful. Essential. It's needed to make sense of sentences. And relationships.*

As always, her wisdom comforted me. I gathered Mary Louise's paintings into my arms.

Back in the director's office, Lorenzo laid the canvases gently in the safe. I closed the door, heartened by the idea that one day the right person would find them. I decided to reach out one last time, and then leave the next steps to my friend.

Dear Mary Louise,

You're the best friend I have ever had. Thank you for all that you've done for me, from coming to Paris and learning a foreign language to encouraging me to apply for the program manager position. Just being with you makes me feel brave and strong.

I apologize for putting myself first, for not giving you credit or time to express your feelings. For always thinking I knew best. Unfortunately, I have even more to apologize for. I stole your paintings from the curb and put them somewhere safe. I betrayed your trust and your wishes. I don't want to lie anymore, even by omission, and I understand if you can't forgive me.

I asked the trustee you met briefly, who is so honest as to be cruel, to appraise the Eiffel Tower tableau you gave me. She loved it, and asked to include it in the library gala's silent auction. As much as I want to keep it for myself, I want to contribute. You see, everyone here puts their heart and soul into the library, and your painting, well, it's my soul.

I include two tickets to the event and hope to see you and

Antoine. I also understand if you've moved on. Thank you for being such a good friend to me. I will always be grateful for the time we shared.

Yours,
Lily

I sent the letter, and waited. Patience had become one of my fortes.

Chapter 21

DECEMBER 1995

Felicity Jenner—fundraiser

The gala had finally arrived. In my bedroom, before the mirror, I donned my diamond studs, the finishing touch to my outfit. In my gold Azzedine Alaïa bustier and long black velvet skirt, I looked damn good, if I did say so myself. It was only 5:00 p.m., but I wanted to arrive early.

As I locked the flat behind me, Franklin exited the elevator.

"Where are you going?" he demanded.

"To the library."

He looked me up and down. "Wearing that?"

I frowned.

"I mean, you're very pretty all dressed up." He lingered in front of the elevator door, blocking my way.

"Can you move aside? I need to set up for the silent auction."

He regarded me dumbly.

"The gala," I reminded him. The last three weeks, it had been all I'd talked about.

"That's tonight?"

Did he even listen when I spoke?

"I took some time off work next week," he continued. "Since Ellen will be home on winter break, I thought we could sightsee in Paris as a family."

Even a year ago, I would have melted, grateful for his scraps of attention. But now I saw that I deserved more.

"The Louvre, the Champs-Elysées, Sacré Coeur," he listed. "All the things we haven't had time to do."

"All the things *you* didn't take time to do. *I* went to all those places when we first arrived. Mostly alone, because Ellen was at school, and you refused to leave work for an afternoon, even on a Saturday."

He stared at me, perplexed, as if I were speaking French instead of plain English.

"How about a romantic getaway on the Riviera, just the two of us?" He tried to put his arm around me.

I stepped out of his way. "I'm busy."

"But I'm here. I'm ready."

"Why now?"

"What do you mean 'Why now?'" He sounded churlish. It's true no one ever asked him to explain himself. "I'm between projects. I finally have a week off."

"A whole week?" I couldn't keep the sarcasm from my voice.

"Don't be cross."

"You think I'm being cross?" I shook my head. He really didn't understand. He would never understand. "I think we should separate."

With Ellen thriving at Oxford, I'd questioned my own future. When she graduated, she would have her own job, her own life, and I'd be alone with Franklin. The thought filled me with dread.

In this Wives of Executives life, there was no "we," only him and his needs. Like Ellen, I was ready to spread my wings and had filled out an application of my own. Jennifer had submitted the documents for French working papers for both David and me. Somehow, she'd expedited the process, and now, we each possessed a *carte de résident*. He'd remain the part-time custodian at the library, with a salary and a nearby studio. Starting in January, he and Tolstoy would attend the Sorbonne. It was wonderful to see their friendship blossom—a reminder that the library was made of more than books. I proudly accepted the position of full-time fundraiser. The pay was dismal, but I felt passionate about championing the ALP and promoting literacy. I'd worked harder than I ever had in my life on the silent auction, calling in favors from all the corporate bigwigs and their wives I'd kept in touch with over the years. Checks poured in. I was overwhelmed by their generosity. The only firm that did not contribute was Franklin's. I'd mentioned the fundraising goal to him five times. My mistake was broaching it with him, not his boss. Wifely courtesy had cost the library a generous donation. Last week over tea at Ladurée, Jennifer and I tallied the contributions. Tactfully, she did not mention that my husband's firm was nowhere to be found on the list.

I double-checked the spreadsheet. "We really raised this much?"

"*You* raised that much," Jennifer corrected.

At the library, I'd found a role that I excelled in, found people who appreciated me. I knew from the W.E.s—the Wives of Executives support group held in the library conference room—that other husbands did value their wives' important projects, despite their busy work lives. I was not expecting too much of Franklin.

"You think we should separate," he scoffed.

"I think we should divorce."

"You're just angry."

"I already found another apartment."

His mouth hung open. For once, I'd rendered him speechless.

"When Ellen returns to Oxford in January," I continued, "I'll move out."

"But—"

"No buts. I must run."

My friendships with Meg and Jennifer as well as the W.E.s had taught me that there were people who would cherish me. I joined the ranks of the E.W.E.s, Ex-Wives of Executives. One member joked I'd upgraded. Another quipped that fortunately, both groups would soon be obsolete—the next generation of W.E.s would be Women Executives. Or A.W.E.s—Awesome Women in Europe.

My new flat was located near the ALP. Of course, with my meager budget, I'd no longer have a view of the Eiffel Tower. However, I'd be the main character of my own life, instead of a "plus one" in Franklin's. For the first time in fifteen years, where I lived would be my choice, not his. This freedom was priceless.

Chapter 22

DECEMBER 1995

Lily Jacobsen—program manager

The night of the gala, the library was transformed into a winter palace. Trustees, potential donors, journalists, and book lovers entered through an arch of holly to find the circ desk decorated with branches of mistletoe. In the reading room, all the books on the shelves were turned around, so the white edges of pages set off the pine trees decked with braids of soft lights. The windows were thrown open, and fresh air wafted in, rustling the red leaves of the poinsettias that lined the ledge. There was an aura of anticipation and industrial-strength disinfectant. To remove the rest of Roth's blood, Hayes had hired a cleaning company; the carpet was still damp. Even so, the atmosphere was enchanting. Two hundred guests smiled and exchanged business cards, ate and drank, made small talk and large donations. Perched on an easel, the painting that Mary Louise had given me was the first item attendees viewed. Next, they perused the selection of books to bid on, which included signed copies of Wendy's novel. Off to the side, more auction items were laid out with clipboards to record bids. Interestingly, it was mostly experiences, not stuff, for auction, from a weekend getaway at the Sour Grapes vineyard to cooking classes to sailing lessons. Attendees gushed over the items and jotted down bids. Round tables were covered by crisp white linens and decorated with charming centerpieces made of antique books, date stamps, library cards, and touches of mistletoe. This was the most glamorous event I'd ever attended.

Lorenzo, David, Tolstoy, and I had signed up to "help out." Of course, we noted that somehow the ALP had enough money to purchase ten cases of champagne but not enough to pay the waitstaff. But this observation seemed insignificant compared to the seismic shift at the ALP—for the first time in fifty years, Meg would not take her place at the welcome table or refreshment stand. She had been invited as a guest. To celebrate her retirement from volunteering, the four of us had pooled our money to buy her a corsage. As I pinned it onto her silky blue dress, which matched her eyes perfectly, I told her that she looked lovely.

"I'm feeling my age," she confided. "But I tell myself that books have lines, and if we're lucky, our faces have lines with stories to tell."

"Exactly." I thought of my mother, who'd died too young to acquire those beautiful wrinkles and white hair. "You've been volunteering a long time. I think you're right to turn the page."

"Thank you. But, Lily dear, you sound exhausted," Meg said.

"I am, a little."

"You work too hard. Institutions are not people. They don't love you back."

"I've learned that."

"When I first met you, I wanted to give you my key to the palace. But now I don't want you to make the mistake of giving too much of yourself to this place. Save your energy for your writing."

I hugged her. "I'm honored that you wanted to entrust it to me."

We both regarded Tolstoy, who circulated among the guests serving appetizers.

"He's thrived here," Meg said.

In life, you could take things easy or take them hard. At the ALP, I took them too hard. With his combat experience, little setbacks wouldn't affect Tolstoy the way they did me.

"He loves this place," I said. "He'd make a great program manager."

Meg nodded. "I'll give him the key tomorrow." She moved to join me behind the refreshment table before saying, "Force of habit," with a chuckle.

I encouraged her to mingle. She was soon swept away by a debonaire book club leader. I glanced at the clock above the door—Mary Louise and Antoine hadn't arrived yet. Maybe they weren't coming. She was certainly angry with me for keeping the paintings. And anyway, there was no guarantee that Antoine would like me. I imagined him with gray hair, not much taller than her, five-seven at most. Divorced with kids her age. Mary Louise was his clean slate, his blank canvas. Someone new to laugh at jokes he'd repeated a thousand times. He wouldn't stop touching the skin of her upper arm, a curl of her hair, the curve of her cheek. I blamed him for her giving up her art, and only hoped that I could hold in my resentment when we met.

If we met.

I took a deep breath and told myself that either way, I'd be okay. I'd reached out, the rest was up to Mary Louise. I respected her feelings and choices.

Writing Odile's story gave me a sense of purpose and made me steadier somehow. It felt important to write about the courageous Frenchwomen who crossed an ocean for love, most knowing that if it didn't work out, they would not be able to afford to return home. Because I'd thought about their plight for so long, I found the words flowed.

After reading a few chapters of *The War Bride,* Wendy had urged me to submit them. I liked Colette Levy so much that I sent them to her first. She said she adored Odile's story and wanted to publish it. The advance was enough that I could finally write full-time, which meant my time at the library was coming to an end. I was another one of those girls who didn't even last a year. I felt a little embarrassed about that. At least I'd forged some relationships with French editors that the next program manager could build on.

At Chris's apartment, curled up on his couch, he and I had celebrated my book deal with bubbly. He'd read Paul's chapter and asked about the character, a policeman who frequented the library during the war. We were both stunned to realize that Chris's grandfather had been Odile's beau. Then again, maybe it made sense: he'd brought Chris to the ALP each Saturday not just to check out books but to glean what had happened to Odile.

"What do you think Paul would say if he knew that you were dating Odile's adopted granddaughter?" I asked.

As he mulled over the question, Chris ran his hand through his hair.

"Grandpa deeply regretted his actions during the war. So seeing us in love, he'd probably say, 'Even though I did wrong, things still turned out right.'"

I liked to think that was true. Tufts of Chris's hair stood up straight. He was my book head, now and always. I loved how we talked about everything, or nothing at all. I loved him. His quiet encouragement. His hands on my hips. His lips on mine. I closed my eyes.

"Thinking about Book Head?" Lorenzo asked, bringing me back to the present. "You have that nauseating he's-ever-so-dreamy expression on your face."

He looked dapper in a blue suit set off by his paisley bow tie. I wore a dress I'd found on sale—an indestructible black sheath, all the better for serving red wine and my favorite gooey cheeses—Maroilles from the North and Munster from Alsace.

Before I could answer, Hayes strode up and inspected the charcuterie board. "No cheddar?"

"I ordered French cheeses for the special occasion."

"So it's your fault that it stinks to high heaven in here."

At this accusation, the old me would have been gripped with guilt. The new me just chuckled to myself as I recalled Lorenzo's mantra: *Always do what makes you happy; if people don't like it, well, that's just a bonus.* I'd learned not to care so much about what

Hayes thought. From booking excellent speakers to "helping out" this last time, I knew I'd done my best.

"Jennifer de Narp is headed this way," Lorenzo told him.

Dread filled Hayes's eyes, and he skulked off.

She was a vision in a pink Chanel gown. The matching clutch was only big enough for a lipstick, a credit card, and a condom. She used it as a pointer while giving a tour to a potential donor. She bragged about our lineup of speakers and statistics, specifically the strong attendance. Appreciative of her praise, I wished I could confess that I'd kicked her to be done with my feelings of guilt and embarrassment, but the gala wasn't the time.

After she handed off the gray-haired gentleman to Pam de Laney, she migrated to me. "You look like you have something on your mind."

Lorenzo gestured for me to zip it.

I didn't want to upset her, and I really didn't want booze thrown in my face. "It can wait."

"I'd rather know now." Her lips pinched together.

"For a while, I've wanted to tell you how we know each other—or rather, how we first bumped into each other."

"Well?"

"It was on the street, when I kicked you." Casting my gaze downward, I waited for her to shout, *What a horrible thing to do!* or *You're fired!* but she remained silent.

"I'm very sorry," I continued, relieved to have the secret out. "I was working through some stuff, but that's no excuse for taking it out on you."

"I knew it was you," she replied in a breezy tone.

My head shot up. "You knew?"

"I figured it out the third time I saw you."

"Why didn't you say anything?"

A smile twisted her lips. "It's fun to watch you squirm."

David passed with a tray of champagne. Ms. de Narp grabbed us each a flute.

She raised her glass to me. "You deserve to enjoy this moment. Cheers."

Twenty minutes later, the couple I was waiting for arrived. Mary Louise! *Merveilleux!* My heart sang. His eyes fixed on her, Antoine escorted her under the arch covered with holly. I had to admit that they looked good together. He was dashing in his tux, and her simple pastel Cacharel dress suited her. As they got their bearings, they took in the pine trees, the champagne pyramid, her Eiffel Tower tableau. While he gazed at her painting, she gave a quick wave. I dove through the crowd, elbowing patrons out of the way. I wanted to hug her but contented myself by saying, "You came!"

"Sorry it took so long to finally get here."

I knew she was talking about not just the library but a place where we could be together.

"You must be Lily. A pleasure to meet you." Antoine shook my hand.

His gaze returned to Mary Louise's painting. "I sensed it was yours immediately," he told her. "Many Parisians are blasé. I love your perception of the city, your love for Paris. I must bid on it." He strode to the table and picked up the clipboard.

I'd been prepared to hate Antoine, but his admiration for Mary Louise's work melted my jaded heart.

Mary Louise asked if readings were always so swanky, and I explained that tonight was a fundraiser with a bigger budget than our usual events.

From afar, I heard Hayes's intake of breath. "Christ!" he hissed. "That's Antoine de Pouvrey. How did I not know he would be here?"

"Lily put him on the list," Felicity replied.

"She wrote 'Mary Louise and Antoine.' How was I supposed to know that she was friends with the CEO of Techtron?" He gathered the trustee posse and prepared to pounce.

"Thanks for not making a fuss over Antoine," Mary Louise told me, perhaps overhearing the conversation herself. "He hates being fawned over."

Suddenly, I understood what he saw in her—the same thing I did, a good-hearted person who was not swayed by money or power. He loved her for the right reasons.

"Sorry about my boss," I told Mary Louise with a remorseful shrug. "I'm sure he means well, but he's the worst."

"He gave you a hard time?" She whipped out a small pad from her purse and drew a quick sketch. "He'll be sorry. Give me a sec."

"You're working on a new series?"

"No, but I might. We could call it bastard bosses." She held up her caricature of Hayes. If anyone deserved to have an exaggerated chin and dollar signs for eyes, it was him.

"That's one hundred percent accurate. You're an excellent judge of character. Have I ever told you that?"

"No."

"Well, I should have. It's one of the things that makes you a great painter. It's as if you see into someone's soul."

"Tonight's the first time I've wanted to draw in ages. Maybe the library inspired me." She regarded me with her doe eyes, and I felt her fragility but also her strength. "I always painted for me. I don't know why I let that snobby gallerist we pitched discourage me. Many people have said they loved my work. Why do I only hear his voice? I'll figure out a way to drown it out."

"I'm glad." I couldn't help it—I hugged her. "I'm sorry. For everything. I'm ready to listen if you ever want to talk."

I'd been so certain. Certain about what Mary Louise should do, who she should date, that we should be artists in Paris. I needed to remember that she had her own strengths and to give her credit for all she was and all she'd accomplished.

"I appreciate your saying that. Thank you for believing in me." She gestured to her painting. "My best work on display at a black-tie event. Thank you for making my dream come true."

She'd forgiven me. I promised myself that I would do better.

In the future, Mary Louise and I would probably make more missteps, but hopefully we'd find a way to talk through hurt feelings.

"I'm really happy for you," I told her. "Antoine seems like a great guy."

"Thank you. And I'm happy for you, too—tonight seems like a big success. Let's debrief over coffee tomorrow. I must hear more about this place!"

I grinned as I considered my end-of-year statistics.

Times I was yelled at: **5**
Times I wanted to give up: **8**
Times I was glad I stuck it out: **8**
Events hosted: **72**
Times I was proud of our literary fellowship: **72**
Total number of attendees (excluding Pam de Laney, who refused to sign in): **3635**
Events Mary Louise attended: **1**
How certain I was that all would be well between Mary Louise and me: **100%**
Number of friends made at the ALP: **countless**

An hour later, the bids were tallied, and Hayes gathered us in the reading room. At the podium, he announced, "Thanks to my efforts, we've raised over ten thousand dollars tonight and secured five million from our sponsors."

This was how it ended? Jennifer de Narp did years of unpaid work as a trustee, Felicity Jenner used her contacts to find funding, and Hayes got the credit? No, he took the credit.

Through the din of lukewarm applause, I told Lorenzo, "I can't believe that Hayes didn't at least thank the trustees and staff."

"I can," he replied. "Jerks like him always get ahead."

Thanks to the hard work of others. "How do you put up with it?"

"I'm considering moving on," he confessed. "I applied for a job in the French library system. I took their exam and aced it. Soon, I'll be a *fonctionnaire*."

A state employee. France's holy grail. "Truly unfireable. Plus, you could torture a whole new set of co-workers."

"And a new set of readers. Expand my reach. I'll miss you, though. You're one of my favorite people to torture."

I elbowed him in thanks. "I'll miss you, too. The gala is starting to feel like a going-away party."

"What do you mean?"

"I just put in my resignation." It was time.

He nodded. "That makes sense. You can concentrate on your writing."

"How?" How was he always a step ahead of everyone?

He gave a little shrug. "My awesome little author, I know *everything*."

Jennifer de Narp took the podium. Applause broke out.

"Thank you all for coming out tonight. *Un grand merci* to our donors for your bids. I have an announcement to make. As of the fifteenth of next month, I will be taking over as director."

Pam de Laney and the other board members moved to stand behind Jennifer. They were the period at the end of her sentence.

"It took time," Meg told Lorenzo and me. "But she got the trustees to vote him out. Her palace coups are brutal, but at least there's no bloodshed."

"The director is dead," I said.

"Long live the director," Lorenzo replied.

"We thank Quentin Hayes for the time and energy he has given, and wish him well in his future endeavors," Jennifer said.

Strangely, Hayes appeared relieved, like a bank robber who'd been in hiding for years, finally busted and able to drop the act. "Another job eulogy," he muttered.

"I'd like to thank Felicity Jenner for her work tonight," Jennifer continued. "And am thrilled that she'll be joining the staff as our full-time fundraiser."

More hearty applause.

"We'd also like to recognize Meg Bauer, a.k.a. Margaret Saint James, for her fifty years of service." Jennifer gestured for Meg to join her and handed her a bouquet. "She is the epitome of kindness, generosity, and warmth. Many of us would not be here without her. I often came to the library more for Meg than for the books. She means the world to me and to the ALP community. I know this isn't a goodbye."

The two women embraced, and patrons advanced to offer thanks and congratulations to Meg.

Wendy strode toward me. "Thanks for the invite. What an amazing shindig. This is my husband, Roberto, who's helping me produce the documentary." She gestured behind her to a man carrying a movie camera.

Pam de Laney had waylaid him and suggested he "help out" by filming our gala for the ALP archives.

"You're so lucky to live in Paris," Wendy continued. "Roberto and I fantasize about staying here for good. We even applied for one of those *compétences et talents* visas. I also put in to be the next writer in residence here. The library is incredible. Just look at the display of patrons' favorite books. The camaraderie makes it so inviting, I could totally write my next book here."

Behind us, Jennifer told Pam, *Time to upgrade. We'll paint these blah beige walls a stark white.* She tapped her stiletto. *We'll pull up this puke-green monstrosity and put down charcoal-gray carpet. We'll only invite heavy hitters who've won the Pulitzer or teach at Harvard.* Pam nodded approvingly and replied, *Instead of the wonky welcome table, we'll install a plexiglass gate that members can open with their card. We're bringing the ALP into the next century. It's exciting to think about.*

The library had a history, and thanks to the dedicated book lovers and money raised at the gala, that story would go on, no matter who worked here, no matter who called the ALP home. Meg had become a dear friend. She'd been taken for granted by

ALP directors, yet the library gave her the greatest friendships and a place she felt at home. The library had stripped me of my confidence, but had helped me find my path to publication and introduced me to Chris as well as to amazing colleagues. We didn't have to work together to remain friends. Life was a book, and I couldn't wait to start my next chapter.

Epilogue

THE LIBRARY

As the gala came to a close and patrons poured out my doors, I heaved a sigh of relief. Finally, Meg and I were alone. We had to laugh. Once again—*even after she'd retired from volunteering*—she stayed to tidy up and was the last to leave. It didn't matter that she wore a ball gown. Here she was, a bouquet in one hand, a Hefty bag in the other, stuffing the trash into the bin on the darkened street.

She nearly ran into a petite woman perched on a red suitcase. Her hennaed bob closed around her eyes like curtains. She looked familiar to me. I hadn't seen her in five decades, so it took a moment to place her. You can't blame me. Each year, thousands of people meander through my stacks. Still, Odile had been one of my favorites.

Stunned at seeing her, Meg dropped her bouquet. The women gawked at each other, perhaps drinking in the changes, perhaps pondering what to say.

Meg spoke first. "How I've waited for this moment."

Odile rose. "I'm sorry. For everything."

"I never should have told you to go."

"I don't blame you." Odile held out her hand. "After what I did . . ."

Meg stared at it. "You shouldn't have left me."

"I didn't know how else to prove I was sorry."

"Like this." Meg embraced her.

Odile ran her fingers over Meg's snowy crew cut. "It never grew back?"

"I prefer it short. After the Liberation, I rid myself of unnecessary things—long hair, syllables in my name, a philandering husband, concerns about what others thought of me."

With a little push to open my door, I beckoned them inside.

"It feels as if I've come home," Odile said as she touched the rickety coatrack, the American and French flags fluttering together, the dewy palmetto leaves, before Meg led her to the director's office. They were soon standing before the safe, where Meg pulled out the manuscript. "I kept Professor Cohen's novel for you."

"I always wondered what became of it." Odile's voice was filled with awe.

"We can start reading tonight."

"Just one chapter . . ." they said together.

"After hours in the Afterlife, like we used to," Odile said.

"I created something for you." Meg opened the jewelry box.

Odile's eyes brimmed with tears as she admired the brooches. "Lily and I read about your artwork in the *Herald*. Such talent."

Meg pinned *Jane Eyre* on Odile's lapel.

Odile stood straighter. "Better than receiving the Legion of Honor medal."

"High praise indeed!" Meg said with a laugh.

In the decades since I was founded, it's been a privilege to be a part of so many lives, so many decisions, so many hopes, so many stories. People have made me what I am: a shelter, a haven, a hideout, a cure for loneliness. There's much I'd like to tell you. Sometimes you do the right thing for the wrong reason. Sometimes minutes pass slower than years. Sometimes tears say more than words. Even the strongest people stumble before finding their footing. But hold on, friend. Hold on.

Acknowledgments

This novel is close to my heart. Its theme of figuring out where we belong and what we are meant to do with our lives is something we all must ponder. There's no age limit on these questions.

I'm grateful for my agent Heather Jackson, as well as my editors Lara Blackman and Peter Borland for their edits, encouragement, and insight. This is my third book with Atria, and on page 231 is a list of the many talented, hardworking, whip-smart people who came together so that you could read or listen to this novel.

My thanks to friends and fellow writers for their support: Luci Baum, Patti Callahan Henry, Pamela Combastet and our AAWE writing group, ALP colleague and AAWE Booknik Andrea Delumeau, Mary Duncan, Carol Fitzgerald, Penelope Fletcher, Brooke Lea Foster, Susan Jane Gilman, Kristin Harmel, Ruth Hogan, Rachel Kesselman, Kaaren Kitchell, Anne Korkeakivi, Anne Marsella, Jane Mobile, Alannah Moore, Anca Metiu, Jade Maître, Mardi Michels, Emily Monaco, Rebecca Plotnick, Anna Polonyi, Paul Schmidtberger, Lori Thicke, Kate Thompson, Jen Tronson, Lindsey Tramuta, Diane Vadino, Yara Zgheib, Laurel Zuckerman.

I'm grateful for the support of my family and in-laws. I grew up on the plains of Montana and am lucky that my family were readers. Thankfully, our town had a library, because the closest bookstore was ninety miles away. I still feel a thrill every time I walk into a library or bookstore. My thanks to librarians, booksellers, book clubs, podcasters, and readers. You keep me going with your kind notes, posts, and invitations to speak.

Dear Friend,

I hope you have enjoyed reading *The Parisian Chapter* as much as I enjoyed writing it. It's always a pleasure for me to return to the world of the American Library in Paris, which I first wrote about in my novel *The Paris Library*. That book originally focused on the main character Odile Souchet's experience as a war bride. In fact, the book was first titled *The War Bride*.

My fascination with war brides began when I was a child in Shelby, Montana. One of my neighbors was a war bride from Rouen, Normandy. I remain in awe of the thousands of courageous women who crossed an ocean to the unknown in order to begin a new life with a GI. I'm grateful to Montana Historical Society members, who interviewed war brides from England, France, Germany, and Japan. Each piece of information I uncovered about them made me want to learn more.

Although I loved the war bride sections of that work in progress, while writing at a convent in Belgium I realized that the book's focus was changing, and I needed to eliminate the scenes that described Odile's journey to the United States with her fellow war brides as well as the first years of her marriage. It's never easy to cut chapters, and these were among my favorite parts of the entire book. So, I'm grateful to be able to share them with you today as a bonus to *The Parisian Chapter*. I like to imagine these as the first pages of the novel written by my character Lily Jacobsen about her beloved friend Odile.

Merci!

Sincerely,
Janet Skeslien Charles

THE WAR BRIDE

LILY JACOBSEN

NORMANDY, JANUARY 1945

Odile

The U.S. Army did not know what to do with me. Or with Marceline or Lucienne or Huguette. Since the autumn, requests for permission to marry mademoiselles had cluttered commanding officers' desks. Some days, it seemed there were as many fiancées as soldiers, and as many awkward conversations. "You barely know the woman!" "You're shipping off tomorrow!" "You'll forget her! She'll forget you!" Nothing doing. The men wanted their brides with them in America.

Naturally, wounded soldiers like Buck got sent home quickly, first-class mail. But the army thought it wouldn't hurt us ladies to sit in a depot in Normandy, sent parcel post if our paperwork came through. While we were waiting at Camp Lucky Strike, Red

Cross volunteers taught us to sew quilts. As we pieced patches of material together, we spoke of our darlings, of the country we would call home.

"What's a 'sharecropper'?" Huguette asked. "My husband said it was his métier before the war, but I was too embarrassed to admit I didn't understand."

"It's like *Gone with the Wind*."

Finally, our ship came in, though we had to pay a hefty price for a one-way ticket. "A sergeant's salary doesn't go far," Buck had warned. I cupped his cheeks in my hands. "I've worked since before the war," I told him. "Between the two of us, there will be enough." In a few months' time, Uncle Sam would gallantly start paying for war brides' passages, but I couldn't have waited.

During the voyage, we women shared photos of our husbands. One was bald as a billiard ball, stout as a beer stein, and we wondered, What did she see in him? This was the problem with pictures, they only showed so much. At night, while we swayed in our bunk beds, each woman's story of how she met her husband—black and white as a photo—poured out.

Marceline said: It was love at first sight. But his commander kept losing our marriage application. He didn't want us to marry because Seth is Black. So we asked my village priest.

Chantal said: In London, the Red Cross organized a dance for GIs. The matrons only let in the "right" kind of girls. They said I weren't good enough and wouldn't let me through the door. When my Luke saw how mean they were, he let them have it, I can tell you! He gave me his arm and escorted me in.

Lucienne said: Michael parachuted into my yard. My family hid him in the cellar.

Huguette said: My mother begged me to give it time. I told her we don't have time. We're at war.

I said: Buck and I met on Saturday, and the army chaplain married us on Friday.

They said: How romantic!

◆ ◆ ◆

Just a kilometer from New York, we stood at the railing. On the horizon, we spied a regal compatriot waiting to greet us. Lady Liberty stood in the fog, torch raised to guide us to our new home. A reminder that our journey was nearly over, but that another would begin. A new day with a new husband. In a daze, I watched reuniting couples clutch each other at the harbor. When a corporal didn't come to collect his bride, she sat on her trunk and cried. I held her hand, comforting her as I could, while a cross Red Cross worker said, "You were asking for trouble when you married a *complete stranger . . .*"

On the train to Chicago, while Chantal, Marceline, Andrée, Huguette, and Lucienne chatted—"What a big country!" "What if his parents don't like me?"—I stared out the window as the immensity of what I'd done rolled by. To escape my husband, I'd left Paris without a goodbye. I would never again see Maman and Papa, would never again return to the American Library in Paris. What must my friends and colleagues all think? Though I was convinced leaving was the right decision, it was painful to look back. The train slowed for Andrée's stop. She cried and laughed and embraced us. In the carriage, we gave her gifts from our handbags: a lipstick to match her one good blouse, a fountain pen to write us letters, a rabbit's paw to stroke when she got nervous. One by one, my companions alighted, leaving me with Lucienne, whose husband came to claim her on the platform of Chicago's Union Station.

When Michael drew her into his arms, the passionate embrace reminded me of the ones I'd shared with Paul. No, I wouldn't think of him. I was married to Buck now. I recalled our wedding in the army tent, a makeshift chapel. Right before the ceremony, the chaplain had asked me to swear on the Bible that I wasn't already married. He'd heard about us easy, bigamous French gals.

Rémy never would lie to a priest. *You're so good,* I thought to myself, to my twin.

That doesn't make you bad, Rémy replied. *It's all right to move on.*

Buck's head shot back. "Of course she's not married."

Unconvinced, the chaplain thrust the Bible at me. "Do you swear on your honor?"

What honor? With my left hand, I reached out to Buck, who enlaced his fingers with mine. I raised my other hand. "I swear I'll be a good wife."

Buck rubbed my bare finger. "I'm sorry I don't have a ring."

I recalled how I'd hurled the plain gold band from my wedding with Paul into the Seine. "I don't want one."

Michael and Lucienne saw me to my train, the Empire Builder. She told him I was traveling on to Buck's hometown, Froid, which means "cold." Turning to me, she said, "French! It's a good omen."

Alone in the compartment, I was lulled by the miles. The grass turned to yellow brush, trees became long stretches of snow-covered prairie, each station one closer to Buck. We would have a cottage with a little garden. A raspberry patch would grow near the fence. His mother would teach me how to make jam.

When the train slowed to a standstill in Wolf Point, I glanced at my reflection in the mirror. My skin was sallow, but my chignon was perfect, not a brittle hair out of place. Gripping my vanity case, I stuck my head out the door into the cold. Buck hurried over to help me alight.

"There's my little gal." The words came out of his mouth, little puffs of mist. He kissed me and held me tight. I melted into his warmth. It had been six long months.

"We'd better get going," he said, gently disentangling himself.

Now that he wasn't in the military, his buzz cut had grown out. I couldn't stop sliding my hand through his hair, relieved to touch his face, his neck, to see the crinkles around his smiling eyes. Seeing his relaxed appearance, even in this biting wind, I realized how pale and tense he'd been in Paris. Perhaps after a few months here, I would look as happy. Noticing me shiver, he placed his coat over my shoulders.

"Is it blustery like this all the time?"

Buck grinned. "If we're not careful, the wind'll blow us into North Dakota."

Everything gleamed, the rails, his pink cheeks, the chrome of his truck. He took my suitcase from the porter and slung it in the back of the "rig." On the highway, I looked out over fallow fields and could see for miles in each direction. Buck had been right about the sky, bigger and bluer than in Paris, and not a single cloud. He reached over and squeezed my knee. I placed my hand on his. Today was a new beginning. We'd have our own home. For our first meal, I'd make potato-leek soup, and why not a roast? The road stretched in front of us, and I could taste the possibilities.

We drove through Froid, a village dotted with charming little homes, in less than five minutes. There were three bars and one church, but no bookshops or bakeries. Buck parked in front of a two-story white wooden house on the edge of town. It had large windows but no shutters. There was no fence, no barrier to keep out strangers, not like in Paris, where we valued our privacy.

"Come meet my parents."

They came onto the porch as Buck opened my door. His father was a smaller, older version of Buck, his hair gray, his face lined with more worries. His mother wore a lavender skirt and blouse, primly buttoned to the collarbone. In my war-worn skirt and cardigan, I felt self-conscious. In Occupied France, we women tried to go on as before, but over four years, our clothing became threadbare. Yes, some Parisiennes received new dresses from their German lovers, but most of us did with what we had, mending holes and fixing frayed hems. Our shabby clothes became badges of honor. However, here in Froid, upon observing Mrs. Gustafson's ensemble, I was certain that it was not chic to be shabby.

"Ma, Pop, this is the woman I was telling you about, my little gal, Odile," Buck said proudly and pulled me to his side.

"Hello, it's a pleasure to meet you," I said, enunciating clearly, like the Countess.

"A deal?" his father said.

"Ordeal," his mother corrected.

Were they doing it on purpose? I studied their faces. Mr. and Mrs. Gustafson seemed genuinely perplexed. It hadn't occurred to me that they did not know.

"*Oh-deal,* and I got hitched in France," Buck said.

They remained on the porch. His father looked at me warily. His mother's vague smile became a bitter pucker. "You keep telling us that," she said. "But how can you be married if we weren't there?"

"What about Jenny?" his father said. "Everyone thought you two had an understanding."

"She's like a daughter to us," Mrs. Gustafson said. "While you were . . . away, we spent the holidays together."

Buck had a fiancée? I stepped away from him.

"How could you do this to Jenny?" Mr. Gustafson said. "She's waited for years."

"No one asked her to," Buck replied.

His father groaned and stepped into the house. His mother eyed me reproachfully, then followed.

"They'll come around," Buck said.

I followed his parents inside. They whispered on the divan, comforting each other as they could. Watching from the doorjamb, neither in nor out, I wasn't sure what to do. Buck sidled up to me with my suitcase.

"How can we face the Millers?" Mr. Gustafson asked his wife, as if Buck and I weren't standing there.

Finally, Mrs. Gustafson turned to Buck. "Jenny waited, faithful and true, while you ran around with this *French* hussy." She made the word "French" sound like more of an insult than "hussy."

I looked to Buck to defend me. When he remained slack-jawed, I replied to her accusations. "I had no idea Buck was engaged. I never would have married him, never would have left France—"

"No offense, missy, but according to the news, you don't have much of a country left."

First, she insulted me, then my homeland? At the library, I'd worked in a world of words, but now I found myself speechless. How could these people be so callous?

"You have no idea what folks in France have been through," Buck shot back. "And I tried to tell you about Odile. You wouldn't listen."

"At church three days ago, you and Jenny were thick as thieves," Mrs. Gustafson said.

"I never asked Jenny to wait," Buck said. "We're just friends."

Mrs. Gustafson took a cigarette from a gold case, and her husband lit it for her. She sucked in greedily before letting the smoke whistle out through her mouth over and over until she snuffed the cigarette out in the ashtray. She muttered something about coffee and strode from the room. I felt it was a test and wondered if I should help prepare the tray. Maman would never allow a guest into the kitchen. I decided to sit in the armchair, folding my hands like my boss, Miss Reeder, did. On the couch, Buck and his father talked football, a completely foreign language. When Mrs. Gustafson returned, pushing a cart with cake and coffee, I offered to serve but was ignored. Buck and his father stopped chatting. No one spoke. I missed the questions Maman would ask to keep the conversation going. I missed Papa and his overbearing ways. I missed my parents, period.

One cigarette after another, Buck's mother puffed away like the Empire Builder locomotive, until the room was black with smoke and I thought I'd pass out. Still she kept on, explaining, "When Buck . . . went away, the doctor prescribed them for my nerves."

Away. She spoke as if he'd gone to take the waters at a spa, not fight in a war.

After an eternity of silence, she looked at me reproachfully and rolled the cart back to the kitchen. I leaned over and whispered to Buck, "When are we going home?"

"We are home."

"You don't have a place of your own?"

"For four years, I moved from one theater of war to the next. When was I supposed to buy a house?"

"You've been back for months."

"Recuperating. My folks wanted me with them. Besides, Froid's a small town. Not much housing to be had."

I didn't want to stay where I wasn't wanted. I rushed out the front door to the park across the street. It was freezing, but the fresh air felt good. Plopping onto a swing, I let my feet dangle over the brown grass. Buck was probably still in love with his fiancée. His parents hated me. The land was barren, the town small. There were no cinemas, no flowers, no library, no life. I knew I was being unfair, but I couldn't be fair. Not just yet.

Rubbing my left foot over my right, I thought of my brother, Rémy, and wished he was here, that he was not lost to me. *Oh, Rémy, I've made a mistake.* I didn't need to open my purse to know I only had twenty francs. And after I'd betrayed Margaret and burned down her family tree, it wasn't right that I could traipse back to Maman and Papa. When my aunt Caro and her husband divorced, my mother disowned her sister. I'd left Paul. The reason wouldn't matter. My parents wouldn't take me back. *The wine is poured, you have to drink,* Papa would say. Americans used different imagery: *you've made your bed, now lie in it.* Both expressions amounted to the same thing—what's done is done. There's no going home.

Buck joined me. He held the swing steady, hands on either side of me, and looked into my eyes. "I'm sorry, little gal. I tried to tell them. Ma only hears what she wants to."

That I could believe.

"The time without you here has been an . . . *ordeal,*" he said, and we laughed together. "Things will get better. Jenny was my high school sweetheart. I'm not a kid anymore. The war . . . She'll never understand like you do. Of everybody, you're the only one who knows."

◆ ◆ ◆

After a tense evening meal, Buck led me up the stairs. Mr. and Mrs. Gustafson followed, and I wondered if I would be sleeping with Buck or in a guest bedroom. I wanted to be respectful of his parents—after all, I was a visitor in their home. I waited for a clue from his mother, whose beige lips remained pursed. Well, then . . .

In Buck's bedroom, badges from his scouting days covered the dark paneling; his shelves held sports trophies, not books.

"Go on and get settled," he said. "I'll be right back."

Unsure of myself, unsure of my surroundings, I perched on the twin bed. I could hear his parents on the other side of the wall.

"We don't even know if they're really married," Mr. Gustafson said. "Why didn't you put her in the guest room?"

"She's French. She's no virgin," came the reply.

I keeled over onto my side and drew my knees to my chest. Hoping to drown out the words, I held a pillow over my head.

When Buck returned, he pulled it away. "Little gal, what are you doing?"

He took me in his arms, and slowly, as he kneaded my back, the tension of the day evaporated. I tilted my head, and we kissed. Through the wall, I heard a cough. I drew back and moved to my suitcase. Kneeling down, I opened it and breathed in deeply, certain I could still smell home—Maman's jasmine perfume, Papa's pipe, the leather of Rémy's satchel. I dug around until I found my nightgown, which had been a part of my trousseau. I imagined Maman bent over the embroidery ring, pulling the pink thread through to create a garden of roses at the hem. My back to Buck, I took off my red belt and dress and slipped on the gown. I loved the flowers that flourished at my feet. For a moment, I felt innocent.

"No need to be shy," he told me. "Let's go to bed."

Groaning under his weight, the mattress sank when he slid in next to me. His warmth seeped into my skin. Tight against his chest, I felt like I'd come home after a long, confusing journey.

"I missed you," he said. "Did you miss me?"

"Yes." I ran my hands along his back.

"You look pretty in your nightie." He inched his thigh between mine.

I kissed his mouth. I tasted the salt on his neck. I opened myself to him. There was so much I wanted to tell him, how much I loved him, how much he'd saved me, how much I loved the feel of his body in mine. We moved together, to a place where words no longer mattered. The bed began to creak. Buck thrust faster and faster, then one last time.

There was a crash as the legs at the head of the bed gave, and suddenly our feet were higher than our heads. We giggled.

"What a performance," I told him. "Isn't there an expression about bringing the house down?"

"I can't take all the credit." He kissed my hand. "You're a wonderful leading lady."

A moment later, he dragged the mattress with me on it to the floor. He flung his arm across my waist and I cuddled up next to him, somewhat surprised to have found a new happiness after Paul. As my eyes fluttered shut, I remembered one of my favorite lines from *Their Eyes Were Watching God*: *Love is like the sea. It's a moving thing, but still and all, it takes its shape from the shore it meets, and it's different with every shore.*

Buck's parents had been surprised by our marriage, but they loved him and would accept his choices. All that mattered was that we were together.

◆ ◆ ◆

In the morning, I slipped on my dress and went to freshen up. When I came out of the bathroom, my mother-in-law jabbed her cigarette in my direction. "Hussy! Can't you control yourself?"

I felt my face flush with mortification, and I sped back to Buck's room.

A few minutes later, he and I joined his parents for breakfast.

"Did you sleep all right?" Mrs. Gustafson asked him. "The doctor said you're supposed to get plenty of rest."

"I guess two of us on the bed was too much. The legs gave way."

“You broke the bed?” she asked, masterfully adding a hint of surprise.

“We didn’t break the bed. It broke.”

I admired the way Mrs. Gustafson handled the situation. Deny any knowledge. Spare Buck any embarrassment. If only she’d been kind enough in my case. But she hadn’t. And if I didn’t have a map of Montana, at least I had the lay of the land.

◆ ◆ ◆

In Froid, there were no lines, not at the post office, not at the general store. I rejoiced. “Expect things to be different, but try not to compare. Tell yourself it’s not better or worse, just different,” the Red Cross matron at Camp Lucky Strike had said. Different. Yes, even the texture of the bread, the salty tang of the butter. The air was drier. So were the people I met on Main Street. Maybe they were kinder to Buck because they’d known him longer. They’d warm to me. Hadn’t the Americans at the library been friendly?

Buck went to work at Mel’s Garage, leaving me alone with his parents. I stayed in the bedroom. If I ventured out, Mrs. Gustafson fired up the Hoover and aimed it in my direction. When he came home in the evening, it felt as if the savior had arrived.

On Sunday morning, Buck and I entered the church. I inhaled deeply. Stale incense—something I knew. When the service started, I recognized the cadence of Latin. Finally, something familiar. *Out of the depths I have cried to thee, O Lord: Lord, hear me. Let thy ears be attentive to the voice of my supplication. My soul hath hoped in the Lord.*

In Paris, I’d hated Mass. In the cathedral, with the sun gleaming through the stained glass, Rémy told me to calm my mind, Maman told me to be quiet and pray. And throughout the war, I had. For Rémy’s safety. For peace. For wisdom. But I’d felt nothing. Today, I bathed in light, as if someone took my hands and told me the terrible things I’d done didn’t matter. I could be a better person. It wasn’t too late. I felt blessed. In a town I did not know, in a church with worn carpet, I was at peace.

Until the final blessing, when I felt the glare of the Millers, Jenny tucked between her parents, the outraged trinity.

From the pulpit, Father Maloney, who'd arrived the same week as I had, suggested that next Sunday people stay after Mass for a potluck. I decided to make an apple tart.

The following week at the hall, parishioners devoured Delores Murdoch's meatloaf and Betty Iver's Jell-O salad made with chopped celery and maraschino cherries. Only two people took any of my pie—the priest and Buck. Even Mr. and Mrs. Gustafson didn't try a slice. Someone joked about the "French tart." At the end of the luncheon, only my dessert remained. To spare my feelings, Father Maloney told me it was delicious in a voice loud enough for all to hear and asked if he could take the rest home. I was so overwhelmed by his kindness, the first in Froid, that I could taste tears in the back of my throat. In the future, to avoid more culinary shunning, he informed his flock that he would order pastries.

Buck

Buck went to the Oasis every Friday after work. He'd been home for over a year and had yet to pay for a drink. At the bar, the men hailed the war hero and celebrated his medals. They slapped him on the back, and after a few beers, asked what it had been like. He never told them that he'd landed on a beach of blood. That he'd never been so scared. That he dreamed of body parts strewn on the floor of the supermarket, in the pews at church, and even in his bed.

He didn't tell them that now he had to force himself to hold his rifle. That when he and his father went hunting, his hands shook. His hands still shook. The only way he could shoot was to lie prone, gun wedged between the ground and his shoulder. He didn't tell them that most of the men in his squad never made it home. He didn't tell them that he wished he hadn't.

He didn't tell them how he'd met the enemy face-to-face, both of them out of bullets. Him or me. He didn't tell them that he strangled the son of a bitch. Him or me. Me. He didn't tell them that twice now in his sleep he'd choked his little gal. She told him it wasn't his fault. But it hurt him. It hurt him bad.

He'd traveled. He'd seen things.

He hadn't wanted to change. But, here he was, different.

Melancholy. That's what they whispered. In church. At the general store. That's what they called the black curtain that came down and caused him to stay in bed. Or punch the wall. Because his shoelace came untied. Because the neighbor's dog wouldn't stop yapping. Because he had done things he'd never wanted to do. Because people called him a hero. When he knew the real heroes were dead and buried.

He loved Odile. Her eyes, still sad after all this time. He knew she was the only one who understood, because she'd done bad things, too. At the hospital, he'd seen it in her eyes. The guilt. The longing. The lost innocence.

The first time they'd met was in 'forty. Back then, he'd been frustrated by the way America sat on the sidelines. The antsy quarterback couldn't wait to get in the game, so he'd crossed the border to enlist in the Royal Canadian Air Force. His squadron had been sent to England, then France, where he'd been hit. At the hospital, he and a bunch of other wounded soldiers slumped along the walls of the hallway, waiting to be examined. Odile arrived to bathe his face. He'd been in pain, but those warm hands and that soft accent soothed him. When he came to after the operation to remove shrapnel from his thigh, hers was the first face he saw. She stayed with him, stroking his arm. When he told her he loved her, she replied, "With everything they pumped into you, you'd love a goat." He smiled at the memory. He'd loved her wide-eyed and sassy.

When he saw her four years later, head bowed on the stoop, he'd loved her even more. Those brown eyes drenched in regret, he'd comforted her the best he could. For some reason, she clutched a red belt. Gently, he pried it from her hand and tied the leather around her waist, even now a lasso he used to pull her close.

There was a before, and there was an after. And before, in France, Buck had never thought about how hard it would be for Odile after. Before, she'd had a full life as a librarian. After, in Froid, she couldn't find a job. Father Maloney took pity on her and hired her as a part-time secretary. She organized a small library in the church vestibule, but with chores at home and on the farm, few people had time to read.

Buck could see she was miserable. He could see she tried to hide it. She hated living with his parents, who, frankly, were no help. He and Odile saved every cent so they could put a down payment on a house. Finally, they moved.

Working at the garage beat being a soldier. The smell of gasoline and grease beat puke and guts. He didn't mind the long hours. He enjoyed the puzzle of a Chevy. He appreciated each part, the peace he found in taking the pieces apart, in putting them back together, to see the engine whole and running. A flask idled in the pocket of his coveralls, for when the day got to be too much. He wished people would leave him alone. His boss said, "I told you to replace the muffler, not dismantle the whole damn truck." His co-workers elbowed him in the ribs each time Jenny brought in her brand-new Cadillac because of a suspicious noise. "There's something 'suspicious' about her coming round so much. Har, har."

She giggled and touched Buck's chest like they were still in high school. She probably knew the guys would tell their wives about her every move. "Tell your folks hello," he'd mutter and get back to changing the oil on a Ford. He needed as much overtime as he could get. He wanted to buy Odile a fancy Louis XIV chair from France. His little gal never complained, but her smile was wistful, and more than anything, he wanted to make her happy.

Sometimes, in the middle of the night, when he felt as if he would suffocate under his memories, under her sadness, Buck eased out of bed and pulled on his jeans and went outside. On the lawn, he hunched over, hands on his knees to steady himself, and sucked in gales of night air. Times like this, there was only one place he wanted to be. He headed down the street to the house on the edge of town. He snuck in the back door and inched up the stairs. Slipping into the bedroom, he undressed and snuggled under the tatty quilt, surrounded by his trophies, his victories, his life before. When things were still right.

Odile

Each morning, I awoke next to Buck, grateful we had our own home. When we'd moved in, the first thing he did was build bookshelves in every room, even the kitchen. Through an army buddy back East, he bought me novels in French. He seemed devoted. Still, I fretted, almost certain I smelled perfume on his work shirt, and last night, he'd slipped out again. Furious that he thought he could fool me, I put clothes near the bed so next time, when he left in the middle of the night, I could follow. It took a week, but eventually, he snuck out. I crept along, hiding behind hedges, following him to the last place I expected him to go.

Once inside his parents' house, he didn't flick on a light. Did they know he was there? What was he doing? After an hour, I shuffled home, feeling ridiculous, and vowed to be sweeter to make up for my doubts. I would pretend I didn't know anything about his odd nights. Anyway, neither of us seemed to get much sleep. In my nightmares, I found myself back in Papa's office at the precinct, reading crow letters denouncing Jewish neighbors and co-workers. *Roger-Charles Meyer is a pure Jew, well as pure as that race can be, and I will not hide the fact that I would be delighted if he were taken away. . . .* I agonized about what more I could have done to help Library subscribers like dear Professor Cohen—destroyed more letters, confronted my father, warned people what was happening.

* * *

In Froid, I no longer had a first name—I was Buck's wife or the War Bride. I tried to befriend the other ladies, but under Jenny Miller's sullen eye, they backed away. When Mrs. Gustafson spoke to me, her voice was still stilted. The meaner they were, the kinder Buck was. He and I didn't discuss the past, but once I showed him a photo of the Library, with its lovely flower bed. The next day, he planted a border of petunias along the walk to the mailbox.

At least I had correspondence from my own kind, women who'd suffered the same traumatic rebirth. And I wrote and wrote. The truth to some, lies to others. But mainly my letters were somewhere in between. I even wrote to Maman and Papa. To ask if they were in good health, to say I was sorry. Shame stopped me from mailing those letters.

My favorite time of day was 2:00 p.m., when the postman brought news from fellow war brides. *My husband gave me a strand of pearls and took me to the opera for our fifth anniversary. My husband beats me and no one here cares. I'm expecting my fourth child, people call me the Rouen Rabbit. I'm still not pregnant—the doctor says it's because of malnutrition during the war. Pray for me. Pray for us. We live with his parents. Still. He hasn't found a job. Yet. Our house has walls made of cardboard covered in newspaper—my parents would like to visit, but I can't bear to have them see how we live. I want to return to France but don't have any money. No one here understands. My husband drinks too much. He jumps when I touch him, and sometimes he cries for no reason. The doctor gave him pills. Suzanne from the ship lives three doors down! Sorry I haven't written in ages, the university asked me to create a French-language curriculum; I'll direct the entire program. My little ones are feisty, I can hardly keep up! I write for the local paper. My in-laws are adorable. My in-laws will never accept me. I'm glad I came here. I never should have come.*

Finally, after seven long years, I had news of my own: I'm with child!

* * *

Buck couldn't keep his hands off my belly. Instead of going to the bar, he stayed home. We sat on the couch and waited for the baby to kick. His flask was forgotten behind a cushion, and his midnight strolls stopped.

When my water broke, he gripped my hand, more scared than I was. Who hadn't heard stories? "Hazel had another stillborn." "Mildred died in childbirth, God have mercy on her soul." "The baby was breech, Stanch had to reach in with both hands and turn things around."

"I wish I could bear the pain for you," Buck said as he drove us to the hospital.

"Je t'aime," I said as he helped me alight from the pickup. "More than anyone."

"I love you, too. You saved my life more than once."

At the front desk, the nurse jumped up and got a wheelchair. In the maternity ward, she helped me into bed. She didn't say much, but stayed at my side. I couldn't stop passing gas, couldn't stop my tears from falling, couldn't blow my nose because I hadn't brought a handkerchief. I wished I knew what to expect. The library had had a book about this—the truth made grown women faint. Why hadn't I read it?

The nurse left, just left without saying a word. I watched the door close slowly, cutting me off from everyone. Homesickness hit me as hard as a contraction. I cradled my belly. "Maman," I whimpered, eyes on the door. I'd never felt so alone.

The nurse returned with an extra blanket. She'd been gone just for five minutes, but it had felt like hours. "We wouldn't want you to catch cold," she said and tucked the blanket around me.

"Thank you." I felt something wet between my thighs. "I think my water broke some more."

The nurse giggled, but when she pulled back the covers and saw the blood, she stopped laughing.

She and an orderly rushed me to the labor room. The pain was so bad that I screamed. I felt a prick of the needle. I felt the next contraction. I felt myself fall into oblivion.

◆ ◆ ◆

After Mass, seated at a table in the hall, Mrs. Gustafson cradled her grandson in her arms. His arrival stirred up old gossip. Buck's mother reminded the other ladies that he and Jenny had never been engaged. She refused to hear another word. After all, the Millers had moved to Missoula.

"We're proud of Buck's little gal," Mr. Gustafson told anyone who'd listen.

Buck's parents showered me with advice, the baby with affection. They called him Marc instead of his given name, Marcel, which they considered effeminate, and worse, too French. When they invited me to call them by their Christian names, I just couldn't.

The townspeople thawed, too, finally forgiving me for stealing Jenny Miller's sweetheart. Their snubs had hurt, but as the years went by, I found I simply had nothing to say to them. I had my family. Buck and I watched Marc learn to walk, we watched him try to roller-skate for the first time, we watched him walk up the aisle for his first communion, we watched every one of his football games. Buck remained at my side, and I knew I'd made the right decision all those years ago.

About the Author

Janet Skeslien Charles is a *New York Times, USA Today,* and #1 international bestselling author. Her novels include *The Paris Library, Moonlight in Odessa, Miss Morgan's Book Brigade* (called *The Librarians of Rue de Picardie* in the UK and Commonwealth), and *The Parisian Chapter.* Her essays and short stories have appeared in the *Chicago Tribune, The Sydney Morning Herald,* and the anthology *Montana Noir.* Her work has been translated into forty languages. Janet was born and raised in Montana. After graduating from the University of Montana, she got a job teaching English in Ukraine. She later went to France, intending to teach for a year, and has been there ever since. Place is at the heart of every story she has ever written. She loves traveling, spending time with friends and family, and researching stories of forgotten people and places. To connect, visit her website JSkeslienCharles.com, @jskesliencharles on Instagram, and her newsletter JSkeslienCharles.substack.com.

Thank you to the **Atria Books** colleagues who collaborated on *The Parisian Chapter,* as well as to the hundreds of professionals in the Simon & Schuster advertising, audio, communications, design, ebook, finance, human resources, legal, marketing, operations, production, sales, supply chain, subsidiary rights, and warehouse departments who help Atria bring great books to light.

Editorial
Peter Borland
Hannah Frankel

Audio
Lara Blackman
Gaby Audet
Lili Feinberg
Sarah Lieberman
Lauren Pires
Allison Light
Sydney Fuqua-Holiman
Hana Matsudaira

Jacket Design
James Iacobelli

Marketing
Dayna Johnson
Morgan Pager

Managing Editorial
Paige Lytle
Shelby Pumphrey
Sofia Echeverry

Production
Mark LaFlaur
Kyoko Watanabe
Briana Skerpan
Vanessa Silverio
Susan M. S. Brown
Barbara Greenberg
Lisa Nicholas

Publicity
Gena Lanzi

Publishing Office
Suzanne Donahue
Abby Velasco

Subsidiary Rights
Nicole Bond
Sara Bowne
Rebecca Justiniano